'"I wish my Bellingham, Finch."'

'Good God, Varley, you cannot expect me to agree to this!' Marcus said, leaping up from his chair to stand with both hands planted flat on the lawyer's desk. His dark eyes blazed. 'It's nothing short of blackmail.'

'Nor will I agree to it!' Amy raged. 'I won't be manipulated in this way.'

'I have merely read you the terms of the Will as Lady Bellingham decreed. And there is one more small paragraph you would do well to hear,' Varley declared. '"Unless my nephew agrees to my wishes, he will inherit nothing. And Miss Finch may choose any two pieces of my jewellery."'

Amy gasped. The Will was watertight. . .

Sally Blake was born in London, but lives in Weston-super-Mare. She started writing when her three children went to school, and has written many contemporary and historical novels under different pen-names. She loves the research involved in writing historical novels, finding it both exciting and addictive.

MARRYING FOR LOVE

Sally Blake

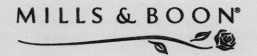

MILLS & BOON®

*MILLS & BOON and MILLS & BOON with the Rose Device
are registered trademarks of the publisher.*

*First published in Great Britain 1997
Harlequin Mills & Boon Limited,
Eton House, 18-24 Paradise Road, Richmond, Surrey TW9 1SR*

© Sally Blake 1997

ISBN 0 263 80501 8

*Set in Times 11 on 11½ pt. by
Rowland Phototypesetting Limited
Bury St Edmunds, Suffolk*

04-9801-68778

*Printed and bound in Great Britain by
Caledonian International Book Manufacturing Ltd, Glasgow*

Chapter One

Amy had been truly dreading this day. It seemed such a short while ago that it had all seemed like a great adventure, and one that she had never imagined. To go on a sea voyage, away from her native Scotland—and all paid for, too—was not the sort of chance that came to an ordinary girl like herself. It might not be travelling to the far distant shores that wealthier Regency folk enjoyed, but to Amy it was still the stuff of dreams. And she owed it all to her employer, Lady Bellingham.

Her face was clouded now as she leaned on the ship's rail with the rest of the eager passengers, so excited to be reaching their destination after the long and wearisome voyage, and longing for the first glimpse of Dublin's shoreline. Amy's hazel eyes blurred, knowing how very different this arrival was for her from the intended one. And knowing, too, how very nervous she was becoming.

Hardly aware of the lump in her throat, she fumbled for a lace handkerchief in the pocket of her respectable travelling dress, whose layers were far too hot for the rising temperatures they were experiencing now in this hot summer.

The elderly Scottish couple, who had befriended her in the last horrifying days, saw the downward droop of her slender shoulders, and moved closer to her. The gentleman cleared his throat awkwardly, but the lady put a delicate hand over Amy's arm.

'This will be a sad time for you, my dear,' she said sympathetically. 'Do you have relatives meeting you?'

Amy swallowed, knowing she meant to be kind. But what hired companion of barely twenty summers was likely to have relatives waiting to greet her in this grand city?

'I do not, ma'am,' she murmured, 'but Lady Bellingham was to have been met by her nephew, and instead of a joyful reunion after a number of years, I will have the task of breaking the sad news of her death to him.'

The lady made understanding noises. 'So terrible for you, Miss Finch. Were the lady and her nephew very close?'

For a moment Amy felt the most appalling urge to burst out laughing. And how very awful that would be, with the thought that poor Lady Bellingham's body would assuredly have been food for the fishes by now in the stormy waters of the Atlantic Ocean.

But for the life of her, she couldn't forget the way Lady Bellingham had denounced her nephew when she had received his latest enthusiastic letters. She had a caustic tongue when she chose to use it, and frequently called the nephew a scallywag. It was a childish term that always amused Amy, since he was no longer a child.

*   *   *

'The foolhardiness of the boy never fails to amaze me, Amy!' she had almost spluttered. 'But this time he's gone too far. Altogether too far!'

Amy waited, knowing her employer wouldn't be slow in pouring out the details of the letter to her. She confided in Amy to the extent of frequently embarrassing her, but although she was a strict employer, and sharp in manner, she was also fair, and Amy had never betrayed a confidence. And from all she had learned in the two years she had been in Lady Bellingham's employ, she felt that she knew the errant adventurer, Marcus Bellingham, quite well.

'What has he done to vex you this time?' she asked, knowing the lady would expect the question.

Lady Bellingham gave an unladylike snort.

'He's had some wild schemes in his time, but this is just throwing money to the four winds. He's gone into partnership—and with some good-for-nothing rogue, I've no doubt; they plan to grow rich on some alluvial gold-mining scheme in the Wicklow Mountains. Apparently, some locals have reported finding some evidence of the metal remaining in the area. So, with his usual enthusiasm, Marcus is quite sure there's gold there for the taking, and that he and his partner will make their fortune.'

To Amy, whose journey to Skye had been the farthest she'd travelled from Inverness in her whole life, or who had done nothing more than kowtow to an elderly employer's whims, it sounded wildly romantic and exciting.

'Perhaps they will,' she offered.

Lady Bellingham's eyes flashed. 'Don't be naïve,

girl. It's far more likely Marcus will come to me for an early share of my fortune to get him out of his latest scrape, if not to save him from total ruin. I know him too well.'

'I don't recall that he normally asks you for money. Does he do so now?' Amy said, knowing the lady liked her to be as bold as herself, but hoping at the same time that this wasn't too much of an intrusion into personal affairs.

'He does not. But I'm perfectly sure that's what he's hinting at, and I'll not sanction such a reckless and ill-advised scheme without protest.' She paused. 'Or at least, not without seeing for myself what the foolish boy is getting entangled with this time.'

Amy caught her breath at that moment, wondering if the lady really meant that remark as it sounded. Lady B. was a real homebody, and had always vowed to resist the idea of visiting far-off places. The worldwide travelling of others wasn't for her. So surely she couldn't mean. . .

Lady Bellingham looked at her young companion with a sudden gleam in her aristocratic eyes.

'Well, would it appeal to you, girl, to voyage to southern Ireland, to examine the pros and cons of this ridiculous new venture of my nephew's?'

'Well, yes, it certainly would, Lady Bellingham. In fact, the very thought of it takes my breath away,' Amy said, flushed with excitement at the imagery it evoked.

She had been shown all the unknown Marcus's letters to his aunt, since she had been required to write the dictated letters back to him, for the lady's hands were too swollen with rheumatics now to make writing comfortable. And Amy knew that

Marcus threw himself with enthusiasm into whatever he undertook, and she envied his adventurous spirit. How lucky to be born a man, when the lives of ladies in the first quarter of the nineteenth century were so much more restricted.

But she reminded herself quickly that she would be travelling—if it all came to pass—as a lady's companion, no more. And when the adventure was over, she would be returning to Skye with a head full of memories and tales to tell. Not that any of it could possibly compare with the most romantic tale of all, when Charles Stuart had escaped from the mainland, disguised as Flora Macdonald's maid, to their mystical and magical island. All of seventy-five years had passed since then, but the romance and eventual tragedy of it all was still strong in the minds of the islanders.

'Yes, I see that it excites you,' Lady Bellingham said drily. 'You know, you can be quite pretty when you daydream, Amy. Most times you look far too intense.'

'That's because I take my duties seriously,' she retorted, and the lady laughed and spoke with a rare fondness.

'Well, you may relax a little more when we are on board ship, Amy. In fact, I insist on it.'

'Then you really do intend to visit your nephew?'

'Of course. You will see about arranging our passage this very day, and we'll inform him as soon as it's settled.'

Amy had thought, then, that it wasn't only Marcus Bellingham who had a spirit of adventure in his soul. It had simply taken his aunt more than eighty years of her life to recognise it in herself. And it had all come to nothing. . .

'My dear Miss Finch,' she heard the shipboard acquaintance saying now, 'do you have a meeting place arranged with Lady Bellingham's nephew? And if my husband and I might be of any assistance, please say so.'

'It was all arranged, ma'am,' Amy said in a muffled voice. 'Mr Bellingham was to meet us on the quay and escort us to a hotel for the night before leaving Dublin the next day for Callanby in the Wicklow Mountains.'

Her voice cracked; of course, such arrangements would be changed now. She had to tell Marcus Bellingham the dreadful news, and she had no idea what she would do then, since there was no possible reason for him to help her. In frustration, she recalled that Lady Bellingham had declined to pre-arrange return passages for the two of them, declaring in her imperious way that she had no idea how long she might be needed here. And Amy didn't have a penny of her own.

So her only option now would be to throw herself on Marcus's mercy, and she had far too much pride to relish the prospect.

But a snippet from one of his letters swept into her mind then, a charming, sweet snippet, which gave her some small hope that he wasn't going to be too unfeeling to help a stranded traveller.

'You would love Callanby, Aunt Maud,' he'd written. 'It's in a green valley with the mountains in the background, and very reminiscent of your beloved Cuillins on Skye, though not so dour and black, I fancy. You and my uncle always loved the mountains, I recall.'

But it hadn't been an invitation to visit him in his green Irish valley. . .

'I'm sure the news will be a shock to Mr Bellingham, Miss Finch,' the shipboard acquaintance continued. 'But if you find yourself in any real difficulties, please don't hesitate to contact my husband and myself at the Continental Hotel in Dublin. I'm sure we could arrange something for you, and I'll give you my card.'

Amy murmured her thanks, knowing she was never likely to do so. The couple were pleasant enough, but she had no doubt that any connection between them would be on a employment basis, and she had no intention of ending up as a lady's companion ever again. Despite her waspish ways, she had grown fond of Lady Bellingham, whose untimely illness and appallingly quick death from a sudden fever had robbed Amy of a pseudo-relative as well as an employer. And she had no others.

The ship was easing into the quayside now, to a blare of hooters and waving flags, and eager passengers looking for familiar faces. Amy strained her eyes against the brilliant summer sunlight, and felt its heat dampening her skin. She looked vainly for a figure remotely resembling the youthful portrait of Marcus Bellingham that took pride of place on the drawing-room wall of the remote house on the island.

He had looked so self-confident in the portrait, with all the arrogance of youth as he posed with his dog at his side. It had been painted shortly before he left for foreign fields as a gift to his aunt. Amy had always thought his dark hair and bold eyes were reminiscent of a pirate of old, and that he was just as dashing an adventurer to have gone wandering the world to seek his fortune. But she had known better than to express such sentiments to his aunt.

He would have changed by now, of course. The portrait had been painted more than ten years previously, and Marcus Bellingham was thirty-two years old now, despite the fact that his aunt had still regarded him as a wayward boy.

Amy was sometimes embarrassed to realise how much intimate detail she knew about him, both through his letters, and from his aunt's memories of her only living relative. But she freely admitted now that she didn't really know him at all. And what was more important, he didn't know her either.

They were strangers who were forced to meet under the most unhappy circumstances and, as yet, Marcus was completely ignorant of the fact. Amy's soft heart quailed at the thought of having to tell him, but there was no one else to do it. She had already informed the ship's captain and doctor that it would be best coming from her. At least the telling would come from someone who had been truly fond of his aunt.

Her heart jolted as she saw a tall, dark-haired man striding along the quayside, and she tried to gauge whether or not he could be the one. Then she saw him being embraced by a woman with a small family of children clutching at her skirts, and knew it wasn't him. She felt suddenly bereft and forlorn, watching all the excited arrivals and greetings. The quayside was flooded with people, jostling and shouting, and to Amy it seemed as though everyone had someone of their own, while she had no one. The enormity of her situation struck her anew with terrifying sharpness.

She saw a member of the ship's crew approaching her.

'A gentleman has been asking for Lady Bellingham, miss,' he said uneasily, touching his cap. 'I didn't rightly know what to say to him——'

'You didn't tell him?' Amy said in alarm.

'No, miss. I just told him the lady's companion would be shortly disembarking, and he's waiting for you near the wharf yonder.'

He pointed in the direction of the busy wharf, and Amy caught her breath. The sun was behind Marcus Bellingham's head, but somehow there was no mistaking that proud bearing, so much like his aunt's. And, although he was older, she knew him instantly from his portrait.

The dark hair was even longer than fashion decreed, and the cut of his clothes was dashingly informal, intimating that here was a man who cared little for the tastes of the day, but went his own way. It was an echo of his own character, Amy thought.

She accepted the crewman's arm as she stepped down the gangplank, and walked rather unsteadily to where Marcus Bellingham waited a little distance away from the ship. She needed to get her landlegs again after the voyage and the inclement weather off the Scottish islands that had delayed their arrival, but it wasn't the only reason she shirked this task so much. How did you tell a man that the one living relative he was expecting to greet had died at sea?

He took little notice of Amy, except to register

the trim figure of the comely young woman walking towards him. But long before she reached him, Amy could see that his eyes were still searching among the passengers for the one face he knew. Amy's heart balked again. But she took a deep breath, and addressed him.

'Mr Marcus Bellingham? You *are* Mr Bellingham, are you not?' she almost quavered.

The dark eyes slowly looked down at her, and a small frown appeared between his brows. They were very *fine* brows, Amy noted, as if such inane thoughts could stave off the moment she dreaded, and almost as aristocratic as his aunt's. Though in this man's case, they could be called arrogant, rather than—

She pulled her thoughts up short, as she realised he was speaking to her impatiently now.

'You suppose correct, ma'am—'

'It's Miss,' Amy mumbled. 'Miss Amy Finch.'

The frown disappeared, and his eyebrows lifted as he seemed to take in her entire appearance now in one sweeping glance of somewhat sardonic approval. But he shook her hand surprisingly warmly. He was definitely as unconventional as she expected, she thought, and careless of the niceties of Regency etiquette.

'So you are the elusive Miss Finch who has been writing me all those scathing letters from my aunt. Somehow I expected you to be older—'

'They were your aunt's words, sir,' she said, ignoring the rest of his comment.

'But not all of them, I suspect. I detected more than one roguish aside that came from a more tolerant mind, and now I see that I was right. I'm pleased to make your acquaintance at last, Miss Finch.'

She hadn't expected this compliment and she was struck momentarily dumb. *How* could she tell him. . .?

Before she could gather her wits any further, the matter was taken completely out of her hands. The captain and ship's doctor had disembarked from the sailing vessel, and were coming their way. The captain gave her a small salute, but the doctor kept right on walking towards them, holding out his hand to Marcus, his voice filled with sympathy.

'My dear sir, allow me to pass on to you my deepest condolences. You are Mr Bellingham, of course, and Miss Finch will have told you by now of the terrible occurrence on board ship. Alas, there was nothing I could do for the dear lady, and the fever progressed with appalling speed. The captain has requested that I assure you that everything was done at the end with all decorum—'

'What the devil are you talking about, man?' Marcus said, his face and manner changing at once from pleasantly welcoming to dark and angry suspicion.

Amy closed her eyes briefly, wishing the doctor to Kingdom Come. Why couldn't he have left her to do the telling. . .but, of course, he assumed that she had already done so. . .

He looked uncertainly at Amy now, and she shook her head slightly as he started to back away.

'I'm sorry. Please forgive me, sir. I've obviously made a mistake in speaking out, and it would be best if I leave Miss Finch to tell you in her words.'

'I think Miss Finch had better do just that,' Marcus said, rounding on her. His voice was hard now, and he had gripped her arm with unwarranted cruelty, she couldn't help thinking. She found herself stammering, and was furious with herself for seeming so inept.

'I—I didn't know how to tell you,' she gasped. 'It was so—so *awful*, you see. And as the doctor said, it—it happened so quickly—'

'Are you telling me my aunt is dead?'

He said it for her, baldly, and unemotionally.

'I'm afraid she is,' Amy whispered. 'I'm so—so terribly sorry to give you such bad news. It was a fever—'

He said nothing at first, and then he spoke grimly. 'So I understand. And did she suffer unduly?'

'Not a great deal, I believe. She became delirious very quickly, and then she—she simply slipped away—'

Perhaps this was the way shock affected some people, Amy thought, seeing the granite hardness in his jaw. His letters to his aunt had been cajoling at times, and they had frequently sparred in them, but she had never believed him to be anything less than fond of Lady Bellingham. Now, still in a state of shock herself, she wasn't sure of anything any more.

She tried desperately to think of something sensible and useful to say while he spent the next few minutes gazing into the distant void. She ventured another few words.

'I have a letter of condolence and explanation from the captain for you, Mr Bellingham. Also the—the death certificate, of course.' She swallowed, still finding the words so difficult to say. 'And all her clothes and personal effects are in her trunk, which I have arranged to be delivered to the hotel that you mentioned in your letter—'

'What possible use will they be to me?' he snapped, in a tone that Amy could only think of as callous in the extreme. 'The clothes will be sent to the poor house, although I suppose we must go through the rest of it together. You'll know more what was important in the woman's life than I.'

She stared at him, and wondered if he had ever had any real feelings at all for his aunt.

'Don't you care?' she burst out, unable to believe that anyone could be so cruel. 'Didn't you want to see her after all this time? She gave a great deal of thought to this voyage, sir!'

He made a moue of sound. 'She gave a great deal of thought as to how she could dissuade me from following my dreams, as she called them. And I've no doubt she would have spent her entire stay here finding fault with everything I did, as always.'

He stopped abruptly, and spoke more slowly. 'As for not caring, you and I probably have different ideas about what constitutes caring, Miss Finch. I have never felt it necessary to show my feelings to others, and nor does it require a man to weep and wail like a woman to feel grief.'

Amy was outraged by his remark. She considered it an indictment against the entire female sex, and she spoke indignantly.

'You do me an injustice, sir. I freely admit I cried at your aunt's demise, just as any normal person would do.'

'And am I not normal?'

There was a *frisson* of arrogance in his voice now, and he looked at her as if seeing her for the first time. Amy felt something like a little shockwave run through her.

He was so very handsome, and so very irritating. If he wasn't so rude, she could probably have found him extremely attractive indeed, but this certainly wasn't a time for letting her heart rule her head.

'I'm sure you're perfectly normal in many respects, Mr Bellingham,' she said, 'but I find your attitude regarding your aunt's death very upsetting.'

He grabbed her arm and walked her swiftly away from the quayside before she could utter another word. She hardly realised how long they had been standing together on the wharf while the rest of the ship's passengers disembarked and went their separate ways.

For a moment she had the fanciful feeling that she was being abducted, and she looked around desperately for a familiar face, but there were none. Even the sympathetic couple on deck were nowhere to be seen, and were no doubt on their way to the Continental Hotel.

'I'm perfectly capable of walking by myself, sir,' she snapped. 'I fear you have lived in a rough environment for too long, since you seem to have forgotten both your manners and the way to treat a lady.'

He stopped walking, and she was obliged to stop too, since he hadn't yet let go of her. She felt quite ill. She had endured an appalling voyage, and now this—this *oaf*, who looked as though he didn't give a tuppenny toss that his aunt had just died, was treating her like a servant.

Which was exactly what she was, Amy reminded herself swiftly.

'My apologies, Miss Finch,' he said gravely. 'And you're quite right, of course. I have lived in what you call a rougher environment than my aunt would have wished for a considerable time, but you would know all about that, wouldn't you? In fact, you know all about me, I seem to recall, including my private business.'

Amy flushed. 'It was hardly my fault that your aunt was unable to write her own letters in recent years, and used me as a kind of secretary—among other things,' she added, remembering how she had frequently scurried about at the lady's bidding.

Marcus's expression relaxed into the smallest smile. 'Oh yes, I've no doubt my aunt got her money's-worth out of you. Well, since you're here, I suppose I'll have to decide what to do with you.'

'I'm sure I don't wish to be a burden to you, and you have no obligations to me—' she began stiffly.

'Don't be ridiculous. Of course I have obligations to you. And I grant that you must be feeling somewhat upset yourself, despite the way I suspect Aunt Maud had you at her beck and call.'

He was unbelievable. . .and yet, his last words were so near the truth that Amy found herself giving the ghost of a smile in return. It seemed a very long time since she had smiled at anything at all, and she bit her lip, hoping he wouldn't think her frivolous. But *he* wouldn't, she thought, revising her ideas at once. He seemed to care as little for anyone else's feelings as his own.

'You needn't pretend with me, Miss Finch,' Marcus went on. 'We both knew my aunt's caustic tongue.'

'Didn't you have any fondness for her at all?'
Amy said indignantly.

'Of course I did. When I was a child and my
uncle was alive, she was a quite lovable person. His
death brought about a great change in her. From
then on, she kept her feelings very much in check,
and taught me to do the same. So you must forgive
me if I don't choose to parade my feelings for all
to see.'

Amy still privately doubted that he had any. . .
though this was a small revelation she hadn't known
before. She didn't know *all* about him, she conceded. But why would he want to parade his feelings
in front of a servant, anyway? For some reason, she
couldn't get the wretched word out of her mind now,
and knew it was because of the speculation she had
seen in the other passenger's eyes at the possibility
of finding a maid so easily.

'I have a conveyance waiting for us,' he
said, abruptly now. 'Do you have no baggage of
your own?'

For the first time he seemed to realise that she
was a person and not just a nuisance. Amy felt
herself bristle, and spoke just as sharply.

'Of course. It's with Lady Bellingham's, and will
be delivered to the hotel. I trust I was not over-
stepping the mark in arranging it, sir.'

They looked at one another with hostile eyes.
His were very dark, and it was difficult to read the
expression in them. Amy was not a simpering
female, and for some reason she felt that she had
met her match here, even though she knew it was a
foolish thought. What possible reason could Marcus
Bellingham have for sparring with *her*, except on

a superficial basis? And they were so soon to part, God willing, providing Marcus paid her fare home.

Her temper subsided, remembering that she was truly dependent on him now. Without the remotest intention of acting the coquette, she put her hand on his arm, and felt the rigidity of it beneath the sleeve of his coat.

'I'm truly sorry about your aunt,' she said in a softer tone. 'This must all be a terrible shock to you.'

He gave a brief nod, glancing down to where her slim fingers rested lightly on his arm. In embarrassment, she drew them away at once. It wasn't done for the hired help to comfort a gentleman in this way.

It was odd, Amy thought fleetingly. Ladies of his own class could be as tender and sympathetic as they chose, while 'ladies' of a far lower class could give a gentleman comfort in a very different way. It wasn't a particularly comfortable thought to know that she came somewhere between the two. . .

'You have a very expressive face, Miss Finch,' Marcus said, startling her. 'I can quite see why my aunt liked having you around. She cared little for the blank faces of idiots, and would have enjoyed your company.'

If it was a compliment, it was an unexpected, and not altogether welcome, one. Amy didn't care to know that her feelings were so often displayed on her face for all to see, and she lowered her eyes quickly.

'Over here,' he said next, and she realised they had neared a row of horse-drawn vehicles, waiting to take the disembarking passengers on their way. The driver handed her inside, and Marcus sat beside

her, since there was no other room. She was aware
of his closeness in the heat of the day that she was
beginning to find so stuffy, and thanked heaven she
had brought lighter clothes with her.

They drove without speaking, away from the quay
and towards the town of Dublin, with its fine,
crowded buildings and green squares. Amy was
pleasantly surprised by its elegance, and leaned
forward to look at the sights. But a rut in the road
suddenly made the carriage lurch, and Marcus held
on to her quickly as she jerked forward.

'You would do best to sit back, Miss Finch. We're
nearly there, and you can admire the town at your
leisure during the next few days.'

She turned to look at him. 'The next few days?
But I—I—' She stopped, for what could she say?
That she wanted him to arrange her passage back
home this very minute? She was in no position to
demand anything. He shrugged and spoke shortly.

'I had booked you and my aunt into the London
Hotel for three days, since I intended showing her
around. Until you decide what you want to do, I
suggest we simply make use of the booking.'

'Thank you,' she said, almost inaudibly. The prospect of spending three days with this man was not
entirely appealing, and she hoped she could see
something of the area by herself, rather than hang
on to his coat-tails.

When they arrived, she saw that the façade of the
pleasant-looking hotel was emblazoned with the
flags of various nations. It was cooler inside
the building, and she found she could breathe a
little easier.

She waited while Marcus registered their names, and then they were escorted to two adjoining rooms on the first floor. Almost immediately Lady Bellingham's trunk and her own modest baggage were delivered to her room. Once the porter had gone, she stood uncertainly, her throat thick. She answered the knock on her door to find Marcus there.

'I'll leave you to unpack and settle in,' he said. 'But I'd be obliged if you would give me the captain's letter that you mentioned, and also my aunt's death certificate.'

'Of course,' Amy said, knowing she should have done this straight away.

She had simply forgotten it in all the confusion, and she fumbled in her reticule for the important envelopes and handed them to him without comment. For he would surely want to peruse them in private, and maybe then he would come to terms with all that had happened, and be able to express his grief in a more natural way.

He paused for a moment, and then went on. 'Perhaps you would sort through the personal effects, and we can go through them together tomorrow morning. Meanwhile, I need to take these documents to my lawyer right away, so I shall not see you again until we meet for dinner at seven o'clock this evening. Good day to you.'

He was gone, and Amy stared at the closed door with a burning sense of outrage. He was impossible, having nothing more on his mind than speeding off to his lawyer with documents to prove that he was now the sole heir to Lady Bellingham's fortune. He was nothing more than a fortune-hunter, she seethed, and any finer feelings she may have had for him vanished in mid-thought.

Chapter Two

Amy was agreeably surprised to find the London Hotel so comfortable, although she acknowledged that Marcus would obviously have found somewhere good enough for his aunt, if only to impress her. She was shown into a suite, with one large bedroom and a smaller one, together with a small sitting-room. Having had no prior warning to change the arrangements, Marcus clearly expected Amy to occupy the entire suite, she thought in confusion.

She still found it hard to rid herself of cynical thoughts about him now. But once divested of her travelling garments and having washed away the grime of the journey in the welcome hip-bath at her disposal, she began to wish she could wash him out of her mind just as easily.

But there was no chance of that just yet. And nor could she afford to antagonise him. In fact, she was very much aware that she should be civil to him if she didn't want him to abandon her entirely.

She gave a sudden shiver. Lady Bellingham had always been a very private person, making no attempt at any kind of social life on the island,

and she had decreed that they kept themselves to themselves during the voyage, and didn't mix with the other passengers.

Apart from the couple who had befriended Amy in recent days, she knew no one in this entire country but Marcus Bellingham. And right now, he was rushing off to his lawyer to set the inheritance in motion...

The disagreeable thought jolted her into action, and Amy rose from the refreshingly warm water so thoughtfully delivered for the more discerning clientele, and swathed herself in a bathrobe before starting to unpack. They had left Skye in a cooler summer than it was here in the south of Ireland, and she knew she would be thankful for her lighter garments now. But what to wear for dinner with this man, to whom she was sure she was a most unwelcome burden?

Dubiously, she considered a soft silky gown in a deep bronze colour that most people would think quite fine for a lady's companion. Her employer had had it made for her as a combined Christmas and birthday gift, with the brusque comment that she supposed a young woman would naturally be interested in such fripperies.

With its flattering style, its high-waisted bodice and the low square neckline that emphasised the swell of her breasts, Amy loved it, and was touched that Lady Bellingham had been so unusually thoughtful.

She had worn it at dinner on several occasions on board the ship, and she decided to wear it this evening in a spirit of bravado. And also so that she wouldn't disgrace Marcus, she admitted. Since she naturally had no mourning clothes with her, and could hardly expect him to have any, it wouldn't seem to be out of place.

Long before seven o'clock, she had taken out all of Lady Bellingham's personal effects and placed them on one side, leaving the clothes in the trunk. It wasn't a task she relished, but she knew it had to be done. And then she attended to herself, seeing the mauve shadows beneath her eyes, and the way her mouth still trembled now and then.

Amy lifted her chin, knowing *this would not do*. She could almost hear Lady B. saying the words to her, when something didn't suit her ladyship. The lady had always been stoical, and she wouldn't expect Amy to go to pieces now.

She pinched her cheeks to fill them with colour, and then brushed a hint of powder beneath her eyes to try to disguise the misery she felt. But *someone* had to mourn the passing of a good lady, she thought, with a spark of anger that was directed solely at the lady's nephew.

She descended the stairs to the foyer of the hotel nervously, wondering where she was supposed to meet Marcus. It wasn't done for a lady to knock on a gentleman's door, and in any case, she had no wish to appear to be on such intimate terms with him. Thankfully, she saw him waiting for her in the foyer, and he looked up as she came down the staircase, and they caught sight of each other at the same moment.

For a second, Amy's heart stopped, for he had obviously returned to the hotel some time ago, and had time to change his clothes and tidy himself. And he was a gentleman of some stature, she thought dumbly, on whom the cut of his elegant attire sat so very well. . .

'Well, well,' he said, as she reached him.

She saw how his eyes took in every inch of her, slowly, and deliberately, from the top of her glossy dark hair pinned up in tortoiseshell combs, to the bronze silk gown that caressed her body in a discreetly sensuous manner, and the matching elbow-length and fingerless evening gloves. 'It seems we have both decided to make an effort to play the part of congenial companions this evening, Miss Finch.'

'I believe that is the way your aunt would wish us to behave, sir,' Amy said swiftly, lest he should think she had made the effort with any devious thoughts in mind. He gave a small nod, and offered her his arm.

'I'm sure she would,' he said, without expression.

They were shown to a secluded corner table in the sparsely populated dining-room, and Amy began to feel increasingly nervous. They were being treated as a rather more intimate couple than was necessary, she thought, and it wasn't what she wanted at all. Nor, she thought, could Marcus possibly want it. As he ordered an aperitif for them both, she sat very still. She was unused to dining in hotels, and she allowed him to choose everything for her.

'I've gone through your aunt's belongings,' she said finally, in an attempt to make conversation. 'There are pieces of jewellery and toiletries that I'm sure you will want to keep or dispose of to someone—'

'What on earth would I want with such things?'

Amy floundered. 'Well, presumably you would keep them for your wife, or a special lady-friend,' she said, praying he wouldn't think her forward or that she was probing into his affairs. It wasn't her fault she was involved to the extent that she was, and she was becoming increasingly irritated with him for making her feel that way. . .

'I have no wife, as you very well know,' Marcus said. 'And as for a special lady-friend, my partner and I have been kept far too busy of late to think about such delightful diversions. Does that answer your question, Miss Finch?'

She felt her face grow hot, and knew she needed no rouge at that moment.

'I assure you I was not asking on my own account—'

'I don't remember implying that you were. But since you know so much about me, I thought it only prudent to fill in the missing gaps.'

She disliked him more and more. He was so arrogant, and she knew it would be best to keep their conversation less personal. He, it seemed, had other ideas.

'But I know less about you, and that seems very unfair, don't you think? I've been rather curious about my aunt's companion and the fine turn of phrase with which you wrote her letters. I was quite convinced they were not written exactly as she dictated. So while we dine, you may tell me all about yourself.'

And if anything was guaranteed to put an end to any discussion, that was it, thought Amy.

'There's nothing much to tell. I've been with your aunt for two years and we usually got along very well, surprising though you may find it,' she said carefully.

'I don't find it too surprising. I imagine anyone would find it easy to get along with you, as you put it.'

She looked at him. If he was trying to put her at her ease, it wasn't working. She put down her glass, and spoke with quiet dignity.

'I hope you are not flirting with me, sir. If you are, I think it's in very bad taste, in the circumstances—'

'Good God, woman, there's no need to look so outraged,' he said, with no apology for his words. 'I'm not about to ravish you. I'm merely trying to pay you a compliment, which you seem unusually reluctant to accept.'

'Then I do accept it, and I thank you, Mr Bellingham.'

'Marcus,' he said abruptly.

'What?' she said, staring.

'For pity's sake, let's drop this formality. You've addressed me informally too many times in your letters for us to be so stiff with one another now. My name is Marcus, as you also know very well. And I prefer to call you Amy instead of Miss Finch, which sounds far too much like a schoolmarm for comfort.'

She felt her shoulders tense and then relax. The way he cut through all the social niceties was at once refreshing and exciting. The word was in her head before she could stop it. Exciting, yes. . .and hadn't she always secretly envied Marcus Bellingham his exciting nomadic life, and taken a vicarious pleasure in sharing it, through his letters to his Aunt Maud?

'That's better. Thank God. I began to think we were to share an unbelievably miserable evening together,' Marcus went on, as he saw her slight smile.

'I'm sorry. I expected you to be more disturbed about your aunt, and—'

They were interrupted by the arrival of their meal, a succulent concoction of chicken and sauces and potatoes. Amy felt her mouth water, realising how hungry she felt.

'I'm sorry if my reaction is not exactly what you expected,' Marcus stated. 'But remember that I haven't seen her for ten years, and my memory of her is as dim as hers was of me. She still thought of me as a reckless youth, and I still thought of her as I last saw her, sternly lecturing me on my foolish ways.

'Of course, I'm sorry about what's happened, and the manner in which she died must have been very upsetting for you. But you can hardly blame me if I do not have the same feelings about her demise as you do.'

As he spoke, she looked at him through the flickering candlelight on the table between them. And, oh no, she conceded. Whatever else was said to describe the arrogant Marcus Bellingham, he was no reckless youth. He was a man, in every sense of the word.

She concentrated on her meal before she let other, unbidden feelings come into her mind. And reminded herself that she was not here as a possible bride, as so many young and hopeful working-class girls might view a handsome and well-connected man. She was here to finish something that had started some time ago, when Lady B. had first had the idea to see for herself what her nephew was up to. Though what Amy, or anyone else, could do to stop Marcus squandering his aunt's money, she had no idea. And, in any case, it was really none of her business.

'So tell me more about yourself. So far, you've only told me what I already know,' he went on, changing tactics as he saw her downcast eyes.

'But really, there's so little to tell—'

'Nonsense. Everyone has a past, so tell me yours. Or did you, like Aphrodite, spring fully-grown out of the foaming waves?'

She looked at him in astonishment, and he laughed. It was the first time she had heard him laugh, and it was a warm, rich sound, widening his mouth and showing the whiteness of his teeth. He put his hand across the table and squeezed hers for a moment, and when he released her, she could still feel the contact of his fingers over hers.

'Oh, my dear Miss Finch,' he said, reverting to mocking formality, 'your lovely face is a picture of disbelief that I would know about such things. Do you think my education began and ended with grubbing about in a river searching for elusive gold-dust?'

'I'm sure it did not, sir! Naturally, I know you are an educated man.'

She stopped. More educated than I, she was thinking, though even she knew of the legend of the beautiful goddess Aphrodite, who had had so many adoring lovers with whom she bathed and frolicked on the romantic island of Cyprus. . .

'And now I've offended you, and you still haven't

told me anything. Is it all part of your enigmatic charm to keep a gentleman in suspense?'

She found his light tone patronising, rather than reassuring, which was what she assumed it was meant to be.

'I employ no such guile, sir, and if you want to know all about me, then I can tell you very quickly.'

'Please don't rush the telling. We have all evening,' Marcus said.

Amy stared at him unblinkingly. 'I cared for my grandmother in her last years, and used to read to her every evening. That's how I came to know the classical works, since she so delighted in hearing about myths and legends. But when she died, I was obliged to look for employment, and since my role in life seemed to be that of companion to an elderly lady, a kindly friend referred me to your aunt who was seeking a female companion. Does that answer your questions?'

He looked at her just as thoughtfully. 'It seems like a terrible waste to me.'

She took offence at his remark. 'I assure you I don't consider my life wasted at all, and I hope your aunt would not have thought so either.'

'You misunderstand me, Amy. Knowing my aunt's finicky ways, I know you must have been as good a companion and comfort to her, as you were to your grandmother. But a lovely young woman such as yourself is not meant to spend all her days and nights catering to the whims of old ladies.'

She flushed again as the conversation became all too personal once more.

'I chose it, and I was perfectly happy with it,' she said stiffly.

'And did you never yearn for other things? I know my aunt was not a social person, and there must have been times when you felt restricted, and longed to dance or to visit a theatre or go to the mainland. And did you never have thoughts of finding a husband, which I understand is every young woman's goal in life?'

Oh, but he was impossible! And she wished she had a better command of words to put him sorely in his place.

'Not everyone is a husband-seeker, sir, just as not every man is a wife-seeker. There's time enough for all that, as you have apparently found out for yourself, since there was never any mention of a lady's name in your letters.'

She spoke daringly, and realised she was almost holding her breath. It didn't matter a jot to her whether or not there was a lady on Marcus Bellingham's horizon, but she knew she would feel oddly betrayed if there was such a person, and that he had kept it a secret from her—or rather, from Aunt Maud, she reminded herself hurriedly.

'I have no need for a wife for the present,' he said coolly. 'My work is my wife, and until my project produces the riches I believe that it will, it takes up all my energies.'

'What a waste,' Amy heard herself retort, and then she slapped her hand to her mouth in shock, knowing she had really gone too far, and wondering if she had really said the words that echoed his. It was so impertinent!

To her amazement, Marcus was laughing again.

'Oh, Amy, thank God you're not as stuffy as you first appeared. I always suspected you had a sense

of fun that was subdued by my aunt, and now I
know you have some spirit too. I like that in a
woman, so if I ever decide to look for a wife, I may
just give you first choice.'

'How very kind of you,' she said, oozing sarcasm.
'And if I'm ever in the position of being at the
workhouse door, I may just accept your crumbs, but
I doubt it.'

She reminded herself of her need to be civil to
him, but it seemed increasingly impossible to do.
They seemed to have crossed so many boundaries
in so little time, she marvelled. He was outspoken,
and so was she, given half a chance. And she knew
how right his assessment of her previous
situation was.

She *had* been subdued by his aunt, and even
though it had been an uncomplicated life, it had held
no sparks. At least, not the kind that were flashing
between herself and Marcus Bellingham now, in a
way that made her feel more alive than she had felt
in a very long time.

And it was all wrong to feel that way, she thought
guiltily, remembering the bereavement that seemed
to mean more to her than it had to him. But she had
to admit that she was getting to understand him a
little more now. Ten years without physical contact
with his aunt was a very long time, and although
he had always done his duty in writing regularly,
he had only ever got disapproval from her.

By the time they finished their meal, Amy wondered awkwardly what they were supposed to do
about the lady's effects. It wasn't done for her to
invite him to her room, but they could hardly bring

down the box and go through it in one of the public rooms of the hotel.

Besides, she really didn't want to do anything more tonight. She was suddenly extraordinarily tired. It had been a long day, and the events of the past had all been leading up to this day when she'd had to tell Marcus such awful news. The reaction to all of it was setting in fast, and all Amy longed for was to go to bed and sleep. In vain, she tried to stifle a yawn, but he saw it, and spoke sympathetically.

'You must be exhausted. I suggest that you have an early night, and perhaps you could make a list of my aunt's effects for me to consider. We'll spend a leisurely morning going through it if you wish, and in the afternoon we have an appointment with Mr Thomas Varley.'

Amy was alerted at once. She knew that name. She had gone with Lady B. to her lawyer's chambers on the island some months ago, and waited in an outer office for an endless length of time while various changes to her Will had been drawn up. And she knew that copies of it had been dispatched for safekeeping to Mr Thomas Varley, a partner in the legal firm of Varley, Lester and O'Rourke, of Dublin.

'*We* have an appointment? But surely there's no reason for me to be involved in this? I can easily find something to do to amuse myself.'

Besides, she had never had anything to do with lawyers, and the very thought of a Will reading— if that was what was implied here—always made her nervous.

'I'm afraid you do. You need to give verbal evidence that the letter from the ship's captain and the medical certificate are authentic. Varley insists that you are to be there. Also I daresay my aunt has left you one or two trinkets in her Will, and if they are among her effects it will be a simple matter to transfer them into your keeping.'

He was so formal again, and Amy swallowed, knowing there was no help for it. She would have to visit the lawyer's chambers with him, and hear the solemn bequests read out. It was a natural thing for someone to want their goods and chattels left to their nearest and dearest, but to Amy it had always seemed so ghoulish, as if the person was reaching out from the grave—or in this case, from the watery deep—to dictate the future of those who were left behind.

In just the same way she had dictated her authoritarian letters to Marcus. . . And Amy tried to squash the guilty memory that sometimes, just *sometimes*, she had fantasised that she was writing to someone of her very own. . .

'I'll say goodnight then,' she murmured, when her thoughts were taking an altogether too-disturbing turn.

He rose from the table and held out his hand. She took it without thinking, and felt his fingers curl around hers. She bit her lip, for it was the first really human contact she had had with anyone for a very long time. And she was suddenly so overcome with emotion at all that had happened, and all that was yet to come, that she would have liked nothing more than to rest her head on his shoulder and weep.

'Allow me to escort you to your room, and I shall look forward to seeing you in the morning,' he said gravely, and she wondered if he had had a sudden stab of remorse at the callous way he had spoken about his aunt earlier in the day, or indeed, if he ever let his emotions get in the way of his ambition. The brief feeling of empathy towards him vanished, and she removed her hand from his.

'I thank you, but there's really no need. I'm quite capable of finding my own way,' she said, and she walked ahead of him out of the dining-room and up the curving staircase. When she reached the landing, she glanced down.

He was still standing there, watching her, and she had the oddest feeling that, however resourceful and adventurous he might be, Marcus Bellingham was still a lonely man. As lonely as herself. And her hands and eyes were damp as she fumbled for her key and let herself into her bedroom.

Amy spent a restless night. She was truly exhausted, but although she fell asleep as soon as her head touched the pillow, her sleep was beset by dreams of being cast adrift in an angry sea. And she awoke in the middle of the night, trembling and fearful of her plight.

Pull yourself together, girl, she admonished herself in a silent facsimile of Lady Bellingham's strident tones. Marcus won't throw you to the wolves, and even if he doesn't give you the fare home, there are other alternatives. You're not spineless, are you? You've worked for your crust before, and you can work again.

Of course she could work. She was young and she was healthy. She could even work here in Dublin. . . The thoughts and possibilities tumbled around in her head, half-formed, and only half-acceptable. She wasn't sure she would ever want to remain here. It certainly hadn't been planned that way.

And it wasn't home. It was a land of strangers with strange ways and quick voices that she didn't yet know. As a door banged somewhere in the hotel, she brought her thoughts up short. What was she even thinking about? She had no intention of remaining here, none at all. As soon as she could persuade Marcus to pay for her fare, and a passage on a ship could be arranged, she was going home.

But home to what? the insidious thought crept into her mind. She had not allowed it to enter there before, but she couldn't rid herself of it now. There was nothing for her to go back to now. No Lady B.; no honourable position as a lady's companion; not even a real home, for unless Marcus intended to live on Skye, she presumed the house and grounds would be sold. . . She shivered in the night, despite the day's heat that still lingered, and punched the pillow in an attempt to find a more comfortable spot to rest her head.

She dressed more soberly in the morning, and when they met for breakfast, she saw that Marcus, too, had donned his more casual wear, rather than the formal clothes of last night. But he had the kind of lean, rangy male figure that would look good in a sack, Amy thought, with mild resentment. If ever he sought a wife, he'd surely have no problem in finding one!

And if it didn't seem a priority in his life, she wondered cynically just how many young ladies would find him an even more attractive proposition when they discovered he had inherited his aunt's fortune.

'Did you sleep well?' he greeted her, once they had taken their places in the dining-room, and had given their breakfast orders.

'Tolerably well,' she answered, 'but I had too much on my mind to relax completely, no matter how tired I was.'

'Understandably so,' he said.

His professed understanding annoyed her. How could he possibly know what worries beset her? He may think he was hard done by in not having received an advance on his inheritance for his reckless schemes, but Lady B. had always been generous in her regular allowance to him, as Amy knew.

'I thought we would take a drive around the town later this morning,' he went on to say, just as if they were ordinary visitors. 'You'd like to take a look at some of the buildings, I dare say, before we go to Varley's chambers.'

'As you wish,' she murmured.

She took a deep breath. Her grandmother had always said there was no point in hiding behind a problem, and thinking it would just go away. It was far better to bring it out in the open, air it, dust it off, and solve it as best you could. Amy looked at Marcus directly, her hazel eyes huge, since she was literally about to throw herself on his mercy.

'I'm embarrassed at being a nuisance to you—'

'You're not,' he said.

'Of course I am, and please don't patronise me by pretending otherwise! I know I would be in your debt by making a request, and you must believe

me when I say that I absolutely *hate* making it—'
Annoyingly she heard herself dithering all the same.

'What the devil are you going on about? If there's
something you wish to ask me, then ask it. I'm not
a complete ogre, am I?'

She looked at him steadily. No, he wasn't an ogre.
Given any other circumstances, she would have
admitted that he was a very personable man indeed.
In fact, the most personable man she had ever met.
But then, she hadn't met too many, she admonished
herself, so she had better not let herself be swayed
by a pair of fine dark eyes and a very kissable
mouth. . . She felt the blood surge in her veins as
the unexpectedly erotic thought swept through her.

'Well? What is this request?' Marcus asked more
gently, seeing what he thought was fright reddening
her cheeks and making her bosom heave painfully
fast in her high-waisted morning dress.

Amy swallowed. 'My—my passage home,' she
whispered. 'I'm very much afraid I have no means
of my own at all, and I was totally reliant on your
aunt. And she—she had refused to purchase return
tickets for us, since she had no idea how long we
would expect to stay.'

Her voice trailed away as Marcus looked at her,
saying nothing. His voice was mirthless when
he spoke.

'You mean until she decided whether or not to
give me up as being a worthless cause, is that it?'

'I didn't mean that at all.'

'Yes, my dear Miss Finch, I believe you did. Your
face constantly gives you away. Did no one else
ever tell you?'

'Frequently,' she said angrily, looking down at

her plate on which a mound of eggs and bacon had arrived, and which she thought she couldn't possibly eat.

'And you shouldn't deny something that is so very attractive. Far too many young women hide their feelings behind a mask of frigidity or a totally blank expression. But I suppose I must apologise for making yet another compliment, since they seem to bother you so much.'

He was taunting her, and she thought how rich it was that he condemned those who hid their feelings. For didn't he do exactly the same thing, and had stated as much with a kind of arrogant pride!

'Compliments do not bother me, providing they are sincerely meant.'

'Then you must believe me, for I never say things I don't mean. Now then, did you make out that list for me to see?' he said, suddenly brisk and businesslike.

Amy welcomed the change of attitude, for there had been a warming in his dark eyes that she didn't rightly fathom. It had sent that *frisson* of excitement running through her veins again, and she had the sense to know it was a dangerous feeling, for he couldn't be in the least bit romantically interested in a lady's companion. Any more than she was interested in *him*. . .

'I have it here,' she said, pulling the piece of paper out of the pocket of her dress.

'Good. Then we'll sit in the hotel lounge when we've finished eating, and go through it together, though you'll have more idea than I what's of value and what isn't.'

Amy wondered what he would do with the jewellery. She knew that some of it was indeed quite valuable, and some was of more sentimental value. She guessed that he'd probably sell the lot and put the money to the rest of his inheritance. She felt a brief sadness for the lady's lovely things, that would end up on a shelf in a jewellery emporium as 'having once belonged to a lady of quality' and no doubt sold off for a bargain price. . .

But when she showed Marcus the list later, he merely frowned, and decided after all that he couldn't make head or tail out of it.

'You need to see it all,' she agreed. 'Should I bring it down?'

'I'd rather we went through it in private, if you have no objection. If some of the stuff is of value, it's best not to have it on public display.'

After a moment, she nodded. The sitting-room in her suite was perfectly respectable, and it could hardly be called an assignation. Besides, she was merely the hired help, and could be disregarded as being almost part of the furniture.

'I've no objection,' she said.

It was a difficult task. Not all the pieces had any meaning for Amy, and most had none at all for Marcus. She couldn't ever remember Lady Bellingham wearing the silver hair ornaments, which seemed far too frivolous for her. But she must have been young once. . . Finally, Marcus put everything back into the box and spoke shortly.

'Let's leave it for now. I need some fresh air, and the morning is cooler for sightseeing.'

Amy was only too glad to agree, and to sit in a hired carriage with him while he pointed out the

sights of Dublin, which she freely acknowledged
was a beautiful old city with its fine public buildings
and parks.

'I hadn't expected it to be so—so civilised,' she
said, for want of a better word.

'Oh, we're very civilised, Amy, though you
would find things rather different in the mountains.'

She took little notice of his comment. Such rugged territory was of no interest to her. Since his
aunt wasn't here, there was no reason for her to see
it at all. All she cared about now was getting back
home. And it struck her that if Lady Bellingham
was leaving her a small legacy in her Will, she might
not need to rely on Marcus's generosity at all. The
thought cheered her more with every moment that
passed, and she was thankful to have it at the back
of her mind.

Chapter Three

At four o'clock that afternoon they arrived at Thomas Varley's legal chambers, and despite her new feeling of anticipation, Amy also felt a mixture of anxiety and distaste at having to go through this ordeal. It was as if Lady B. herself was hovering in one of the dark corners of the room, watching and waiting to see what reaction her legacies would produce. . .

Were all lawyers' chambers blessed with the same musty smells of ink and sealing wax, old tomes and airless interiors?

Amy tried to shake off her mounting anxiety as they were invited to sit down in Varley's office, while the lawyer himself sat behind a vast desk and cracked his fingers ever so slightly from time to time as he shuffled the papers in a file. She was mesmerised by that finger-cracking, and tried to stave off her nervousness by speculating as to whether or not they would eventually snap. . .

The two men were already acquainted, since Varley acted for Marcus in whatever capacity was required, which included forwarding his regular allowance from his aunt. Amy began to wish she didn't know so much about the situation already. Considering that Lady B. had chosen to keep so much of her life private, Amy had been obliged to become her confidante in most matters. Except for the contents of her latest Will.

'Now then, my dear sir,' Varley said in a clipped accent with more than a hint of Northern England in it. 'Please allow me first of all to offer you my sincere condolences once more, and also to extend my sympathies to your aunt's companion. It must have been a most trying time for you, Miss Finch.'

'It was. Thank you, sir,' Amy murmured, keeping her eyes lowered. *A trying time*? Was that the only way a cold-blooded lawyer could describe the horror of the latter part of that voyage? But having made a token gesture, and confirmed the ship's captain's letter and death certificate, she realised he was paying her scant attention now.

'You know why you're here, of course, Mr Bellingham, and I suggest we waste no more time.'

'That would be best,' Marcus said curtly. 'I've no wish to remain in Dublin any longer than necessary, and will be glad to get back to Callanby and my own affairs.'

He showed such little concern now for being in any way responsible for Amy's plight, she thought indignantly. All he cared about was getting his hands on his aunt's money and ploughing it into his mad scheme. And probably losing the lot, she thought, with a cynicism that would have done credit to Lady Bellingham's.

The lawyer opened a bulky envelope and spread it out on the desk in front of him. Amy could see the ornate heading on the top sheet, announcing that this was the last Will and Testament of. . .

'Lady Maud Bellingham,' Thomas Varley stated, 'was a wealthy woman, as you are well aware, Mr Bellingham. And as her only living relative, you would naturally have expected everything to go to you on her death.'

'Naturally,' Marcus said, but his eyes narrowed at the odd phrasing. Surely the cantankerous old dear hadn't left the bulk of it to one of her pet charities, or something equally futile?

For though he knew she had despaired of him and his ambitions, there was a strong sense of family loyalty in Marcus, and he'd hoped to make her see that he was no ne'er-do-well, and had really succeeded in this venture to which he'd given such time and thought. That day would never come now, and he felt a real pang of regret.

Amy, too, realised her heart was beating faster, trying to read something in the lawyer's words. A sixth sense told her there was going to be something unexpected in Lady B.'s Will, and for the first time she wished she'd been privileged to see it before now.

Some surprises in life were less than welcome, especially if they were destined to incur the rage of the man sitting beside her. And she could see by Marcus's clenched hands and rigid demeanour that he was prepared to be displeased, if not downright furious.

Amy was briefly sorry for him. Lady B. had frequently been scathing about what she called her nephew's folly, but Amy had always had a soft spot for a young man who had the will to follow his

dream. And he was certainly not reckless, she
acknowledged. He gave everything considerable
thought.

'Will you get on with it, man?' Marcus was saying testily now. Varley looked at him coldly, and
then shrugged.

Marcus had been his client for a long time; Varley
had dealt with the more-than-handsome allowances
that came from Skye for him on a regular basis, and
had suggested to his aunt long ago that it would be
advisable for him to keep a copy of her Will in his
chambers. That advice proved to be sound now.

Varley also knew Marcus for a hot-tempered man
who spoke plainly and never minced his words. If
there was something that had to be said, Marcus
Bellingham would say it. And if it didn't need saying, he could be equally obstinate and impatient. But
there were procedures to adhere to, Varley thought
doggedly, and he droned through the normal flowery
wording that the said lady was of sound mind,
and was stating her wishes in the presence of
witnesses. . .

' "To my loved nephew, Marcus Bellingham, I
leave the bulk of all my worldly goods and chattels.
My house on the Island of Skye is to be sold, and
the proceeds added to the residue of the estate. All
dealings will be done through my lawyers on the
island, and Mr Thomas Varley of Dublin." '

He paused, while all this was digested, and Amy
saw Marcus's hands visibly relax. There would be
nothing to stop him going ahead with all his plans
now. But he was too astute not to have noticed a
certain word that the lawyer had stated.

'You say the *bulk* of the goods and chattels, sir.

What exactly does that mean?' he demanded.

Varley held up his hand. 'Pray let me go on, sir. There are several smaller bequests for Lady Bellingham's household staff, and one other, rather more unusual one.'

Amy thought he looked less than easy now, and hoped it wasn't some outrageously large gift to herself that would incense her nephew. Though she couldn't imagine why the lady would do such a thing. Amy had been a loyal companion and useful confidante to whom Lady B. could rant and rage whenever she felt the need, but never a close friend.

' "To every servant in my employ, save Miss Amy Finch, I leave the sum of twenty pounds to spend as they wish." '

Amy's eyelids flickered at hearing her name, and waited with growing anticipation, too agog now to care what Marcus might be feeling. Within minutes she might learn of the means of her passage home; the fact that Lady B. had singled her out must mean more than the handsome sum of twenty pounds. . .

'Lady Bellingham has dictated the remainder of her Will in more personal terms,' Varley went on. 'If you will permit it, I will read it out in its entirety, and I would be obliged if neither of you interrupted until I have finished.'

'Pompous oaf,' Amy thought she heard Marcus mutter beneath his breath, but he gave a curt nod and folded his arms. The lawyer continued reading.

' "I am extremely fond of my nephew, though he may not believe it, since he knows full well that I have never approved of his bohemian way of life, and made no bones in telling him so. Nevertheless, that does not detract from the affection I have always felt for him." '

Amy didn't dare look at Marcus, unable to guess at his feelings at this unexpected declaration of affection. But as if it did him any good now! People should show their feelings while they were alive, not when it was too late. . .

' "I wish for nothing more than my nephew's well-being, and have given considerable thought to my final words. They are these: within six months of my death, unless circumstances have changed between the parties concerned, I wish my nephew, Marcus Bellingham, to marry Miss Amy Finch." '

He ignored the audible gasps from his listeners and went on relentlessly.

' "My reasons for this are sound. Miss Finch is a respectable and sober young woman, who will exercise a sensible restraint on my nephew. Their marriage will also prevent some gold-seeking and quite unsuitable person from getting her hands on the Bellingham fortune." '

'Good God, man, you cannot expect me to agree to this!' Marcus said, leaping up from his chair to stand with both hands planted flat on the lawyer's desk. His dark eyes blazed. 'It's nothing short of blackmail.'

'Nor will I agree to it!' Amy raged. 'I won't be manipulated in this way.'

And to be referred to as such a dull frump was the ultimate indignity.

'I have merely read you the terms of the Will as your aunt decreed, Mr Bellingham,' Varley said, waving him to sit down again. 'And there is one more small paragraph you would do well to hear.'

Marcus glared at the man, and Amy realised that he had never once looked at her since hearing his aunt's dictum. She was awash with misery. She might not be his choice of bride—indeed, she had never even considered such a thing as being remotely likely, or desirable—but he needn't be so ungracious as to make her feel she was the last woman on earth he would want to marry!

'Read it, and then I shall tell you exactly what I think of this outrageous suggestion,' Marcus snapped.

' "Unless my nephew agrees to my wishes, he will inherit nothing but the continuing allowance he already receives, and half of my remaining fortune will go to an animal sanctuary and other good causes. He may only inherit the residue when he marries some other suitable person of whom my lawyer approves. In this event, the said Miss Finch may choose any two pieces of my jewellery that she so desires." '

Amy gasped. The Will would seem to be watertight, and she could sense the fury that seemed to have struck Marcus dumb for the moment. Thomas Varley handed him a copy of the Will.

'You may study this at your leisure, sir, but please understand that I will need confirmation of your decision before I can release any of your aunt's fortune to you, other than your monthly allowance.'

He was very much in control now, and apart from anything else, Amy was acutely embarrassed at having to listen to this. It put Marcus in an impossible and humiliating position, and of course he would never agree to it. . .and yet, if he did not, he would lose everything he needed so badly. . .

She swallowed, wondering if he would stoop low enough to marry for money, which was the very thing his aunt was guarding against in her choice of his bride. The whole situation was bizarre, and she had no idea how he was going to react.

'I daresay you'll want to talk things over carefully with Miss Finch,' Varley was saying, pointedly glancing at the clock in the corner of the room. 'And I suggest you both take your time in giving the matter serious thought.'

Marcus stood up, almost knocking over his chair in his anger. 'I shall return tomorrow, sir.'

'I'm afraid I already have a full day of appointments, Mr Bellingham—'

'And I will remind you that I leave for Callanby the day after tomorrow, and have no intention of changing my plans. I will be here tomorrow at noon. If you expect your lawyer's pound of flesh for the miserable work that you do, I suggest that you see to it that all other appointments are cancelled at that time.'

He turned on his heel, and Amy threw Varley an apologetic glance as she followed Marcus quickly out of the chambers and into the street below. To her horror, he rounded on her at once.

'Did you know of this?' he snapped. 'Was it something you and Aunt Maud cooked up between you, with the intention of coming here and worming your way into my affections?'

She couldn't believe his arrogance, and her eyes flashed angrily.

'I most certainly did not know of it! And nor would I ever have agreed to something so underhand. How dare you accuse me of it!' She drew a deep breath. 'And let me tell you another thing. I wouldn't marry you if you were the only man left on earth!'

Several passers-by looked on in amusement at these two apparently quarrelsome lovers. Marcus grabbed her arm and almost bundled her into the waiting hire carriage. He told the driver to drive them anywhere he chose, while he and the lady conducted their business in private.

He didn't speak for a long time, but simply stared at her, his eyes as darkly gleaming as ripe chestnuts. The intensity of his gaze made her squirm, but she hoped savagely that it served some purpose. Because if he couldn't see the genuine distress and outrage she was feeling at this turn of events, then he was the most insensitive man in the world. But didn't she already know that?

'I'm truly sorry for the predicament your aunt has put you in,' she said stiffly. 'But I assure you it was none of my doing, and was as much a shock to me as it was to you. You must believe me, Marcus.'

'Why must I?' he said.

Her eyes flashed at him. 'Because I'm an honest person, that's why. Knowing your aunt as you did, do you think she would have hired anyone whom she thought was less than trustworthy? And did you ever know her to do a devious thing in her life?'

At last he shook his head. 'No. So, supposing I do begin to accept that you knew nothing of this—'

'I did *not*,' she almost shouted, feeling as foolish and helpless as a naughty child accused of stealing apples, and furious at the feeling.

'Then what are we going to do about it?' he said, his rage changing to calm with lightning speed.

'Why, nothing, I should think. It's hardly something either of us wishes, and no doubt if I choose two pieces of jewellery as she wished——' she swallowed painfully, because it all seemed so terribly calculating '——then I can sell them and buy my passage home, and we need never contact each other again.'

'That's true,' he conceded. 'And it would seem to solve your immediate problem, which hadn't even occurred to me. But it doesn't solve mine, does it?'

'Yours?'

He leaned towards her, and in the confines of the carriage, his face was necessarily close to hers. She could see the faint afternoon shadow on his chin, so noticeable on a dark-haired man, and said to show virility, though Amy had no experience of it. She could see the texture of his skin and the outdoor ruggedness of it that came from long hours of hard work, and she knew instinctively that whatever Lady Bellingham had thought of him, he wasn't a shirker.

'I mean, my dear Miss Finch, that unless I do as my aunt dictates and marry you within six months, I will undoubtedly lose everything I've ever worked for.'

Amy ran her tongue around her dry lips.

'I'm sorry,' she mumbled.

'Why should you be? It's not your fault a madwoman saw a way of curbing her nephew's reckless ways by marrying him off to a——what was it?——a respectable and sober young woman?'

Amy flushed. 'I assure you I deeply resent such a description!'

'Which part? Being respectable or being sober? Or do neither of them apply to you?'

He seemed to delight in taunting her, she fumed. In the last few minutes his tone had altered to what she could only call calculating, and she felt a new alarm. Did he think he could get round her in some way? Though, in what way? There was only one. . . The next minute, she felt his arm slide around her shoulders and give them a gentle squeeze.

'We both need time alone to think, Amy, and we'll discuss it more thoroughly over dinner this evening. Meanwhile, I suggest you consider all the possibilities carefully, as I intend doing.'

As far as she was concerned there was nothing to consider, except which pieces of Lady B.'s jewellery would fetch enough to send her home and give her a little to live on for some months. She bit her lip as such a mercenary and demeaning thought entered her mind, but it was far better than the alternative. . .

'D'you want me to go round again, sir?' they heard the driver shout out, and they both realised they had approached the London Hotel for the second time.

'No. You may stop here, driver,' Marcus said.

As they alighted, Amy somehow knew that if life had been simple before, it was never going to be simple again. When they entered the hotel, Marcus lifted her fingers to his lips and kissed them.

Over the back of her hand, her eyes met his in great suspicion, sure that this gesture of affection was all for the benefit of other guests in the foyer. Though why it should matter what impression they had of this unlikely couple, she couldn't think.

Unless. . .unless it was to establish that they were indeed affectionate towards one another, so that should any future announcement be made. . .

Outraged, she snatched her hand away from his.

'Until this evening then, Amy,' Marcus said coolly, quite aware of her reaction. He turned away on business of his own, while she mounted the stair-case angrily, feeling as if she had aged a hundred years in the last fateful hour.

She sat down heavily on her bed. She supposed she had been as close to Lady B. as anyone was permitted to be during the last two years, yet she had been left nothing but two pieces of jewellery... though she knew very well that this was a far more valuable legacy than the twenty pounds each of the household servants were to get. It was more per-sonal, more special... Without warning, the tears slid down Amy's cheeks.

She had never been covetous, and in the normal way it wouldn't have mattered if she'd been left nothing at all. But suddenly she could imagine Lady B. thinking hard about what to leave her 'respectable and sober' companion...and instead of annoying her, it was a strangely endearing compliment, coming from a lady who rarely made any.

But Amy was also a very feminine young woman, and whereas she had bundled the jewel cases into the box with the rest of Lady B.'s effects, she took them out now, assessing them very differently. Some of them were very fine indeed, and had hardly been worn.

Amy knew they had been given to her by her late husband, and that since his death she had discarded any idea of fine dressing or bedecking herself with jewels, and had gone into virtual seclusion.

When she had learned of this, Amy had found it odd to associate her austere elderly employer with a young and passionate wife who had once loved and been loved. . .but these jewels had so obviously been given in love. She picked up one necklace after another and held them against her slender throat, where they sparkled and shone. And they all spoke of a love too great ever to be repeated.

Amy was unable to imagine how it felt to be loved like that. Love hadn't touched her yet, but she was young and romantic enough to want it with all her heart. And an arranged marriage of convenience, to a man who stood to gain an inheritance with which to further his ambition, was *not* the stuff of romance. When Amy married, she would be marrying for love, and nothing else would do.

By now, she realised she was standing in front of the dressing-table mirror with clenched hands, her heart beating fast. Lady B.'s gold-and-sapphire pendant was around her neck, and she saw how it rose and fell against her throat. And the treacherous thought swept into her mind that if only things had been different, and if only they had met in other circumstances, then Marcus Bellingham could be the one. Oh, yes, he could so easily be the one. . .

She removed the pendant with shaking hands, for it would be the worst foolishness of her life to fall in love with such a man. An adventurer, who was presumably capable of letting money slip through his fingers like grains of sand in pursuing dreams. . . She forced herself to repeat his aunt's words, rather than thinking that now she had met the man, he didn't fit her earlier image of him.

But he was undoubtedly attractive to any gullible young girl. And she had better keep that description of herself uppermost in her mind too, Amy thought grimly.

By the time she had dressed for dinner that evening, she still hadn't made her choice of jewels, and she descended the hotel staircase with more nervousness than on the previous evening. But she had made her resolve, and she had to be true to herself. She could never enter into a loveless marriage, no matter how persuasive Marcus Bellingham might be. And in any case, he would probably be as totally resistant to it as she was herself.

He was waiting for her again, and it was almost a repetition of the previous evening. But not quite. This time, there were things they had to discuss, however difficult. . .

'You look stunning,' he said, as he came forward to greet her. His eyes were frankly admiring, though she wore the same dress as she had worn before, and she was immediately suspicious of this sudden charm.

'I thank you, sir,' she said icily. 'But you must be mistaken, since I've been feeling sorely put out ever since this afternoon.'

And if that wasn't enough to deter any red-blooded man, she couldn't think what was. But she had reckoned without Marcus's single-mindedness. And she should have remembered it.

He reached for her hand and kissed it again, but this time he turned her hand over so that his lips touched her palm. And the contact sent a shiver of desire running through her so swiftly that Amy felt her eyes dilate. He curled her fingers over her palm, and spoke softly.

'That's for you to keep and to remember. Our business is a long way from being concluded yet, Amy.'

He escorted her into the dining-room. Several other guests glanced their way as they were seated, smiling at the solicitous gentleman and the lovely young girl, and obviously seeing them as a loving and handsome couple.

But Amy saw his plan immediately. He intended to seduce her into this cold, loveless marriage, simply to get his hands on his aunt's money. It was despicable. . .but it was far more than that. It was humiliating. It made her feel less than a woman. And although she admitted that he had all the right words, they were only words, and they meant nothing.

'I think it best if we conclude our business, as you call it, as speedily as possible, sir.'

'Why are you afraid of me, Amy?'

She flinched, wishing he wasn't so blunt, and perfectly aware that he wasn't far wrong.

'I'm not afraid of you—'

'Then stop calling me sir, and keeping me at a distance. We've already come too far for such nonsense.'

'I don't know what you mean—' she said.

'I think you do. Don't tell me that you haven't spent the last couple of hours debating the alternatives in your mind. But you're far luckier than I, of course.'

'Really? Because I'd be getting a husband I don't want, and a lifestyle that certainly doesn't appeal to me!'

Her words ran away with her, and she was angry

with herself for letting him know that she had indeed
let the possibility enter her mind, if only for the
briefest moment. But also because she had spoken
as if she had really toyed with accepting the
preposterous idea.

'No. Because you have choices,' he said quietly
now. 'And when you look at it logically, I do not.
My entire future, and everything that I've worked
for, depends on you. It's a heavy responsibility,
wouldn't you say, Miss Finch?'

Oh, but this wasn't fair! Until this afternoon, she
had hoped he'd see her as his responsibility, and
would simply pay her passage home. Now that responsibility had shifted, and he was putting all the
onus for his future on to her.

'I don't see that I have any choice at all,' she
said hotly. 'You surely cannot expect me to agree
to your aunt's proposal—and nor do I imagine for
one moment that you would want to go through with
it. What honourable man would?'

She knew she was throwing him a challenge, and
also implying that she would think very little of a
man who put riches before honour. She didn't look
at him as she spoke, but when he said nothing, her
gaze was drawn to his face.

'Do you think me a man of so little honour?'

'What else can I think, if you can even contemplate this idea of Lady Bellingham's—'

'But can you honestly tell me that you have not?'

She felt the painful flush in her cheeks again,
because in her wildest moments, she knew that, oh,
yes, she had imagined being this man's wife. She
hadn't even been aware that the thoughts had been
conscious ones, but they had been there just the

same, insidious and evocative. And perhaps they had always been there. . .

'I see that you have, and I think you forget how your face gives you away, Amy.'

She didn't like the arrogant satisfaction in his voice, and she replied curtly.

'I hardly think the idea can appeal to you, anyway. I'm sure there must be some other lady you would far rather marry than someone of your aunt's choosing. Someone who wasn't simply *respectable and sober* enough to keep you in check!'

She tried to think back. And, yes, he *had* occasionally mentioned various names in his letters to his aunt, but there was never one that occurred often. And she also recalled that he'd once told his aunt he was enjoying life far too much to think about taking a wife. Which probably underlined his entire attitude to matrimony, Amy thought scornfully.

'There's no one else,' Marcus said, 'and I don't believe you are otherwise attached, either.'

It was a great temptation to tell him there was a fiancé waiting for her back on the island, but she knew he wouldn't believe her. She'd never make a convincing liar, and besides, her face would give her away. . .

They ate their meal in uneasy silence, and when it was over, Marcus placed his napkin on the table, and looked at her thoughtfully.

'So what are we going to do about it?'

She was still defiant. 'I've no intention of being a pawn in your affairs, Marcus, and I'm afraid I can't agree to your aunt's wishes. I'm sorry, but there it is.'

'So we must think about the alternative. Have you chosen the pieces of jewellery you want to keep?'

She started, not expecting this. She had expected anger, or cajoling, and instead he was perfectly calm. Far too calm. But if this was the way he intended to accept her decision, then she was prepared to answer him just as coolly.

'Not really. It's difficult. There are some lovely pieces, of course, and I know they were your uncle's gifts to his wife. He must have loved her very much.'

'He did. She wasn't always the woman you knew,' he said. 'She was far livelier and more tolerant in her younger days. And yes, my uncle loved her very much.'

'And that's how it should be for married people,' Amy couldn't resist saying. 'Which makes it all the harder for me to understand why she made this proviso in her Will.'

Marcus laughed. 'Can't you? She made it plain enough. It was to safeguard her foolish nephew from the clutches of some fortune-hungry female. At least she was right in her belief that you don't fit into that category, otherwise you'd have had no hesitation in agreeing to it.'

'Well, thank you for that,' she said.

'And I'm sure you've realised that while you may choose any two pieces of jewellery that you wish, and live handsomely for a while on the proceeds if you chose to sell them, you could also have it all.'

Amy frowned. 'What do you mean?'

'I don't believe you can be that naïve, my dear Miss Finch. If you marry me, then as my wife you would naturally have all my aunt's jewels and personal possessions. I would have no possible use for diamonds and pearls, other than to see them around your pretty neck.'

His glance went lower, to where the deep neckline of her dress was bare of jewellery, and revealed the creamy swell of her breasts. Involuntarily, she pressed her hand to her throat, and felt the pulse beating wildly there.

'I'm sorry,' she murmured almost inaudibly, fighting down the sudden surge of excitement in her veins. She had never felt like this before. Never been assessed so blatantly, or been made to feel so much like a desirable woman. And she had to remind herself that it was all a ploy, that he had his own reasons for seducing her with his eyes and his voice, and his sheer animal masculinity. . .

Marcus sighed. 'Then it seems we have reached stalemate for the moment. It's a pity, but I don't give up easily, as you very well know. And I promise you it would be whatever kind of marriage you choose. One that was as loving and fulfilled as my aunt's, or a marriage in name only, or—'

He paused, and she swallowed, wondering if he really meant the words he said. A loving and fulfilled marriage. . . There were plenty of arranged marriages among his class; some unions were frequently happy and successful. . .and probably just as many others failed miserably.

'Or what?' Amy said.

'Or there's another way. But we'll leave it for now, and I suggest we discuss it in the morning.'

Chapter Four

By the time Amy reached her bedroom, she saw that a maid had already lit the oil-lamp on the little side table and turned back the quilted bedcover. She sat down heavily on the edge of the bed, wondering just what devious plans were going round in Marcus Bellingham's head right now.

For didn't she know well enough that he possessed the capacity for lightning changes of mood and direction? Hadn't she found herself filled with admiration as she read his letters to his aunt? Lady B. had been so scathing, and yet his ventures certainly hadn't all been disasters. Amy had often thought his aunt would like nothing better than for Marcus to come home and live with her as the man of the house. And that would certainly not suit such a fearless spirit.

And hadn't she become aware that his quick mind always considered the maximum range of choices, even of a kind that others might never even see as possibilities? So why did such a thought alarm her so?

She answered her own question. It was because

Amy Finch had never been personally involved in his ventures before. And whatever he was scheming now, she knew she was bound to be an integral part of it.

She was aware of a miserable headache at her temples, and she had no sedative powders to ward it off. The only solution was to turn the lamp down low when she had undressed and put on her cotton nightgown and robe, without needing the encumbrance of the heavy quilt over her in the warm night air. She lay flat on the bed with her eyes closed, and tried to relax completely.

But as soon as she closed her eyes, all she could see was the image of Marcus's face in front of her. His eyes and his voice were soft, and oozing seduction. And one remembered phrase from his persuasive tones seemed to be the only thing that was filling her head. . .

'. . .a loving and fulfilled marriage. . .'

Amy moved restlessly on top of the bedcovers, trying to slow the quickening beat of her heart as her treacherous imagination took over. To her, such a marriage as he described had always meant a loving partnership, with children to bless it. And since there was no love between them, he surely couldn't seriously have meant any such thing.

But just for a moment, she allowed herself to dream. . . In the waking dream she was swept up in Marcus's arms, and he was kissing her mouth with a true lover's passion. And she was responding so readily, and so wildly, and giving herself to him in ways that were totally unknown to her innocent heart as yet. . . And the touch and the taste of him was so vivid in her mind that she could almost believe it was real. . .

Her eyes flew open in alarm. Her palms were damp, and her shallow breathing had become a painful gasp, as she recognised where her wayward thoughts had been leading her. She had never known a man in the physical sense, nor had she been awoken to the ways of seduction. There had been few men in her immediate circle for many years, and no man's lips had ever touched her own. In that context, Lady Bellingham's assessment of her being a 'respectable and sober young woman' was all too miserably correct.

But she was not without normal and healthy longings, either. And from certain guarded information gleaned from the garrulous scullery maids, there was a whole world of knowledge and unknown experiences awaiting her and every young girl who stepped over the threshold of marriage. She wasn't even sure whether or not those nubile girls even waited for the sanctity of marriage.

Her thoughts switched direction from such meanderings, to encompass the most fanciful option of all. So what if she did agree to Marcus's outrageous suggestion? What would the future hold for her then? For a moment more she disregarded all other considerations, such as the undoubted advantages of becoming a married woman, and the rightful placement of Marcus's inheritance, and simply tried to imagine how it would be to be Marcus Bellingham's wife.

She had a sudden sharp recollection of a few months back, when she and Lady Bellingham had been obliged to attend the wedding of a near neigh-

bour on Skye, since it would have been seen as a
snub to refuse. Lady B. had been as reserved as
ever, but Amy had been enchanted by the beautiful
simplicity of the occasion, and the love that seemed
to flow between the young couple had been as bright
as an aura. Amy had so envied them that love as
they made their vows for all to hear. The words they
had specially written for each other had remained in
Amy's mind like a litany.

'I take thee to wife, Katrina Mairi, for the sole
reason that I love thee more than life itself, and
therefore I cannot live without thee. And as God is
my witness, I shall cherish and champion thee till
the end of my days, and with this pledge I offer
myself to thee.'

And the young girl, in her simple white gown,
with a crown of spring flowers in her hair and adorn-
ing her wrists, had replied in an emotional whisper,
'I accept thee as my husband, Jamie, to be all that
I love and respect, and I vow to love thee until the
sun shines no more, and the sea no longer ebbs and
flows. And from this day forth I offer myself to thee
for all eternity.'

The beautiful words had seemed more dignified
and more meaningful than any set piece from a
prayer book, and there were few dry eyes in the kirk
that day as the young man had placed the heavy
gold ring on his bride's finger. If they had shouted
it from the rooftops, it couldn't have been more
obvious that this was a true love match.

Amy drew a deep, shuddering breath now,
remembering that lovely, poignant occasion, and
how radiant the couple had been as they sailed away
on the ferry to the mainland for their honeymoon,

with the blessing of the entire island.

That was the way a marriage should begin, she thought in sudden anger. With a love that was pure, and a need to share all the days of their lives together, and not in the underhand manner Lady Bellingham had decreed it. And no matter how persuasive her nephew might be, she resolved to resist any temptation to enter into a sham of a marriage contract.

She had become so restless with remembering that she thought she would never get to sleep that night, but she knew she must have done so, for she was suddenly awake with a strong smell of oil in her nostrils. She realised that her lamp had gone out of its own accord, and the room was unpleasantly pungent.

She slid out of bed and walked quickly across to the window in her bare feet, pulling back the curtains and opening the long windows wide to breathe in some fresher air.

As she did so, she felt the breath tighten in her throat, for she had rarely seen such a glorious night since leaving her native Inverness. The island of Skye was beautiful in its own right, but to Amy there was a different kind of sensual beauty about a still, moonlit night, when a great city was slumbering in darkness, and the silhouettes of the buildings formed a backdrop of manmade hills and mountains.

By now, everyone in this hotel would be slumbering too, and she moved out on to the small balcony outside her window, breathing in the night scents of flowers and foliage from the gardens below. Somewhere in the night an owl hooted softly, and as she turned her head to catch the sound, her gaze caught the glow of a cigar from the balcony adjoining hers, and her heart leapt.

'Don't be afraid,' Marcus said quietly. 'It seems that we both have too many things to consider to sleep easily tonight.'

'You startled me,' Amy said, flustered. 'And it's most improper for a lady to be seen in her night attire.'

She couldn't see his face properly in the darkness, but she could hear the amusement in his voice when he replied.

'I hardly think the voluminous garment you're wearing is going to be a threat to your honour, Miss Finch!'

She glanced down at herself. It was true that the white embroidered cotton robe she wore over her nightgown, with its long full sleeves and high neckline, was hardly going to entice a lover. She felt her face grow hot at the thought, for that certainly wasn't her intention. And she registered that he was still fully dressed, despite the late hour.

'Nevertheless, it's unseemly for us to be standing here like this,' she said, moving back a pace.

'Is it? I think it's rather charming.'

He moved closer to her balcony, so that there were only the two sets of railings separating them. The balconies were not joined together, but any unscrupulous man could surely vault the gap between the low railings if he chose. . .

'I have no wish to be compromised, sir,' she said, trying to sound more indignant than nervous, and desperately trying not to betray the undoubted rush of excitement that she felt. If it wasn't exactly

Romeo and Juliet, it was just as intimate and daring to be alone and unchaperoned when the rest of the world was sleeping. . .

'I would never dare to compromise you, Miss Finch. From all that I know of you, any such move would soon be given short shrift.'

She stared at him. He was half in shadow from the direction of the moonlight, but her eyes had become accustomed to the gloom now, and she was well aware from the smile in his voice that he was trying to provoke her. And she was simply too curious not to take it further.

'I'm sure I don't know what you mean,' she said, inviting him to tell her exactly that.

Amy was aware that they were automatically keeping their voices low, so as not to disturb any other guests on the floors above or below.

But that only added to the intimacy of the situation, she thought in alarm, and she couldn't rid herself of the wretched word now. She stepped back further so that she was nearer to her open windows than to him. But there was still a very small distance between them.

'You've lived with my aunt for too long, Amy, and some of her stuffiness has rubbed off on you. But beneath it all I'm fully aware of the fiery spirit that would soon throw off the ties of convention, given half a chance. Tell me I'm not right, if you dare.'

Her mouth had become dry, for he had put into words a longing that was not accepted as being a woman's prerogative, and one that she had long kept secret in her heart. To be as free as he was, to roam where the heart dictated in a man's world, and to follow a dream. . .she pulled herself up quickly.

'I think you forget yourself, sir. If I am too stuffy for your tastes, as you call it, then I would remind you that I still grieve for a lady who was good to me, and would have expected at least a pretence of grief from her only nephew!'

As she went to turn back into her room, Marcus reached across the railings and caught at her arm. He was very close to her now. He had discarded his cigar, but the fragrance of it was not unpleasant on his breath. Amy felt a *frisson* of fear, wondering if she had gone too far. But now his voice was quiet and deliberate, and she couldn't doubt its sincerity.

'I've always believed that when a life is over, those who are left should remember the person with affection, and celebrate all that she brought to that life, instead of wallowing in useless misery. We all have private memories, Amy, and I am not totally insensitive to grief.'

'I'm very glad to hear it,' she said in a muffled voice. 'Now, will you please let me go?'

For a moment she thought he was going to say something more, and then, before she could guess his intention, he leaned across and touched her cheek with his lips.

'Then for what's left of this night, I'll bid you goodnight again, my dear Miss Finch.'

The way he spoke her name was as caressing as a warm embrace, and she shivered visibly. The night air had gone decidedly cooler now, and she moved back into her room, closing her windows firmly, and snuggling back between the bedcovers without removing her robe

Nor did she give a thought to the fact that, in

effect, she was covering herself from unbidden and seductive thoughts about a man she thought she knew, and who could still surprise her, and touch her romantic heart so unexpectedly.

She deliberately shut out such thoughts. She tried to make her mind a total blank, imagining herself sinking into soft, dark velvet, as her wise grandmother used to advise when she was a restless child, unable to sleep. But the childish nightmares that had prevented sleep in those green-apple days had no comparison with the grown-up dreams that beset her now.

'I have a proposition to put to you, Amy,' Marcus said the following morning, as brisk and businesslike as if the closeness of the encounter on the bedroom balconies had never happened.

She was relieved at his attitude. She didn't care to remember how much in retrospect she had enjoyed the clandestine meeting, nor how it would have scandalised respectable society, no matter how innocently it had begun.

There had been nothing innocent about the way it had continued, Amy thought keenly, though she accepted that she was probably making mountains out of molehills. A more sophisticated person than herself would have simply relished the excitement of it all.

'What proposition is that, sir?'

Breakfast was over, and they had retired to one of the small sitting-rooms in the hotel; for the present they had the room to themselves. She was seated on one of the deep arm-chairs the hotel provided, and Marcus sat on another close beside her.

At his words, she was suspicious at once, and prepared to be on her guard for whatever he was about to say. Any proposal of marriage to comply with his aunt's Will was definitely *out*, Amy reminded herself, ignoring her rapidly beating heart.

'It was understandable that we both reacted in the same way to my aunt's outrageous bequest, and I would have expected nothing else from you,' he said calmly, and she seethed at his choice of words.

He didn't really have to call the idea of marrying her *outrageous*, she thought contrarily.

'And rightly so,' she said, just as cool.

'And I take it that under no circumstances would you agree to going through a form of marriage that was dictated by a third person?' He didn't wait for a response, but continued, 'But as you already know, I have dire need of the inheritance that is rightfully mine, and I spent a good part of last night walking, and trying to think of a way around it.'

So now she knew why he had been out on the balcony, still fully dressed, and as sleepless as herself.

'I can't see that there is any way around it, save for the one that we both refuse to consider,' Amy said quickly.

'Please hear me out. What I have to say may not appeal to you, but I pray that it will. As I've already told you, I have many debtors knocking on my door, and mostly through the gambling idiocy of my partner.'

Amy tried to keep her face impassive, unsure how much truth there was in the statement.

'When I purchased the property and the large stretch of land that I needed along the stretch of river

in the Callanby valley, I admit that I too gambled on
meeting the payments,' he said stiffly, and Amy
could see how much he disliked confessing his own
failings to a virtual stranger. But they had already
come too far to be called ordinary strangers. . . She
waited without comment.

'The upshot of it all is this: I believe I can hold off
the debtors if they believe the money is eventually
forthcoming. That is, if they are assured that the
inheritance will be mine.'

'Go on,' she said grimly now, as he paused.

'All right. No more prevaricating. What I'm asking you to do is to agree to a mock engagement,
and that we should go through a form of marriage
that would naturally be in name only, within the six
months stated in the Will. In fact, the sooner, the
better, if you agree to it. Then, once the money is
secure, the marriage could be annulled. I would pay
you a handsome sum of money to enable you to
go back to Skye, or wherever in the world you
wanted to be.'

Amy's heart was hammering so fast in her chest
now that she couldn't speak. If his aunt had made
an outrageous proviso in her Will, then how much
more impossible and despicable was this! It was the
ultimate in cheating and deceit. . . And then, before
she could stop it, the only thought surging around
in her head was that the only place in the world she
wanted to be, was with him.

The blood had rushed to her face, and she saw
him look at her uneasily. He spoke quickly, as if
clearly realising he had now gone beyond the
bounds of proper behaviour and shocked her totally.

'Of course, if you had been able to prove that

you were already affianced to another man, it would
make the conditions of my aunt's bequest null and
void. But we both know that wasn't the case, do
we not?'

Of course he would know it wasn't true. If she
had been promised to someone else his aunt would
have also known it, and been obliged to delete the
clause from her Will. But for one tempting moment,
she knew how much she would have liked to prove
him wrong, if only to let him know that Miss Amy
Finch was no man's plaything, but a desirable young
woman whom any gentleman could love. She
pushed the thought well out of her mind, and spoke
with stiff disdain.

'If you're prepared to enter into the kind of deceit-
ful arrangement as you have suggested, then perhaps
we should also pretend that I am engaged to some
fictitious suitor. Then Mr Varley would have to see
that the conditions of the Will no longer applied.'

They stared as defiantly at one another as if they
were the pieces on a chessboard, knowing they had
reached stalemate. Then she heard Marcus laugh
shortly.

'Oh, Amy, I think the man who captures your
heart will be kept very much on his toes! You have
a mind and will of your own, and are far from being
the kind of simpering young woman on the look out
for a husband at every opportunity.'

'I suppose that's intended as a compliment,' she
retorted. 'Even if it does make me sound like some
strident Amazonian female.'

'And we both know you are not. So what are
we to do, Amy?' Marcus said, leaning back in his
armchair. She glared at him, not too sure what this

sudden change of mood and attitude implied.

'I thought I had made my feelings clear enough.'

'But would you really want me to lose everything? You know me too well. You've had access to all my letters for the past two years, and you know of my ambitions as well as I know them myself. Would you really deny me this last chance to prove to my aunt's memory, at least, that the Irish gamble paid off?'

He was taking an unfair advantage of her, and they both knew it. His change of tactics in appealing to her good nature, and his reference to his aunt's memory, together with that softening in his voice, were all having an effect on Amy that she didn't want. Before she could think of a suitable reply, he had leaned forward to catch hold of her hand and looked earnestly into her eyes.

'Amy, hear me out for a moment. Would it be so impossible to pretend to an attachment for one another for a little time? A short engagement is all I ask, then a quiet wedding to comply with Aunt Maud's request, and after that, the arrangements will be as I have already outlined, and I promise that you'll come out of it handsomely.'

'Please don't add insult to everything else by making me sound like a fortune-hunter!'

His eyes sparkled angrily at her curt response. 'All right. But don't take too long giving me your answer. I am anxious to get this business settled, and as you well know, I'm an impatient man, and not well disposed to dithering.'

'I do know it,' she said sarcastically, speaking as freely as he did. 'It was one of the very things Lady Bellingham held against you. Perhaps if you had dithered a little more in your various ventures, you might not be in such a fix now.'

His hold on her hand was stronger now, and she snatched her fingers away, knowing she had been unfair, and also knowing how very much she was attracted to him. And it would be fatal if she were really to fall in love with him.

'But I know exactly what I want now, and I'll await your answer with as much patience as I can muster.'

She had to curb herself from being uncharacteristically reckless. She had never taken chances in her life, but what were her choices? Even with Lady B.'s two pieces of jewellery, she would still have to make her own way in the world. If she agreed to this engagement and farcical marriage, she would at least have some decent capital with which to rebuild her life.

And an engagement didn't have to end in marriage. There was still a way out for her, if the situation became impossible. . . There was still her own legacy to claim.

She took a deep breath. 'Then I agree to it.'

There was complete silence for a moment, and then Marcus's face broke into a wide smile. This time he took both her hands in his and squeezed them, and she felt totally limp with the stress of these last moments.

'My dear girl, I promise that you won't regret it. We'll inform Varley this very afternoon, and then I shall arrange for the local newspaper to send someone to the hotel to interview us—'

'Surely that's not necessary?' Amy said in alarm.

'I think it is, if only for authenticity. And there's

another thing, which is of a rather more delicate matter. I'm sure you remember that my aunt wore a particularly fine sapphire ring, given to her by my uncle on their engagement. If it's among her effects, Amy, I would very much like you to wear it.'

Her first instinct was to say no. Of course she remembered the ring, and knew how fond Lady B. had been of it. She was surprised that Marcus should remember it too, after all this time. Perhaps there was a touch of romance in his soul after all, she thought grudgingly. And it would solve many problems, for there was no way she wanted to visit a jeweller's establishment with him, and go through the farce of buying a ring.

'Very well,' she conceded.

'Wear it this afternoon, when we visit Mr Varley, and naturally, he must believe that we have gone into this voluntarily and happily. You do understand that?'

'I do,' she said solemnly.

He raised her hand to his lips, as he had done once before, and her eyes were blurred as she looked at him. For this certainly wasn't the way she had envisaged becoming betrothed to the man of her dreams. This wasn't the way at all. . .

'Then I'll just say one thing more, Amy. I had no thoughts of marriage before now, but if I had been looking for a bride, I couldn't have chosen better.'

There were other guests entering the sitting-room then, and they smiled at the apparently loving couple sitting so closely to one another. Marcus's words threw her off-balance again, and she sat in stunned silence at the way fate had thrown her together with this man. And wondered desperately, even now, if she was being every bit as foolish and hot-headed as his aunt had always considered Marcus to be.

That afternoon they were to revisit the lawyer's chambers, and when they met in the hotel sitting-room once more Amy was wearing Lady Bellingham's heavy sapphire ring on her engagement finger. It felt odd and unfamiliar, although it fitted well enough, for Lady Bellingham had not been a large woman. Marcus had seen the ring on Amy's slender finger at once, and he had kissed it quickly.

'Thank you,' he said simply. 'One day I shall buy you a more personal one.'

'That will certainly not be necessary, and I think you forget yourself, Marcus! Please remember that this is no more than a mock engagement, followed by a brief marriage of convenience. We are both agreed on that.'

She spoke in some agitation, for if she once sensed that he meant to persuade her to remain married to him for any length of time on those terms, or any other, she already knew she couldn't go through with it. She couldn't live in close proximity with a man of such energy and panache whom she had admired for so long, and not be drawn ever more into a more ardent regard for him. She knew it as surely as she breathed.

'Of course we're both agreed on it,' he said. 'I was merely voicing my appreciation in a way that I thought would please a lady. But I would suggest that you do not show your displeasure if I go out of my way to be attentive to you, Amy. As my fiancée, people will expect a certain amount of fondness between us, and it would be a poor lover who did not show admiration for his beautiful bride.'

He was so smooth, Amy thought. So logical in everything he said. . .and so annoyingly right as well. If they were to enact this charade for the lawyer, and to everyone else with whom they came in contact, then they must put on the pretence of being enamoured of one another. For her part, she was beginning to realise how easy it would be for that condition to be true.

'So, if you are ready to beard the lion in his den, shall we go?'

She gave a half-smile. The simile suited the grizzled lawyer, with his thick sideburns and fleshy cheeks into which his keen eyes almost disappeared.

'I'm ready.'

'And when we return to the hotel, we shall entertain a gentleman from the local newspaper with afternoon tea.'

He gave her his arm as they walked out to the waiting carriage, and once they were seated inside Amy turned to him.

'I still don't see why we have to do that, Marcus. No one will be interested in us—'

'People are always interested in a man who inherits sudden wealth, especially when it arises from such unhappy circumstances. My aunt's death at sea has already aroused interest, and we will give them the story they want to see.'

She had to be content with that. Besides, her heart was pounding too much for her to ask any more questions. She had given her word to him, and betrayed her own instincts in doing so, and there was no going back now.

Thomas Varley's eyes seemed to penetrate right through her as Marcus calmly stated that he and Miss Finch were now officially engaged, and intended to be married within a couple of months.

As if to underline his words, he took Amy's hand in his, where the sapphire ring blazoned between them.

'And is this your wish too, Miss Finch?' the lawyer said. 'Have you agreed, without undue persuasion, to marry Mr Marcus Bellingham in order to comply with his aunt's bequest? I urge you to think carefully before you answer, young woman, for your reaction yesterday led me to think otherwise, as did that of the gentleman himself.'

He held up his hand as Marcus started to speak, and continued to stare fixedly at Amy. His eyes had never left her face all the while he was speaking. And for once, Amy was thankful for the ponderous legal verbosity, for it gave her time to compose herself, and to glance at Marcus.

'Yesterday I was too startled by the terms of the Will to think sensibly, sir, and I believe Mr Bellingham felt the same way. But we have both had time to consider since then. He has asked me to be his wife in a very proper manner, and I have accepted.'

She heard Marcus draw in his breath, and she didn't dare to look at him now. Perhaps she was a better actress than she had ever guessed, to put all the dreaming romance of the young *ingénue* into her voice for the lawyer's benefit, Amy thought.

Perhaps Marcus had begun to wonder if she intended holding him to the long-term result of his proposal after all: that when the time came, she would reject the idea of having the marriage annulled. Perhaps. . .

'Then I must congratulate you both on a successful conclusion to a most unorthodox suggestion,' Varley said abruptly, and Amy wasn't sure if he was being sarcastic or merely tactless.

'Thank you,' Marcus said. 'In the normal course of events, I would not have dreamed of marrying so soon after my aunt's death, but she has dictated the circumstances, as you are well aware.'

'Quite so,' Thomas Varley said, knowing there was nothing more to be said.

'And it would be much appreciated if I could be advanced a portion of my inheritance forthwith,' Marcus went on relentlessly. 'There are many expenses involved in my project, as you are also well aware. A wedding incurs further expenses, and I would not have my aunt's memory besmirched by thinking it was done hastily and cheaply.'

Amy was aghast at this piece of gall. There seemed to be no end to his deviousness to obtain money, although she conceded that it was rightfully his, and that this old miser of a lawyer looked as if he would hold on to the purse-strings until the last possible moment. She could hardly blame Marcus for wanting what was his, and Varley evidently knew when he was beaten.

'Very well, sir,' he said coldly. 'I will see to it that a portion of it is available in the Dublin Bank by the end of the week.'

*   *   *

Once they were outside again, Marcus suggested they took a walk in a nearby park to recover their equilibrium. And it was only then that Amy realised how she was trembling at the ease with which she had lied to Mr Varley. Apart from any other considerations, the necessity to do so offended her innate sense of honesty. More and more, she felt as though events were rushing past her at an alarming rate, and she could do nothing to stop them.

'I thank you, Amy,' Marcus said, when they were strolling through the fragrant, flower-filled gardens of the park, already absorbed into the transient scene of ladies and gentlemen enjoying the summer air.

'I could hardly do otherwise than support our decision,' she said curtly. 'But it did not please me to lie.'

He looked at her without speaking, and she knew how churlish she had sounded. But she simply couldn't help it. The situation fell so far short of her own dreams. . .

'Then I'll do my best to make it all as easy as possible for you,' he said coolly, 'and as far as outsiders are concerned, we'll be the best and most loving of couples.'

She hated this whole deceit, but her eyes prickled, unwilling to admit how much she could have longed for his words to be true.

Chapter Five

'Do you have any objection to being interviewed in your private sitting-room?' Marcus asked her later, as they walked the short distance back to the hotel.

She had already forgotten the interview for the wretched newspaper. By now, the whole affair was taking on such an air of strangeness that she could hardly think sensibly at all. And just why Lady Bellingham had thought her a suitable bride for her nephew, she couldn't imagine. They were most unsuited, she thought crossly; she with her own romantic dreams, and he with his ambitious ones. They were poles apart. . .

'So, do we greet him privately, or in one of the hotel's public rooms?' Marcus persisted.

'Privately,' Amy said, nettled at the way everything seemed to go his way, and taken out of her hands.

He nodded. 'Then I shall await him below, and bring him to your sitting-room in due course. I suppose we'd best order afternoon tea for the fellow.'

Amy gave the glimmer of a smile. 'Do I detect

that you don't care for newspaper reporters
very much?'

'I do not. They are far too ready to embroider the
truth for any sensational story.'

She just managed to resist saying that there could
surely be no more sensational and false story than
the one Marcus Bellingham was so glibly about
to tell!

When the two gentlemen arrived in her sitting-room
in due course, Amy immediately disliked
O'Donnell, the ferrety-faced reporter, with his
constant sniff, and his flourishing importance with
pencil and notebook. But she reminded herself that
this meeting would soon be concluded, and she was
hardly likely to see him again.

They talked of generalities until a maid arrived
with a tray of tea and biscuits, and once Amy had
dispensed it for them all, O'Donnell licked the end
of his pencil several times and looked enquiringly
at Marcus.

'Now then, sorr,' he said, his accent so broad that
Amy could hardly follow it. 'If you'd care to tell
me all the details of your young lady and yourself
for our social page, shall we begin? Our lady readers
always love to hear of a romance happening right
under their noses.'

Amy squirmed at his ingratiating smile. But
Marcus came to sit beside her on the small sofa,
tucking her hand inside his arm, so that the sapphire
ring was prominently on display. Amy didn't miss
how O'Donnell's eyes almost popped at the
size of it.

'Will you let me do the telling, my love?'

Marcus said, looking directly into her eyes.

She lowered her own so that he wouldn't see the sudden fury in them, wondering again just what madness had led her into this.

'I think it would be best,' she murmured, with what O'Donnell obviously saw as womanly modesty.

'As I told you earlier, Mr O'Donnell,' Marcus said, 'Miss Finch was accompanying my aunt on a visit to Dublin from the Isle of Skye.'

'Go on, sorr, please,' the man said, as Marcus paused while he scribbled furiously. 'I'll keep up, never you fear.'

'Miss Finch and I have corresponded for a very long time, and have grown to have a great regard for one another during that time, though we had never met. It was my aunt's dearest wish that her young friend, and her nephew, should have the opportunity of putting that situation to rights.'

Amy was so stunned by this cool bending of the truth that she couldn't look at either of them now. And yet there was substance in the telling too. They *had* corresponded for a very long time, albeit with Lady B. mentally looking over their shoulders, and knew one another through their letters.

'Unfortunately, my aunt died from a fever during the voyage, and had to be buried at sea, to the great distress of Amy—Miss Finch—and myself, naturally.'

'And you didn't hear about the death of your aunt until Miss Finch arrived here in Dublin, I understand?' O'Donnell probed.

'That is so. But in our mutual grief, Amy and I discovered that what had begun as a warm regard for one another through the exchange of numerous letters blossomed very quickly into something else. And I'm deeply honoured that she has consented to become my wife.'

'Knowing it was what your aunt would have wished,' O'Donnell obligingly prompted.

'Of course, and she had hinted as much many times. It's one reason why we don't feel the need to have a prolonged engagement. We travel to my home in Callanby the day after tomorrow, where Miss Finch will be suitably chaperoned, and the wedding will be arranged as soon as is decent. It will be a tribute to my aunt's memory.'

Amy's mouth opened to object, but the arm squeezing hers was holding her very tightly, and the reporter's ferrety little eyes seemed to be looking right through her. He looked from one to the other, and slurped the remainder of his tea.

'So I would be right in telling my readers that your young lady travelled from one end of the British Isles to the other in order to marry her sweetheart. Is that so, sorr? It would charm the ladies to read such a romantic tale.'

'I think you have it just about right, Mr O'Donnell,' Marcus said smoothly. O'Donnell looked at Amy.

'Miss Finch? Is that the happy circumstance?'

'Of course,' she said, knowing she could say no different. Both the reporter's, and Marcus's, colourful bending of the truth incensed her. But she could hardly dispute it now, after letting herself be sweet-talked into the deception. In the eyes of the sceptical, she was as guilty as he was, in going into this for gain.

Before she could think what he was about, Marcus leaned towards her kissed her cheek, as if he was completely enamoured of her. When he sat back, she could still feel the touch of his lips on her skin as he turned to address the reporter.

'You may also add, for your readers' benefit, that I consider myself the most fortunate of men. And now I think you have heard enough, Mr O'Donnell.'

'Just one thing more, Mr Bellingham, sorr,' he said, as smooth as silk. 'Is it right that you've a stake in the old alluvial gold diggings south of the Wicklow mountains?'

'I can't see that that has any bearing on the news of my betrothal to Miss Finch——'

'Not at all, sorr, not at all. It's just that our readers are always interested in a man's prospects and fortunes——'

'What I do in Callanby is no one's business but my own,' Marcus said coldly. 'Now I'll bid you good day, sir.'

He stood up, drawing Amy with him, and O'Donnell had no option but to back out gracefully. But they all knew there would be some additional reference to the project in his reporting. It was what sold newspapers. Once he'd gone, Amy rounded on Marcus.

'That odious little man!' she raged. 'Why did you have to make it all sound so——so——'

'So what? So loving and believable, as we both agreed was necessary? Would you have had me behave in any other way?'

She supposed she would not. But the fact remained that she felt even more that she was plunging headlong into a situation she couldn't control.

Her hands were clenched by her sides, and she was stiff with anxiety. And then Marcus gave a smothered oath.

'For God's sake, don't look at me like that, as if you think I'm about to ravish you at any moment. Not that the idea of it is so very unattractive.'

She drew in her breath. She had never been so close to him, or any man before. She was in his arms, and she could taste him and breathe him. . . and *want* him. The erotic sensation rushed into her without warning. She was aware that her eyes had widened, and the blood had surged into her cheeks. Her breath was coming very fast now.

'And if a man cannot kiss his fiancée, then who can he kiss?' Marcus taunted in his usual manner.

The next second his mouth had fastened over hers, but the kiss was not a gentle one—it was filled with all the fire of a passionate man. She was held captive in his embrace, and her own arms were wrapped around him now, if only to give her support. But not only for that. . .

A furious sense of shock at her own feelings came to her rescue, and she finally pushed him away from her. He took unfair advantage, and she had no intention of being his plaything until he claimed his inheritance and then discarded her. She had too much pride for that.

Nor would she dare to let him know for one second that those sweet moments when she had heard herself called his sweetheart, come from one end of the British Isles to the other to marry him, had touched her heart so much that she could almost wish it had all been true.

'I think you presume too much, sir,' she gasped.

'I may be your fiancée in the eyes of the world, but please remember that this is a business arrangement between us.'

'I'm never likely to forget it, as long as you continue to act as my Lady Outrage,' he said, his mood changing at once to one of sarcasm.

'And what did you mean by saying we travel to Callanby the day after tomorrow?' she demanded. 'I assumed I would remain here in the hotel—'

But the moment she said it, she knew it wasn't feasible. Nor was it what had been intended for Lady Bellingham and herself. Lady B. had wanted to see everything about Marcus's plans at first hand. . .

'Of course you will not stay here. As my fiancée, you will live in my house until the wedding. I have a housekeeper, and as I said, you will be properly chaperoned, Amy, so you need have no worries on that score.'

He was easily taking charge again, making her feel young and foolish. He had got what he wanted, and tomorrow the whole city and surrounding area would read in the newspaper the romantic story of Marcus Bellingham and his future bride.

'Incidentally, I came to Dublin on horseback, since I wanted to sell the nag,' he went on casually. 'But my partner will have my carriage here some time tomorrow. I had no intention of letting my aunt travel in discomfort, and neither will you. We'll be obliged to stay overnight at a halfway hostelry, but you'll be quite safe with two bodyguards.'

It was infuriating. Whenever she began to find him almost human, he always managed to annoy her with his sarcasm and his arrogance. But perhaps it was better so. There was obviously no real future for them together, and the less she thought of him in that respect, the better. And then he smiled, releasing her from his embrace, and holding out his hands. Without thinking, she placed her hands in his.

'Can I suggest that we forget all about business for now, and simply enjoy this evening in Dublin together? I'm told that a troupe of Irish dancers is going to entertain the hotel guests later, and if you've never seen them before, I think you'll enjoy the performance.'

Amy's interest was caught. And if there was a performance to watch, then it would relieve the embarrassing intimacy into which they had been thrown.

'Well, I agree about forgetting business for this evening, and the entertainment sounds very agreeable. So yes, let's call a truce.'

He laughed out loud now. 'I wouldn't have put it quite like that. I wasn't even aware that we had been at war.'

Among Lady Bellingham's clothes was a very fine silvery shawl. She had once told Amy that her husband had bought it for her some years ago. She had rarely worn it, but had thought it might be suitable for a shipboard dinner. She hadn't worn it, and Amy looked at the shawl now, fingering the delicate fabric, and wondering whether she dared to wear it herself.

It would look so lovely worn over the bronze dinner gown, providing Marcus didn't find it distasteful if she wore it. . . She hesitated as the thought struck her. Reluctant to wear it without asking his opinion, and before she changed for the evening, she tentatively knocked on his door, with the shawl draped over her arm.

He asked her inside at once. She hesitated, and then complied, since it was preferable to talking in a corridor where other guests might overhear. He had discarded his jacket, and Amy was fully aware of the compromising situation. But betrothed couples were allowed a certain leeway, she reminded herself swiftly.

'I can't think to what I owe the honour of your company,' Marcus said. 'But sit and admire the view a moment, while I pour you a glass of wine.'

Before she could decline, he was already pouring it out and handing it to her. As the silky shawl slid to the floor, he picked it up and draped it around her shoulders. It was no more than a simple act, yet Amy felt an odd little tugging at her heart at his courtesy.

'My aunt's, I believe,' he observed, indicating the shawl. 'I seem to remember it from long ago.'

At his words, the reason she was here suddenly seemed shameful. She moved away, nearer to the window, taking a gulp of wine, and feeling its warmth coursing down her throat.

'I wondered if you'd mind if I wore it,' she said nervously. 'Would it offend you too much?'

He came to stand beside her, and put one hand on her shoulder. The small caress of his fingers made her catch her breath, and she prayed he wouldn't kiss her again. She wasn't sure if she could bear it, and she didn't care to guess why.

'I'd love you to wear it, and to take anything else that you wish from my aunt's belongings, though I fancy that much of it is too elderly and sedate for your taste. But anything that you like you must keep, and I will arrange for the rest of it to be sent to the poorhouse in the morning.'

'Thank you. Though I must say that the poor will be wonderfully served by such elegant clothes.'

'And why should they not?' he said. 'The poor devils have little enough to brighten their lives.'

Amy took another sip of wine, though it was already making her head spin more than she liked.

'I hadn't expected you to have such compassion in your soul,' she said, half-expecting him to take offence at the remark. Instead, he spoke evenly.

'As I told you before, I'm not the ogre you seem to think me, Amy. I cared for my aunt, even though we rarely saw eye to eye, and I'm sad for her. But life must go on, and if others can benefit from what was hers, then so be it.'

And that included himself, and Amy, as well as the poor, she thought ruefully.

She put down the half-empty wine glass, knowing she couldn't cope with drinking it all before she had some food in her stomach.

'I don't think you're an ogre at all,' she said, her voice wobbling just a little.

'Then I thank you for that,' Marcus said, his gaze holding hers for a longer moment than was necessary.

'I think I should go and get ready for dinner,' she said, her voice hurried. 'Thank you for the wine, and for being so understanding.'

'It's my pleasure, and I hope I will always be able to please you as much.'

She fled from the room, fully aware of the renewed mockery in his words. But it wasn't necessary for them to carry the playacting to extremes, she thought angrily, as she reached her own room. Not in private, anyway. . .

She caught sight of herself in the mirror, and she felt even more annoyed, trying to decide whether she looked as confused as an idiot, or as flushed as if she had just been kissed by a man she adored. . . but she hadn't, and she didn't. . .

She knew she should keep such thoughts out of her mind, and stick to practicalities, for it was perfectly clear to her that Marcus Bellingham could switch on the charm just whenever it suited him. And right now it suited him to keep her sweet, Amy thought irreverently, since there was so much at stake that depended on their marriage.

They were given the same table at dinner that evening, and when it was over, they remained seated while the far end of the room was made ready for the entertainers.

There was a troupe of six young people, three men and three women. The men wore dark green plaid trousers and dark jackets, and the girls wore long skirts in the same dark green plaid, with simple white blouses and a long sash worn crossways from shoulders to waists. On their feet they all wore soft dancing pumps of a kind Amy had seen once in the Highland dancing. The troupe was accompanied by a small group of musicians who struck up a tune on fiddles and drums.

The dancing was intricate and fast, and Amy was enthralled by the way they all kept their hands rigidly by their sides as they danced. All the movement and expression came from those swiftly-moving feet, and there was great applause each time a dance came to an end.

'They're so accomplished! And so clever to remember so many different steps,' Amy said, thankful that this was something she could show enthusiasm about.

Marcus leaned towards her across the table, smiling into her eyes and taking her hand in his for a moment.

'And I am so enjoying that look of pleasure in your face, Amy, that I almost wish they would go on dancing for ever. But even more, I wish that look was for me.'

She looked at him mutely, wishing he wouldn't say such things. Not that she didn't like being flattered. What woman wouldn't—and by such a man! But she knew all too well that it was all meaningless. It was said for effect, for anyone who might be listening, to further establish their relationship with one another for authenticity.

She saw a lady and gentleman at a table nearby glance their way and smile fondly at the apparently intimate moment between the attractive young couple. And it merely underlined Amy's own thoughts. Marcus did this for effect, and for public consumption, and not out of any real feeling for her.

He didn't immediately let go of her hand, and she let her own lay impassively in his. But when the dancers dispersed to a round of applause, she quickly withdrew her fingers.

'I'm sorry it's ended,' she said, disappointed.

'It hasn't. But it's a very energetic exercise, and they need to take a breather, as you can imagine. They'll return in a little while.'

And meanwhile, there was renewed applause as a rather buxom lady stepped out into the centre of the room. From her reception, she was evidently known to the guests, and Marcus murmured that she was a singer of some repute.

Amy didn't know what to expect, but she was instantly entranced as the woman's clear soprano tones began to fill the room. She sang a haunting, plaintive song, and the fact that the words were all in Gaelic only added to the mystical quality of the voice and the music. There was sadness and joy in the melody, and as it died away there was no other sound in the room for a few moments, then the applause was rapturous.

'That was truly beautiful,' Amy said huskily.

As she spoke, she realised that Marcus was watching her, and in retrospect she registered that he had been watching her all the time the soprano had been singing.

'And I could say that you're the most beautiful woman in the room,' he said. 'But you're sure to think I've a devious reason for saying it.'

'I probably would,' she retorted. 'You've no need to say such things to me.'

'I know that. So why is it so hard for you to believe that I mean them?'

'I think I would prefer it if you did not make such personal remarks. It only embarrasses me.'

And it pleases me far too much. . .

'I think you have not been in a gentleman's company too often, Amy,' he went on. 'Am I right?'

She felt herself flush. 'Do I disappoint you by being so obviously unsophisticated?'

'Not at all. It's charming and refreshing to find

a woman who doesn't respond to every ounce of flattery with a flirtatious response.'

'Well, I'm hardly likely to do that,' she replied with a flash of spirit, 'since I've no wish to flirt with you in the least.'

At least that much was true. Not unless it was the sweet flirting of lovers who truly meant something to one another. . .

The dancers were returning to the floor now, and Amy turned her attention to them. But she was beginning to wonder more and more if she had done a very foolish thing in allying herself to Marcus Bellingham. And even worse, if she would ever be able to break free of him, emotionally, if not physically.

She concentrated hard on the intricate figures the dancers were performing, and applauded with the rest of the audience. But her mind was no longer on them, and all she could do was wish she'd never agreed to come to Ireland with Lady Bellingham in the first place. If she had cried off, then perhaps the lady herself wouldn't have come, and she would still be reasonably hale and hearty in her island home.

And Amy would probably have been out of a job, she thought, more shrewdly, for Lady B. had never been able to abide spinelessness.

'You've been deep in thought for some minutes,' she heard Marcus say a little while later.

'I'm sorry. It was very rude of me,' Amy said, hastily showing a more interested face to him.

'Not at all. It's rare to see a lovely woman in repose. And you are a very lovely woman, Amy.'

She clenched her hands together beneath the table.

'I've already asked you not to make such statements.'

He gave a heavy sigh. 'And I would ask you not to be so namby-pamby. It doesn't suit you, and I'm quite sure it's not your usual mode of behaviour.'

His dark eyes challenged her, and she knew her own must be sparkling in return.

'Furthermore,' Marcus went on before she could speak, 'I'm well known in Callanby now, and am known for a man of some spirit. I would not have my friends believe that I chose to marry a simpering creature.'

Her mouth dropped open a little. 'Are you so particular what friends and acquaintances think of your choice? It seems rather ironic to me, since I am not your true choice at all!'

'But they will not know that, my dear, and nor must anyone else, if our story is to be believed.'

She detected a hint of steel in his voice now, as if to say she had already given her consent, and she must abide by it. And she knew that, of course, he'd be thinking how his entire future depended on keeping up the pretence of true affection in public.

'So you do not even intend to confide in these friends of yours—or even your partner?' she said.

'Most certainly not my partner! Ronan Kelly is not the most reliable of confidants, especially when he's roaring with the drink.'

To Amy he sounded a most disagreeable companion. 'So you do have other friends, then?' she couldn't help saying.

He looked at her thoughtfully. 'A man without friends is the poorer for his loss, Amy. I've lived in Callanby for well over a year, as you well know, and naturally I have made many friends there. In fact—'

He paused, and then went on glibly.

'Yes, I think it would be a very good idea for us to have an engagement party soon after our return to Callanby, just to put our relationship on a properly respectable footing. We must be sure to invite Thomas Varley to it.'

And that just about summed up his reason for suggesting it, Amy thought indignantly. It had nothing to do with introducing her to friends and acquaintances. It was all to do with confirming in Thomas Varley's mind that this liaison was mutually desired, and the quicker Marcus would receive his inheritance.

'Oh, yes, he must certainly receive an invitation,' she said with heavy sarcasm. 'Don't you intend to invite that revolting little newspaper man as well? And don't you think it's in very bad taste to be holding a party so soon after your aunt's death?'

'I certainly don't envisage dancing and jollity,' he said coldly. 'But an acknowledgement of the lady in my life would be expected. Perhaps you don't fully understand the sense of it, but I'm doing it as much for you as myself—'

'Oh, really? Do you think I'm so very interested in Lady Bellingham's fortune?' she said, keeping her voice as low as possible so as not to be overheard.

But the musicians had taken over from the dancers now, and there was a general hubbub of noise as the hotel guests chatted among themselves while they were being entertained.

'I think you should be interested in keeping a

sense of proportion,' Marcus said. 'And in suggesting a discreet gathering of friends, since the word party obviously offends you, I intend to show the world that our intentions are honourable.'

He really was impossible! There was nothing remotely honourable about their situation, Amy thought, but he had a canny knack of cloaking every underhand act in a semblance of respectability.

But the thing that annoyed her most, was that everything he said was so logical. She *did* want to appear completely respectable, and loved, and cherished, the way a newly engaged girl should appear.

'Very well,' she said, capitulating. 'And yes, I prefer to call it a gathering of friends, if I'm to be paraded for inspection. I'm sure it would be expected, if you're as well known in the community as you say you are.'

'Trust me, Amy,' he said with a sardonic smile. And she had no answer for that.

There was much to do the following morning. Lady Bellingham's unwanted clothes and belongings were ready in boxes to be delivered to the poorhouse. Marcus declined to go through them, saying that Amy would have a far better idea of what to keep and what to despatch. There was precious little she wanted for herself.

The personal jewellery and effects would all be taken to Callanby to be put into Marcus's safe, until such time as he married for love, and gave them to his true bride, Amy thought defensively, as if saying the words to herself would clarify the situation properly.

Marcus oversaw the despatch of the boxes to the poorhouse, and then went out for a while.

When he returned, he found Amy in the hotel sitting-room, and she saw that he'd purchased a newspaper. Her heart jumped as he pointed out the headline on the social events page: 'A True Love Match.'

And beneath it came the gushing report on the so-called romance of Miss Amy Finch, who had travelled south by sea to marry her sweetheart, only to endure the crushing sadness of her benefactor's death on board ship.

'My benefactor?' she murmured, glancing at Marcus, and wondering how he would take such an outright lie. Lady Bellingham had been nothing of the sort to Amy, and Amy had been no more than a paid employee, like the rest of the household staff.

'O'Donnell had no reason to think you were anything else to one another,' Marcus remarked, and she knew immediately who had put the idea of the benefactor into the reporter's mind. She tightened her lips, hating the thought of being so continually manipulated, but feeling increasingly helpless to combat it.

The report went on to say a little about Marcus and his home in Callanby, but only hinting at his entrepreneurial lifestyle. But the surprising restraint from the man only had the effect of making Marcus sound very dashing indeed.

'I suppose it could be worse,' Amy said at last.

Marcus laughed. 'For a newly engaged woman, who should be bubbling over with happiness, you make the most understated comments.'

'That's because I don't *feel* the way a newly

engaged woman should feel, and I'm hardly bubbling over with happiness at acting out such deceit,'
she said angrily.

He sobered at once. 'Amy, I'm sorry. I didn't
realise what an ordeal this was going to be for you.
It seemed such a simple solution at the time.'

And if she had been another kind of woman, it
would have been simple for her too. If she had
been a calculating fortune-hunter, or a woman of
the world, or a born actress, things would have been
very different. And if she hadn't been toying with
the stupid idea of falling in love with him, knowing
it was all to end as soon as he got his birthright.

'You don't have to worry,' she said. 'I won't let
you down. I've given my word, and I won't go
back on it.'

'Thank you,' he said.

The apparent sincerity in his voice made her suddenly feel near to tears, and she lowered her gaze
quickly before he could see the naked misery
in them.

'Marcus, me boy! By all the saints, what the devil's
all this I've just had shown to me in the Dublin rag?'

Amy was jerked back to reality by the sudden
sound of the thick Irish accent, and she snatched
her hand away from Marcus's quickly. She looked
beyond him to where a man of around forty years
was striding, loose-limbed, towards them. He was
handsome enough, despite his rather fleshy, dissol-
ute appearance, with unruly black hair and bold,
roguish eyes, and he looked Amy over with frankly
blatant approval.

'Ronan. Come and join us, though I didn't expect

you just yet,' Marcus said, his tone considerably flatter and cooler than his partner's. 'Allow me to introduce you to Miss Amy Finch, my fiancée.'

'So it's true, then, is it? I thought 'twas all a mistake, but if your good lady aunt perished on board ship like the report said, then you have me condolences.'

'Thank you—'

'Still and all, it seems you've a fair compensation here, Marcus,' he said, the grin returning. 'And aren't you the devilish one to have kept this little lady hidden away all this time!'

Chapter Six

Ronan Kelly was far brasher than Amy had expected, and she couldn't imagine how Marcus came to be connected with him. She'd have thought him far too uncouth for a gentleman's tastes. Though, remembering Marcus's own sometimes bohemian ways, and the unorthodox places where he'd travelled over the years, she supposed she shouldn't be surprised at anything.

She had already learned that when it came to sniffing out gold deposits, Kelly was supposed to be something of an authority, and it was he who had proposed that the two men should go into partnership. And Marcus being Marcus, she assumed he hadn't been able to resist going into a new venture that might bring him untold riches.

The three of them ate a light lunch in the hotel dining-room, and Marcus explained briefly what had happened regarding his aunt. From the shortness of his tone, Amy could tell he wanted no flowery comments from the other man.

'You have me condolences, naturally, me boy. And it must have been a very upsetting time for you, Miss Finch,' Ronan said, turning to her immediately.

'It was,' she said, remembering the horror of that time all too vividly.

But after Kelly's brief attention to the proprieties, and an interest in her person that made Amy inwardly squirm, his greedy mind had obviously turned to the possibilities that the situation presented. He leaned towards his partner now, his black eyes caculating.

'The saints preserve me from sounding indelicate at such a time, Marcus, and you'll forgive me bringing it up, but does this mean that funds are going to be forthcoming in the very near future?'

Amy saw Marcus's lips tighten. In an instant, she knew that all Marcus had said about his partner was true. It was all there, etched in the man's face. The look of avarice, the scheming ways, the so-called eye to the main chance. And it was a debauched gambler's face if ever she saw one. . .

She immediately chided herself at the thought, for she had never knowingly been in contact with such a person in her life. But she also knew that sometimes, basic instincts could be as sound as facts.

'That's between me and my lawyer,' Marcus said, his voice sharp. 'But you may rest assured that some of our debtors will shortly be paid.'

'I wouldn't have thought there was a need for secrets between a man and his partner, Marcus,' Kelly said lazily.

'Nor would there be, if the money didn't run through one partner's fingers faster than the other can count it.'

There were more secrets than Ronan Kelly dreamed about, Amy thought keenly. But she was becoming embarrassed at witnessing the animosity between them. Each of them was a man who readily spoke his mind, and it was clear to anyone that there was no love lost between them. Marcus sounded sorely put out now, and the other still had that calculating look on his face. But then he laughed, slapping Marcus on the back in what was evidently meant to be a show of camaraderie.

'Here we go again, me boy, at loggerheads the minute we meet, and your lovely Miss Finch will wonder what kind of ruffian you have for a partner. What say we forget our squabbling and enjoy a few jars together?'

'I think not,' Marcus snapped. 'I've more business to attend to this afternoon that requires a clear head.'

Amy was more than thankful for his good sense. And from the unsteadiness of the partner's hands, she guessed that Ronan had already been drinking, though it was barely midday. Her first instinct of mild dislike for the man was quickly turning to something far stronger.

But Kelly merely shrugged and muttered that he'd find plenty of business of his own for the rest of the day.

Thankfully, she saw nothing of him again until the following morning when the luggage was being loaded on to Marcus's own carriage, which he and the groom had brought from Callanby. By now, Amy suspected that the horse Marcus had ridden to Dublin had been sold to raise immediate funds for himself during his aunt's visit. If so, it was to his credit. But it was something she would never enquire about. In the circumstances, the sale of the horse had not even been necessary. . .

She was also realising anew how important she was to the whole future of Marcus's venture. Receiving his aunt's entire fortune depended solely on her. It was a responsibility that weighed heavily on her mind and also on her conscience.

Amy still couldn't imagine why Lady Bellingham had evidently wanted this union between them. But through their plotting they were debasing the lady's final wishes, and however misguided the order, it shamed Amy to know it.

Marcus spread a tartan travelling rug over her knees as they prepared to leave the London Hotel in Dublin. Ronan sat outside the closed carriage with the groom, while the two of them were seated more comfortably inside.

'Please don't fret, Amy. Everything will be all right if we stick to our plan,' he said quietly, just as if he could read the turmoil going on in her head.

'Will it?' She spoke with sudden passion. 'I'm unused to deception, and I'm still not sure I can go through with it without giving myself away at every turn—'

He put his finger against her mouth, and she knew her voice had risen, though she doubted that those outside could hear against the clattering of horses' hooves on the cobbled Dublin streets.

'Always remember that you don't have to go through anything alone, Amy. I will be by your side, and if it pains you to speak falsehoods, then you may leave all the telling to me, since I am undoubtedly more adept at it than you.'

She couldn't tell if he was being facetious or not, but she gave a small nod, and he removed his finger from her lips and held it beneath her chin for a long moment.

'And would it pain you so very much to pretend an affection for me?' he said, taking her by surprise.

She kept her eyes lowered, and held her hands tightly in her lap. How could she answer this, when she already felt such an unwilling attraction towards him!

'I'm sure I shall do my best not to let you down, since it's so important to you,' she said at last.

'That's not what I asked you. And why do you not look at me?'

She raised her eyes slowly, and she heard him draw in his breath as their gazes met and locked for a long moment.

'Lord, but you are so very beautiful,' he muttered. 'And I am doubly conscious of what I am asking you to do, and the sacrifice you will be making.'

'Sacrifice?' Amy said in a cracked voice.

He took his hand away from her face, and she swallowed deeply, suspicion filling her mind at his words. What new devilment was this? He spoke without expression.

'You have agreed to be my fiancée, and to go through a marriage ceremony with me. Is that correct?'

'You know that it is.'

'And in due time that marriage will be annulled. You will then depart with a handsome reward, and it will be as if it never happened. Is that also correct?'

She couldn't understand why he was making

these cold, stark statements that wounded her with every word. If he was calculating in his scheme, then he made her sound no less calculating in her acceptance of it.

'It is,' she said in a small voice.

She felt him tightly clasp her hand.

'And do you not realise the implications such an annulment will have on your future chances of marrying a suitable husband?'

She was startled, for she had given it no thought at all. She had been unable to get beyond the plan they were hatching, and the anxiety to carry it through convincingly. She stared at him now, her face a painful red.

'You mean no one will care to marry a woman who has already been discarded by one husband?' she asked, as brutally frank as he.

'Something like that,' he said quietly.

She had been half-jesting, but she saw instantly that he was not. She fought to keep her pride intact.

'I hardly think I need be concerned with that prospect for some time, sir. After all, I will be handsomely rewarded, as you put it, and can live as I please for as long as I please. As for finding another husband,' she added with a short laugh, 'my first experience of marriage may well put me off the idea for life.'

'Don't be ridiculous, Amy. You're young and beautiful, and with money at your disposal, there may be many men eager to marry you. But they may not be so keen when they discover you already have one unfortunate marriage behind you. An annulment is sometimes viewed with some suspicion.'

'Then what would you have me do? Pretend to
be a widow, and add more lies to those I am already
obliged to tell?' she flashed at him.

The conversation began to distress her far more
than she might have expected. She didn't want to
consider the future, nor to think of those unknown
young men in line for her marital favours. One step
at a time, she thought feverishly. She removed her
hand from his, only just realising she had been holding on tightly to it all this time.

'I would be obliged if you would change the sub-
ject, Marcus. I've no wish to discuss it, and there
is quite enough to think about presently.'

She turned away from him, and he didn't answer.
They travelled in virtual silence for several hours.
They had left the confines and outer suburbs of
the city behind them, and were travelling steadily
southwards.

In the far distance ahead of them now, Amy could
see the hazy blue outlines of the Wicklow Mountains, rearing up into the summer sky, and at last
she felt a sliver of pleasure at the sight. Mountains
and streams and wild, rugged country were all so
reminiscent of the Island of Skye where she had
spent the last relatively happy years. She loved the
bustle and heat of the city, but she acknowledged
that here there was a sense of space and freedom,
and a closeness to God and nature more infinite than
anything man could produce.

'You have a very serene expression on your face.
Do I take it that you've forgiven me?'

She heard Marcus speak abruptly. It was such a
long while since they had had any communication

at all, that she didn't readily comprehend his meaning. She gave a deep sigh.

'I'd rather not answer that, but life's too short to bear grudges. And since we have to be in one another's company for the foreseeable future, I would much prefer that we at least try to tolerate one another.'

His voice was dry as he replied, 'Thank you for that small concession. And I have no wish to be your enemy. Far from it. And if we can be nothing else to one another, except in name, then I'll be honoured to accept your friendship.'

Amy was greatly suspicious of such apparent sincerity. As if he would have no objections to making this marriage a more meaningful one, rather than the sham it was destined to be. And she just didn't believe he felt the same emotions as she did. . . She remembered again that lovely ceremony on the island for those two young people who truly loved each other. It had touched her heart, and she had hoped so much that one day she would find that kind of love for herself.

'We shall be coming into the village of Rossleigh in another couple of hours,' Marcus went on. 'There's little of any consequence there, except a few houses and a staging-post, and a hotel for travellers where we shall stay for the night. I want to make an early start tomorrow morning, since we still have a good distance to go and it's best done in daylight hours. The hotel staff will provide us with food and drink to take for the rest of the journey, since there's no other hospitality between there and Callanby.'

'You make it sound rather alarming,' Amy

murmured, realising she would be the only woman travelling with three men through what sounded like very isolated country.

If it wasn't for the fact that she was with her fiancé, her champion and protector. . . The irony of it all struck her anew, for there was no more love lost between herself and Marcus Bellingham than between him and his other partner! In fact, she was as much a business partner to him as Ronan Kelly.

'You have no need to be afraid. We follow a well-known track and my groom is an excellent driver. We skirt the lower slopes of the mountains for much of the way, and the only difficult part is the high pass as we approach the descent to the town. But I think you will be agreeably surprised by everything you find in Callanby.'

'You forget how much I already know about it,' Amy said. 'Your letters were always very informative and visual. Though I always wondered if the valley could possibly be as green and fertile as you described, or if you were colouring it for the benefit of your aunt.'

He laughed more naturally than of late, and she could see that he was becoming more comfortable the farther they travelled. Cities were not to his liking, she guessed, and he would be happy to be back in his chosen environment.

'You obviously know me too well,' he said, while she thought wryly that she really didn't know him at all.

'But in this case,' he went on, 'I did not exaggerate. Ireland is beautiful and it suits me well. Callanby lies in a valley within the protection of the mountains, but when it rains, it seems as if all the water in creation is concentrated on that valley.'

'I see,' she said, her face revealing that she didn't find the thought particularly attractive. Marcus smiled at her doubtful expression.

'But it gives us certain advantages. The river rushes through my land when it's in flood, instead of being a meandering stream. It becomes a virtual torrent then, so that any mineral deposits from the surrounding area will settle there. And when it stops raining, the valley is as green and verdant as you will ever see. Not for nothing is this country called the Emerald Isle.'

She couldn't deny that he had a way with words. She had always thought so, from his letters, and she liked and admired a man who could put those thoughts into speech, which so many couldn't.

'Then I can't wait to see it for myself,' she said, 'And I wish so much that your aunt could have seen it too.'

'So do I,' Marcus said, sobering at once. 'But I console myself with the fact that if she had been here, you and I wouldn't have been in the happy state we find ourselves in now.'

Before she knew what he was about, he had raised her left hand to his lips. Lady Bellingham's sapphire ring still sat heavily on her third finger, but she was becoming used to its unfamiliarity now. Just as she was becoming used to thinking of herself as Marcus Bellingham's fiancée, and future bride. And she didn't deny that there was a certain danger in believing in it too much.

Amy discovered that the small village of Rossleigh was little more than a hamlet. The only two buildings of any consequence were just as Marcus had said—a staging-post and a hotel.

When their carriage drew up in the hotel court-yard, she alighted thankfully with the assistance of Marcus's hand. She was stiff and aching after the journey from Dublin, and she didn't anticipate a whole day of travel tomorrow with any great enthusiasm.

It was even worse when she found that the hotel had little to offer in the way of city comforts. Her room was spartan in the extreme, and she longed for the luxury of a long soak in a proper bath-tub, but she had to make do with a hip-bath and the pails of hot water hauled upstairs by a couple of sullen maids.

Marcus had said they would dine at seven o'clock, so she had an hour to make herself presentable. She was hot and tacky, and thankful to bathe and change into fresh clothes, though she hardly thought it necessary to look too fine in this outlandish place.

Would Callanby be the same? she wondered now. And what would Lady B. have thought about this awful hotel? For the first time, Amy was almost glad the lady wasn't here to see it, for she'd probably have turned turtle by now and insisted on going straight back to Skye, and home comforts.

While Amy. . . Once she had recovered from the first rigours of travel, Amy was aware of the strangest feeling of pioneering spirit seeping into her veins. With a little shock of pleasure, she now knew exactly what Marcus found in seeking out pastures new. It was a sense of adventure that gave him such charisma and dash, and kept him so vitally alive. It was something Amy realised she could identify with as well.

She looked at herself in the cracked hotel mirror, seeing her sparkling eyes, and the way her breasts rose and fell, just by thinking of the adventure that was still ahead. For this *was* an adventure, going into unknown territory with a man purporting to be her betrothed, and sharing a secret known only to them.

She turned away from the mirror, before her telltale eyes revealed far more to her than she cared to admit. Because, for one stunning moment, she found herself wishing so desperately that it was all real. That she and her lover were pioneering together, seeking out the elusive gold that was reputed to have been found in this area since time immemorial. . .that they were truly partners in mind and body and spirit. . .and love. . .

She wore a blue, long-sleeved gown this evening, and almost without thinking she tugged at the demure neckline to pull it a little higher, as if to disguise the wanton thoughts in her head. She had no wish to appear provocative, especially since they would be obliged to share the dinner-table with Ronan Kelly once more. When Marcus knocked on her door, she opened it at once, and he took in her appearance with a small smile.

'Most suitable,' he said. 'My aunt would be pleased with you, Amy.'

'You mean because I now look more like the lady's companion I always was?' she said.

He tucked her arm inside his as he closed her door behind them and went towards the stairs.

'No. Because any man would be proud to be seen with such a lovely young lady.'

His words took her aback, and her eyes smarted a little at the simple compliment. But she forced herself to remember that if she was playing a part, then so was he. And the pretence of affection was as much for the eagle-eyed Ronan Kelly as for anyone else.

If he once guessed that their impending nuptials were not all they should be, Amy suspected he was the type who would not be above informing the Dublin newspaper of the fact, providing they paid him a healthy sum for the information. Already, and on such short acquaintance, she knew how much she mistrusted him.

'How can you stand that odious Mr Kelly?' she whispered to Marcus, as they descended the hotel stairs.

His answer surprised her. 'He wasn't always as you see him now, Amy. But for his expertise and my sympathy for his plight, I would have dissolved the partnership long ago.'

She knew exactly what he meant. *Once he had his inheritance. . .* but her curiosity was aroused now.

'You can't leave it there, Marcus! Tell me about this so-called plight of his!' She knew she sounded flippant, but the brashness of the fellow didn't seem to bear out Marcus's suggestion of any deeper feelings in the man at all.

'His wife and child were both killed in a fire at their home. Kelly had been reasonably sober until then, but the event turned his brain, and he sought any solace he could. You can't turn against a man when he's lost everything.'

'Oh, how terrible,' Amy whispered, ashamed of her prejudging. It still didn't make her like him, though, and she wasn't looking forward to sharing this evening with him.

Throughout their meal, Amy was aware of the unsubtle probing from the Irishman. But it was purely for the amount of Marcus's inheritance, and not for the sudden engagement between the other two. Finally, when Ronan's voice was heavily slurred, Marcus could stand the irritation no longer.

'I'd be obliged if you would keep your nose out of my personal business,' he snapped.

'I'd have thought it was my business too,' Ronan said.

'Then you thought wrong. And while you continue to fritter away what assets we have until things are settled with my lawyer, I shall continue to keep my hands firmly on the purse-strings.'

Kelly glowered at him. 'By all the saints, Marcus, you can change colours faster than a chameleon. You never used to be as pernickety as a woman—'

'I'll thank you to keep your voice down, and remember that there is a lady present. As for your ridiculous comments, I don't consider them worthy of a moment of my time.'

He could be withering enough to squash the brashest opponent, Amy thought. Except for a hot-headed man like Kelly, who seemed unlikely to be squashed by anyone. But she was hot with embarrassment at having to witness this little scene between them, and she didn't find it hard to surmise that such a confrontation was a frequent occurrence.

And after Marcus's words, the man's attention

turned to her once more. She squirmed at the way his gaze slid over her appearance. He was insolent and hateful, she raged, as his gaze finally rested on the ring on her finger.

'It came as quite a shock to find that you and Marcus were so cosy, Miss Finch. It must have been a very sudden attachment, though you would have been quick to see the advantages, of course, when the old lady died. But I congratulate you. It's quite a jump up from being a lady's companion to the wife of a man with such prospects—'

Before Amy could get her outraged wits together, Marcus had leapt up and dragged Ronan to his feet by the scruff of his neck, his hands closing cruelly around the man's throat. The fact that no one gave them no more than a cursory glance was enough to tell her that this was no unusual happening in this transit establishment, and she was fervently glad that Lady Bellingham couldn't witness it. She would have been completely scandalised, and washed her hands of her nephew completely.

'You will retract those words, you bastard,' Marcus said savagely. 'You may insult me as much as you wish, but you will not insult my future wife.'

Amy's shock at hearing him blaspheme was tempered by the way the other man's eyes bulged in his purple face now, as much as by Marcus's championship of her.

She heard Kelly croaking out the words, 'All right, you pompous bugger, I'll retract them if you give me breath to do so.'

Marcus let him go, and he rubbed at his sore throat, while his colour gradually assumed a redder hue than the appalling purple it had become. For a moment, Amy had thought he was about to expire.

'My apologies, Miss Finch,' he snarled in an exaggerated tone. 'I hereby retract all that I said. Does that suit your lordship?' he hissed at Marcus.

'It will do,' Marcus said coldly. 'And now I suggest that you get to bed and sleep it off, for we're to be away early tomorrow morning.'

Without another word, Kelly lurched off in the direction of the stairs, and they both heard him blaspheming and muttering, while clinging on to the banister rail as he hauled himself off to bed.

'I'm sorry you had to witness that, Amy. Unfortunately, his drinking and gambling habits only came to light after his wife and child died. Had I suspected it, I'd never have gone into partnership with him.'

From the stiffness in his voice, Amy guessed how hard it was for him to admit that he'd been so very wrong in his choice of partner. Marcus was a proud man, and he wouldn't take lightly to being so deceived and cheated. Which was ironic, she thought swiftly, since the two of them were currently in the business of deceiving and cheating. . .

'Amy? I hope you're not really upset,' she heard him say with concern. 'Can I get you something to calm your nerves? A glass of brandy, perhaps?'

She shook her head vigorously. 'I'm no milksop to need brandy just because I heard two grown men arguing,' she said, stung that he should think her so feeble.

He gave a faint smile. 'A milksop is the very last thing I would call you. You have all the fire and spirit of a man—and I mean that as a compliment, for there's nothing unfeminine about you.'

He stopped abruptly, and she didn't know how

to answer him, or even if an answer was necessary or required. But her silence served to emphasise the words he had spoken, and she knew her breath was quickening as his gaze flickered over her as if he had no way of stopping it.

But it couldn't have been more different from the way the hateful Kelly had raked her body with his eyes. There was blatant admiration in Marcus's eyes, as if he truly liked what he saw. . .and Amy told herself swiftly that she would do well to stop such wild imaginings.

'Marcus,' she said determinedly, 'when we are alone I insist that we remember our business arrangement. I agree that we must show a public face, but in private, I want no more compliments—'

Her voice stopped abruptly as she saw the annoyance in his eyes, and she knew she had said the wrong thing. She might be an innocent compared with more worldly young women, but even she knew that no gentleman cared to have his compliments thrown back in his face. But she didn't want to hear them if they were only meant to curry favour and keep her sweet.

'So you prefer to call our relationship a business arrangement, do you?' he said, his voice several degrees cooler than before.

'Well, isn't it?' she countered, honest enough to face the truth of it.

'For the present,' he said, 'and apparently I was mistaken in thinking that the tone of your letters led me to believe that in many respects there was a certain empathy between us.'

'But they weren't *my* letters, were they?' Amy said, almost in tears at the way this conversation seemed to be degenerating into an argument. 'They were your aunt's words, and I was merely the interpreter.'

'Yes, of course. My aunt's words,' Marcus said thoughtfully. 'And I'm wondering if perhaps I should take a little more notice of Ronan's words too. One rash partner is one too many without my adding to the foolishness.'

'I don't understand you, sir,' Amy stammered, seeing that his look was definitely calculating now, where before it had been almost tender.

'I mean, my dear Miss Finch,' he said, leaning forward and taking her hands in his in what might be seen as a gesture of affection—except that from the tightness of his grip, she knew it was not, 'that I wonder if there is not the smallest amount of substance in what my partner said?'

She had become so disturbed that she was not following his train of thought at all.

'He said or implied so many offensive things—'

'And one of them was that a lady's companion, who could assess just how wealthy her employer was, might have seen all too clearly the prospect of marrying her heir. My timely proposal might have been all too tempting to my lady's ears. It might even have been engineered between my aunt and your sweet self!'

Amy gasped, pulling her hands away from his.

'How dare you think that of me, and you demean your aunt's memory by even suggesting such a vile thing,' she said, her voice vibrant with rage. 'You go too far, Mr Bellingham, and I'm not sure that I care to go on with this charade—'

She was on her feet, her hands clenched tightly

at her sides now, and he stood at once, his hands on her shoulders so that she was held by him. She felt too stricken to move for a moment, even though all she desired right now was to get as far away from him as possible.

'Amy, if I do you a grave injustice, then I apologise from the bottom of my heart. But I had to be sure. You do see that, don't you? A more unscrupulous woman than yourself might very well intend to hold me to the marriage vows—'

'I can assure you, sir, that that will never be my intention. The sooner the marriage can be annulled and I can forget that it ever happened, the better it will please me.'

She swept away from him and rushed up the stairs to her room, just resisting the urge to slam the door behind her. She trembled all over. And realised instantly that with her own words, she had sanctioned that the sham of a marriage would go ahead—and her dearest wish in all the world, was that it wasn't to be a sham at all.

And that was the most foolish thought she had had yet. Because he obviously had a doubt in his mind about her now, which he would never be able to forget. Besides which, she was too constant a reminder of his own vulnerability and his need for his inheritance.

Amy had never felt more depressed than she did at that moment, and she found herself blaming everything on Ronan Kelly, and inelegantly wishing him to Kingdom Come.

Chapter Seven

After a restless night on a less-than-comfortable bed, Amy awoke aching in every limb, which boded ill for the journey ahead. But once they were on their way, she resolved to make no complaint that would mark her down as a sensitive female. She simply gritted her teeth and tried to ignore the bumps and ruts in the track as the swaying carriage took them ever southwards and on to the lower slopes of the mountains.

It was a tedious journey. The fact that the sun beat down brilliantly overhead did nothing to lessen the boredom of it, and Amy quickly became lethargic from watching the same kind of mountain scenery. She leaned her head back against the squabs, and had been lulled into a kind of stupor long before they paused for their first rest. When she was gently awoken, she was amazed to discover it was already past noon.

One minute it seemed she had been letting her eyelids droop, and seemingly, in the next, Marcus was rocking her shoulder, and the groom was shouting at the horses to whoa.

'Have we arrived?' she murmured.

He laughed. 'Hardly. But it's time to stretch our legs for a while and take some refreshment. The horses need to be fed and watered as much as ourselves.'

She accepted his hand and stepped carefully down from the carriage, feeling as unsteady as if she had to find her sea-legs. Her mind veered away from a thought that would be forever associated in her mind with Lady Bellingham's sad end.

By now Kelly and the groom were some distance away from them, jawing together and attending to the horses. Amy slowly looked around her and her breath caught in her throat.

'Oh, how beautiful,' she said involuntarily. 'How absolutely *splendid* and—and—and sort of *holy*.'

She blushed madly as the word escaped her lips, but it was truly a scene of silent, cathedral splendour that could only have been created by a heavenly hand.

They had ascended steadily while she had been dozing, travelling through the mountains, and they had stopped now on a small plateau. The more distant slopes circled them, soaring upwards in ever more grandiose fashion, but on these ledges the short tufty grass was green and sweet, and wild flowers grew in profusion.

The air, too, was as sweet and temperate as wine. It was such a trite expression, but never more apt to Amy as now, when she breathed in the clear, fragrant atmosphere.

'Did you think I would have considered bringing my aunt to a place that was *un*holy?' Marcus said unexpectedly, just as if he saw nothing odd in what

Amy had said. 'Did you think I cared so little
for her?'

She looked at him, and saw the sincerity in his
eyes. Whatever else he did now, or had done with
his life, she knew he had felt a true affection for
that contrary old lady. And that he found it just as
difficult to admit it as to show it.

'I know you cared for her a lot,' she said. 'And
I know how she would have loved this. She always
said the island of Skye was her spiritual home, but
I think all of this must compare with it.'

She illustrated her thoughts with a wide sweep of
her arms as if to embrace the universe. Marcus
caught one of her outstretched hands and squeezed it
tightly for a moment before touching it with his lips.

'I thank you for that, Amy.'

The sweet moment was broken by a raucous shout
from Ronan Kelly as he approached with the basket
of food and drink the hotel had provided for their
journey.

'Are you two love-birds thinking of eating and
drinking at all, or shall Will and meself drink all
the proceeds of last night's fling at the gaming
tables?' he said with a grin.

Marcus glared at him. 'Don't tell me you actually
won for a change?' he said sarcastically.

Kelly laughed nastily. 'The trouble with you, me
boy, is that you don't have enough faith in your
uncle Ronan. Sure, we won, and handsomely too,
so we did.'

He held out a flagon of ale towards Marcus, who
declined it quickly.

'You'd do better to keep off that stuff while the
sun is high. And, Will, I'd be obliged if you'd refrain

from drinking too much during the day while you're driving the horses. We want no accidents when we come to the high pass.'

'Have no fear, Mr Bellingham, sir,' Will said, in an accent as thick as Kelly's. 'I ain't planning to hurl us over no mountain edge. I'll take a small drop of ale just to whet me thirst, and then I'll stick to the water.'

'Good man,' Marcus said.

There were bottles of water in the basket, together with the cloth-wrapped parcels of pies and fruit, and he handed a bottle to Amy with a smile of apology.

'We're obliged to be bohemian in our drinking habits while we're on the road, I'm afraid. The transit hotel won't spare us cups or glasses, and Ronan isn't in the habit of remembering to bring them.'

'What would be the point? They'd only get smashed in the travelling,' Kelly jeered, moving away from the pair of them to sprawl out on the grass with Will.

Amy ignored him and turned to Marcus. 'I've no objection to drinking from a bottle,' she said quietly. 'I've not been accused of being a hot-house flower yet.'

She raised the bottle to her lips, welcoming the refreshing water that coursed down her throat. When she had finished, Marcus took the bottle from her, and without wiping the neck of it, he drank from the same bottle. As he did so, his eyes never left her face, and she felt a rush of sensual pleasure at such an intimate gesture.

After they had eaten their fill, Marcus stretched out full-length on the ground, his hands behind his head, suggesting that Amy might also care to relax for half an hour before they continued their journey.

'I think I'd like to walk about a little,' she said. 'I've been sitting for long enough already.'

'Then be sure to keep well back from the edge.'

She looked at him in exasperation, and he laughed and held up his hands in apology.

'All right! You're no hot-house flower—but you're very precious to me, Amy, and I don't want to lose you.'

She turned away, her eyes blurred, wishing he didn't come out with these unexpected praises. For someone who professed to be unable to show his feelings, she thought, as she promenaded back and forth along the plateau, he was quite adept at saying the right thing at the right time. And she had better be more keenly aware of that skill, she thought, for it might not always be as sincere as it seemed. It was to his advantage to keep her sweet, and she would do well not to forget it.

While she was deep in thought, she realised she had walked a little near to the edge of the plateau, and she stepped back quickly. But not quickly enough to prevent a pair of male arms from closing around her as if to pull her back. From the smell on his breath, she knew instantly who it was.

'Careful, little lady, we don't want to lose you,' Kelly said, and although his words were almost an echo of Marcus's, there was a world of difference in their intonation.

Amy shook herself free of him, trying desperately to suppress a shudder at his touch.

'I thank you for your concern, Mr Kelly, but I am quite all right, as you can see.'

She had also seen Marcus stand up on hearing Kelly's loud voice, and he strode quickly towards the pair of them, clearly annoyed at seeing them stand so close together.

'What's all this?' he said, his eyes narrowing.

'Mr Kelly thought I was too near to the edge, and kindly came to my rescue,' Amy said quickly, not wanting to be the cause of yet more antagonism between the partners. 'I assured him I was in no danger, as you see, Marcus.'

He didn't make any further comment, but spoke coldly to his partner.

'I think we've lingered here long enough and should be on our way. We've still a fair distance to go, and I'd prefer it if we reached the high pass before the evening mist starts to come down.'

His words made Amy shiver, and took her mind away from the intriguing thought that for a moment he had seemed almost jealous of Kelly's attentions to her. That would have been a fine twist to their situation, indeed!

Once they were on their way, she turned to him anxiously.

'Is it dangerous to negotiate this high pass that you speak of?' she asked.

'Not for an experienced driver at this time of year, and Will knows the route backwards,' he assured her. 'Later in the year it's best avoided, and anyone travelling to and from Dublin during the winter months is advised to take the longer route around the foot of the mountains.'

He gave her a speculative smile.

'But none of that need concern you, Amy, unless

you're thinking of leaving Callanby as soon as the summer is over.'

'At present I have no idea how long I shall be staying there,' she said without expression. 'It depends on a number of things.'

'Name them,' he said.

She looked at him in exasperation. 'I hardly think I need to do any such thing. You know as well as I do the terms of our agreement.'

'Ah yes. Our business agreement. And no doubt one of the things to keep in mind is the amount of the reward you will be paid for your services.'

'Please don't demean my part in this!' Amy said angrily. 'None of it was my idea, and I only agreed to your vulgar terms because—well, because I cannot live on fresh air, and after the unsettling times I've had recently I shall probably take a sea voyage to decide on my future plans—'

Even as she said the unthinking words, she knew she would not. She never wanted to set foot on board a ship again. . .with the thought came the shock of realising that, if she ever wanted to leave this Emerald Isle, as Marcus called it, she would have no other choice.

She bit her lip, feeling as trapped by Ireland's glorious sun-kissed day, as by the man sitting beside her.

'I hardly thought a sea voyage would appeal to you,' Marcus said, reading her mind in the irritating way he had.

'It does not, now I come to think of it, but since sea travel is the only means of leaving here, then—' She left the sentence unfinished.

'Oh, Amy,' Marcus said in mock sorrow, 'will

you be so anxious to get away from me? Did nothing
I said in my letters ever show you a more convivial
side to me than the reckless fellow my aunt considered me to be?'

'You know that they did,' she muttered. 'And
Lady Bellingham never thought you as bad as she
may have had you believe. Underneath all that scorn,
I believe she had a grudging softness for your devil-
may-care ways. It was just that she considered it
high time you settled down.'

Dear Lord, she thought in some alarm, listening
to herself as she practically lectured a gentleman on
the way to behave. What on earth must he think of
her? To her amazement, she realised he was laughing, and it was a genuine, throaty laugh that forced
her to smile shamefacedly in return.

'Oh, my sweet, sweet Amy, no wonder my aunt
thought you would be a suitable wife for me to settle
down with. You have the knack of putting a man
in his place in the coolest manner, but with such a
becoming blush on your cheeks that only a fool
would take offence.'

'And you're anything but a fool,' she retorted,
not too sure if these were compliments or not.

'Shall I tell you one of the things I like best about
you?' he went on.

'I'm not sure I want to hear it—'

'Why on earth should you not? As my fiancée,
you must expect me to whisper sweet nothings in
your ear from time to time, and to pay you extrava-
gant compliments,' he teased her, but at her glare,
he went on quickly.

'We'll play a game to while away the tedious
hours of travelling. I'll tell you what I like about

you, and you will say what you like about me. There must be *something* to vindicate my wicked character,' he said drily. 'And then we will do the reverse. I will say what I *don't* like about you, and you will do the same about me.'

'What you *don't* like about me?' Amy echoed, forgetting all the rest.

Marcus laughed again, and squeezed her hand, letting it rest comfortably in his while the carriage trundled on.

'Your comment gives me the very hook on which to begin, for what I like very much about you is your femininity, and only a very feminine woman would have picked up on my remark and felt affronted by it.'

'That may be your opinion, sir, but I fear that in reality it makes me sound impossibly vain, to want everyone to like everything about me, when I know that such a condition cannot be.'

'One of the rules of this game is that you are not allowed to argue with the player,' Marcus said sternly. 'You must accept the compliment or the criticism for what it is.'

'And I think you make up your own rules—'

'Naturally. It's my game, after all.'

She didn't quite know what to make of him. She thought she knew so much about him, but he constantly surprised her. And she found herself liking that about him. Her mouth curved into a smile as she glanced at him from beneath her lashes.

'Is it my turn now?'

'It is. If you can possibly find something you like about me, that is,' he said, with an unusual show of humility that Amy was certain wouldn't last.

'I like the way you can always surprise me. I thought I knew so much about you from your letters, and just when I try to anticipate your actions, you say or do something that makes me realise you're human after all.'

His laugh was practically a guffaw this time.

'Good God, Amy, have you only just discovered that? Have I always seemed so very wicked to you then?'

'There are to be no arguments or discussions on the player's remarks,' she reminded him. 'Those are the rules, remember?'

'All right. Any discussions we think necessary can come later,' he agreed. 'So now to the next part of the game. What do I dislike about you?'

She realised she was holding her breath, knowing she was woman enough not to want him to dislike anything at all about her. And from the time it took for him to speak, she thought he must have a very long list in his mind from which to choose.

'I dislike the fact that you're so very young,' he said, after what seemed an interminable time.

She looked at him in astonishment.

'What? How can you dislike a person for being young? No one can help being the age they are, and it's not an acceptable statement. I demand that you erase it immediately.'

He laughed, clearly delighted that she had entered so unwittingly into the spirit of the game.

'No arguments, remember? You must accept what I say.'

Amy shook her head. 'I cannot. If a comment makes no sense, then it must be explained before we continue. That's only fair.'

He looked at her thoughtfully, and before she could guess what he was about, he leaned forward, cupping her chin in his hands and and kissing her lightly on the mouth. She breathed in the scent of his male skin, and the gentleman's toiletries he had used that morning, and felt a weakness in her bones.

'Very well. I dislike the fact that you're so very young, because I know I've taken unfair advantage of you, and you don't have the sophistication to oppose it. I need your compliance in this engagement and marriage, for obvious reasons, but I dislike the fact that I've been obliged to force you into it and perhaps ruined your chances of a more suitable marriage. An older woman would have known how to cope with it all far better.'

'And do you think I will be unable to cope when the time comes?' she said, unsure whether to be outraged at this dismissal of her as an adult, or to be confused by the passion in his voice and the apparent concern for her well-being.

'I think and hope that you will, but it will always be on my conscience that your good name may have been damaged by my desires.'

She flinched from his words. She was unwilling to accept that they were true, but she knew full well the demands of genteel society for a chaste bride to go to the marriage-bed, and even more, that an annulled marriage was always viewed with the highest suspicion.

'I see by your face that you understand the situation I have placed you in,' Marcus said quietly. 'But perhaps you were never fully aware of it before this moment.'

'I think I was,' she said. 'I may be young, but I am not stupid, Marcus.'

He inclined his head in acknowledgement of the fact. Without her being really aware of it, his arm had slid around her shoulders in the last few minutes, and as she leaned against him, she felt a *frisson* of pleasure at the contact.

'My turn, I think,' she said, more huskily than before. 'I have to say something that I dislike about you.'

As if anticipating the worst, he withdrew his arm, leaving her with a sense of disappointment. It had felt so warm and intimate inside the closed confines of the carriage, to be circled within his arm, and feeling the beat of his heart matching the beat of her own. She swallowed thickly.

'I dislike the fact that you think you know everything about me. You can't possibly know my deepest reasons for accepting your outrageous proposal, nor how I will behave when we inevitably go our separate ways. You really don't know me at all, and I dislike your superiority, and the fact that you think me such a child!'

She tried to ignore the pang she felt at her own words. What charismatic gentleman would want to throw in his lot with a child when he could choose someone from the whole world to be his wife?

'That's at least two dislikes,' Marcus said. 'It's not allowed for a player to throw a double at the same time.'

'And I thought Mr Kelly was the gambler—'

'I do have an inkling of a gambler's methods, and I see that you yourself are conversant with the dice.'

'Only in childhood games, sir,' she said with

heavy sarcasm. 'As might be expected from one so young.'

'Perhaps we should abandon this game for the time being. It seems to bring out the worst in us both,' he said with a faint smile.

'On the contrary,' Amy said. 'I think it brings out the truth. I am quite ready to continue if you are.'

'Just one more throw then,' he said, continuing the gambling analogy. 'Let's finish up on something we like about one another, so we can at least travel in harmony instead of resentment.'

'Your turn then,' she murmured, delving in her mind for something she could say about him that wouldn't sound gushing, or flirtatious or compromising. . .

'I like everything that you are. Your freshness, your youth, your fearlessness in standing up to me, your spirit, your natural beauty, the very essence of you—'

'For pity's sake, Marcus, please stop!' Amy gasped. 'You're supposed to say one thing only, and you're describing an absolute paragon, which is something no woman could ever live up to!'

He smiled. 'But I did say one thing. I said I like everything about you, and then I merely elaborated on what goes into that statement.'

'And how do you account for the fact that you say you like my youth, when it's the very thing you said you dislike about me?' she demanded. 'You can't have it both ways.'

He gave a heavy sigh. 'I like it very much, and I only dislike it because it disturbs me so.'

'Why does it?' she said, determined to find out the truth from this irritating man.

'Because I'm so much older,' he said simply.

It stopped her in her tracks. She flushed deeply. If theirs was to be a proper marriage, then maybe such a remark would have some substance, though as far as Amy was concerned he wasn't too old for her at all. He was in the prime of manhood, she thought poetically, and he was as dynamic and handsome a man as she had ever known, and one that any woman would be proud to call husband. . .

'I demand that we retract such statements that we think are invalid,' she said, almost inaudibly.

He leaned towards her, his face very close to hers now. He was almost touching her with his lips once more. . . They were so tantalisingly close to hers, and she could no longer deny the longing for him to press them on her mouth.

'For everything there must be a reason, Amy, and I find you a most discerning young woman,' he said softly. 'So tell me your reason for that remark. Is it that you do not think me too old for you, or that you are too young for me?'

'I think that the ages of two people do not matter a jot, if they love one another,' she said, floundering. 'In this case, of course, it does not apply, but I truly believe that spring and autumn can be perfectly compatible as long as love is there.'

'And we are hardly as far apart as spring and autumn, are we?' he said, before he placed his mouth against hers in a long, sweet kiss.

'Nor are we in love,' she felt bound to remind him when they broke apart. If she had not done so, she thought desperately, she would be in danger of giving away her turbulent feelings completely.

She pushed him away from her, and he half-smiled.

'I should have added that I also like your honesty, even though it can sometimes emerge at the most inopportune times.'

'Well, that's far too many likes about me, and I don't care to hear any more.'

'So let's finish the game. You have to find one more thing you like about me, if you can possibly do so,' he challenged her.

She looked away, to gaze through the carriage window, where the slopes of the mountains were becoming more rugged now, as they climbed steadily towards the high pass. For how could she say what was in her heart?

That it was dawning on her with every hour that passed, that he was a man she could love with all her being, that she had found her soul-mate, and that she had been unknowingly fantasising these things about him all these months when she had felt his letters were for her alone, and not for his aunt's benefit at all! How could she possibly say any of that?

'I see you are finding it difficult,' he said at last.

'Not at all,' Amy said swiftly, not wanting to offend him. 'If I'm as honest as you believe me to be, then I have to say I have always liked and admired your pioneering spirit in following your dreams, despite what your aunt may have thought. Her opinions were not always mine,' she added with a faint smile. 'Does that satisfy you, sir?'

'It will do for now,' he said, and she turned away again, lest he should see the warmth in her eyes that had nothing to do with mere admiration and liking, but a far stronger and deeper emotion.

They stopped for a second time for refreshment before they reached the high pass in the late afternoon. Amy thought Marcus had been exaggerating when he mentioned an evening mist descending from the mountains, but now she saw that he had been right, and that the first gauzy fingers of mist had begun to appear long before the sun began to set.

'Is it quite safe?' she said nervously, glancing through the carriage window. In some places the clouds and mist seemed to join together in a shroud above and below them, enclosing them in an isolated white world. It was appreciably colder too, and Amy shivered, and pulled up the wool knee rug to cover her upper body and arms.

'It's quite safe,' Marcus assured her. 'Will knows this route like the proverbial back of his hand.'

'But what if something is coming the other way?' she said in alarm, her imagination leaping ahead of her.

'It would be a rare coincidence to meet another carriage or even a horseman at this precise spot,' he said, thankful that the presence of the mist prevented her from seeing the narrowness of the pass, and the steepness of the gorges on either side below them.

'All the same, I shall be glad when we're beyond it,' she murmured, unwilling to show how very fearful she felt, and with a need to keep on talking to try and overcome it. 'And I feel obliged to say that your aunt would have hated every moment of this, too. She was not fond of heights, and I fear the air would have been too thin for her comfort.'

It was a little thin for Amy's. She was beginning to feel decidedly light-headed, and whether or not it was all in her imagination, it did nothing to lessen the discomfort.

'My aunt would have survived it all magnificently, just as you are doing,' Marcus said. 'I promise you there is nothing to fear as long as I'm here beside you.'

He might have been making a double-edged remark, Amy thought. It was bitter-sweet to her now, and although she had never truly believed in love at first sight, she was sensible enough to know that that hadn't even been the case here. She had known too much about him long before they met. She had been intrigued and envious of his life, even though she had never fully admitted it, and she had defended him in her soul whenever his aunt ranted against him.

She felt his hand take hold of hers again beneath the rug, and although she knew it could be construed as scandalous familiarity, she felt totally unable to remove it. The clasp of his fingers intertwined with hers felt so right, and so very reassuring.

'How long does it take to negotiate this part of the journey?' she said in a dry voice, when the horses seemed to go ever slower as Will continually shouted at them to guide them carefully.

'Not much longer now. And once we begin the descent, we'll come out into the sunlight again, and you'll wonder what all the fuss was about.'

'I'm trying very hard not to make a fuss,' she objected, and he squeezed her hand tightly.

'I know you are, but I promise you it will all be

worth while very soon. The difference between this area and the valley below is breathtaking.'

She couldn't quite credit the truth of that. But at last she felt the carriage begin to dip a little, and realised they were indeed descending. For a few wild moments she had thought they were destined to remain on the high pass for ever, lost in the mist, and chided herself for the foolishness of such thoughts.

And then it was just as Marcus had said. The clouds and mist seemed to roll away as if they had been gathered up by some almighty hand, and far below them was the widest, greenest valley Amy had ever seen. It was sheltered by mountains on either side, and the river meandering through it sparkled blue and silver in the sunlight.

'Does it please my lady?' Marcus said with a smile as she gazed open-mouthed at the panorama below.

'It's truly beautiful,' she said. 'But there are no houses, or signs of habitation—'

'Be patient. We drive through the valley to the far end, and Callanby lies around the corner. My house is the last one we come to, and all the land around it, including much of the river valley that you see below us now.'

She couldn't deny her astonishment. If he owned as much as he said he did, he was certainly no pauper who had been totally dependent on hand-outs from his aunt. Amy recalled how he'd always told Lady Bellingham he'd made good in many small ways, and had invested where he could. But as usual, Lady B. had scoffed at the very idea of Marcus investing wisely, or even at all.

If Lady B. was here now, she might very well have to eat her words, Amy thought. But she decided to keep her own counsel on that until she saw exactly what kind of house she was being taken to. It might be a palace and it might be a hovel...

But whatever it was, circumstances had decreed that she was destined to take up residence in it with Marcus Bellingham, at least, for the present. Circumstances being the whims of his aunt, and the persuasiveness of Marcus himself...

Chapter Eight

As they descended into the fertile valley, the coolness of the mountain air was left behind them, and the air grew sweet and warm with the evening scents of wild flowers and foliage. Amy was charmed, and not a little relieved by the contrast, and she concentrated all her attention on the winding river valley ahead, gazing eagerly through the carriage window to catch the first glimpse of the small town set in such unexpected and spectacular surroundings.

'How long has Callanby been established?' she asked, turning to look at Marcus, and finding that disturbing gaze fixed on her again.

'There was a hamlet here for centuries, which gradually grew into a village of modest proportions, and then a small town when some city gentlefolk discovered the advantage of spending time in the mountains. Some regularly come here for their health, even in the winter months, for as you must already have realised, the air is extremely invigorating.'

'I do realise it,' Amy agreed. 'It has a strange

effect on a weary traveller, giving one a sudden sense of energy.'

She blushed as she spoke, and hurried on. 'I'm sorry. That must seem like a very naïve comment to you—'

'Not at all. It's a charming one, and a true one. I always feel that sense of renewed energy when I return here, and it has nothing to do with wanting to get back to business. It's as if something in the very air enlivens the blood, and wiser men than myself have discovered it.'

'Then don't you ever envisage a day when the place will become overpopulated, with visitors hoping to find a kind of elixir of life in Callanby?' she asked.

'I pray that day will never come,' Marcus said grimly. 'But if it should, we need have no worries, for our estate is well away from the more populated end of the town.'

She refused to make any comment to his familiar reference to it being *their* estate. It was a slip of the tongue, and no more, she told herself sternly, while another part of her brain cautioned her that nothing Marcus Bellingham ever said was uncalculated.

They travelled through the one main street of the small town, with its cottages and hostelries, its church, and the glimpses of larger properties well away from the main thoroughfare. And when they had left most of the habitation behind and were seemingly at the far end of the valley, a large, double-fronted stone house, mellow in the evening sunlight, came into view.

It was very well aspected, and would do credit to a gentleman's city dwelling, but here it was made more magnificent in its setting of long-established trees and well-attended grounds. Together with the backdrop of the mountains, and the meandering, quietly bubbling river at its foot that was fed by mountain streams, the house exuded a sense of tranquillity that couldn't ever be bought. Speechless for a moment, Amy looked at Marcus.

'Your face betrays you, Amy,' he said. 'Did you really think I would bring my bride to a hovel?'

She blushed wildly again, knowing it had been one of the words in her mind whenever she had wondered so scathingly about his abode.

'I think you forget that, before you met me in Dublin, you had no intention of bringing a bride here,' she flashed at him. 'It was your aunt's good opinion you sought, not mine.'

'And now I seek yours.' He caught at her hand as it lay limply in her lap. 'So does it please you, Amy? Does it enhance your opinion of me?'

She knew he was teasing her, and she felt a brief annoyance.

'I assure you, sir, that the style of a man's house is of far less importance to me than the honourable behaviour of the man himself.'

He laughed openly now. 'Oh, Amy, you give yourself away so readily that it's a shame to tease you, though I must confess it gives me a damnable feeling of pleasure when you rise to the bait so well.'

'What do you mean?' she demanded, dragging her hand away from his.

'I mean that if anyone had honourable intentions in this world, it's you. Do you think I believed, even for one moment, that you entered into this arrangement of ours solely for your own gain?'

MILLS & BOON®

AN IMPORTANT MESSAGE
FROM
THE EDITORS OF MILLS & BOON®

Dear Reader,

Because you've chosen to read one of our romance novels, we'd like to say "thank you"! And, as a **special** way to thank you, we've selected <u>four more</u> of the <u>books</u> you love so much **and** a mystery gift to send you absolutely **FREE!**

Please enjoy them with our compliments...

Tessa Shapcott   Editor,
Mills & Boon

P.S. And because we value our customers we've attached something extra inside...

EDITOR'S
FREE
GIFT
SEAL
THANK YOU

PEEL OFF SEAL AND
PLACE INSIDE

HOW TO VALIDATE
YOUR
EDITOR'S FREE GIFT
"THANK YOU"

1. Peel off the gift seal from the front cover. Place it in the space provided to the right. This automatically entitles you to receive four free books and a mystery gift.

2. Send back this card and you'll receive four specially selected Mills & Boon® Historical Romances™. These books are yours to keep absolutely FREE.

3. There's no catch. You're under no obligation to buy anything. We charge you nothing for your first shipment. And you don't have to make any minimum number of purchases - not even one!

4. The fact is, thousands of readers enjoy receiving their books by mail from the Reader Service™. They like the convenience of home delivery and they like getting the best new romance novels at least a month before they are available in the shops. And of course postage and packing is completely FREE!

5. We hope that after receiving your free books you'll want to remain a subscriber. But the choice is yours - to continue or cancel, anytime at all! So why not accept our no risk invitation. You'll be glad you did!

6. Don't forget to detach your FREE BOOKMARK. And remember... just for validating your Editor's Free Gift Offer, we'll send you FIVE gifts, ABSOLUTELY FREE!

We all love mysteries... so as well as your free books, there's an intriguing gift waiting for you! Simply return this card and when we send you your free books, there'll also be a gift enclosed specially for you!

She looked down at her hands now, feeling the dampness in her palms and the stab of guilt in her heart.

'But that's just what I did do,' she said slowly. 'However you try to couch it in different terms, Marcus, I stand to gain by our—our arrangement, as you call it, just as much as you do. Well, not as much in the monetary sense, of course,' she went on, floundering, 'but in a way that no ordinary girl could ever have hoped for. Not a girl whose role in life was only ever destined to be a lady's companion, and nothing more.'

He leaned towards her, taking her in his arms, and stopping the uneasy flow of words with a kiss.

'No one's future is written in stone, Amy, and I believe we make our own destiny, for good or bad.'

'And would the rest of the world consider our association for good or bad?' she said, knowing she shouldn't ask, but far too curious to resist the question.

He moved fractionally away from her as the carriage trundled them ever nearer to the estate. She could see hazel flecks in his dark eyes that she had never noticed before, and the faint shadow on his chin that always emerged by the end of the day. She was still so close to his mouth that she felt as if she shared his breath.

His next words were so soft that had she not been so close in his embrace, she would not have heard them at all.

'Since I'm reputedly a man of fortune, I care not what the world thinks of me, but I do care what it thinks of us. So I'll defend your reputation to the death, if need be. Does that answer your question?'

She nodded, touched by such a statement. They broke apart as the carriage slowed to a halt, and Ronan Kelly jumped down with his travelling bag slung across his shoulders, and came to peer inside.

'I'll be gettin' back to me own place now, Marcus, and see you good folks tomorrow,' he said brashly.

'Leave it for a day or two, man,' Marcus said instead. 'Miss Finch needs a day or two to settle in, and I aim to show her around and introduce her to a few acquaintances before we get back to business.'

'Aye, and I'll wager that a few acquaintances will have mixed feelings when they hear your news,' the man said with a sly wink. 'I wonder how the Chapman sisters will react. They'll have seen the Dublin newspaper by now, I daresay, as will most of the folk around here.'

'Then I hope all of them will be as pleased by my good fortune as I am,' Marcus snapped, 'and if they're already aware of the circumstances, it will save me the necessity of going into too much explanation myself.'

Amy stared into the distance, knowing that only a fool would miss the unmistakable innuendo in Kelly's voice, and the annoyance in Marcus's. And she didn't dare speculate just who the Chapman sisters were.

As if Kelly realised he was to get no more out of his partner, he stood back and shouted to the groom to drive on. The next minute the carriage continued its journey, and with every turn of the wheels, Amy felt as if she was being drawn into a net from which there was no escape.

* * *

Even before they reached the house, having traversed the well-attended lawns and gardens, Amy could see the bustle of servants emerging outside, to line up as the carriage approached. Her mouth felt dry, hardly expecting this small army of welcome, though in truth it was a very modest contingent.

It was headed by a buxom woman in a dark dress and cap, who was clearly the housekeeper. She bobbed at once as Marcus alighted. He helped Amy down, and kept her arm firmly tucked in the crook of his arm as they stepped forward together.

'Welcome home, sir,' the woman said, 'and since we've all been acquainted with your news, may I say how very sorry we all are to hear about Lady Bellingham, but how very pleased to hear your happier news.'

Marcus answered her gravely. 'Thank you, Mrs Monahan. Naturally my aunt's death was a great shock, but Miss Finch has done much to alleviate my sadness. As you are obviously aware from the newspaper report, Miss Finch has done me the signal honour of agreeing to become my wife.'

Amy drew in her breath a little. To her, his choice of words were those meant for a truer relationship than theirs, and they struck a chord in her heart; she wished they could be all that they implied.

Mrs Monahan was smiling at her approvingly now, and Amy forced an answering smile to her lips as the housekeeper addressed her.

'It's a real pleasure to welcome you, miss, and if I may make so bold as to say so, it's more than a pleasure to see Mr Bellingham so happy in his choice. I wish you both every joy for the future.'

Amy murmured a suitable reply, hoping that her

lack of response was being construed as natural shyness. It was all so *wrong*, and so farcical, she thought miserably. And looking at the smiling faces of the household staff, she realised how many other good people they cheated, as well as each other.

But she was quickly learning that once a course of action was decided on, there was no way of stopping it. Not when a man like Marcus Bellingham was the instigator. The deceit merely gathered momentum, until the two of them were as enmeshed within it as if they were caught in a spider's web from which there was no escape.

She swallowed thickly, wondering if Marcus would be as loath to disentangle himself from the silken chains as she knew she would be herself when the time came. But of course he would. He would have no further use of her once his inheritance was assured. He would have everything he needed, while she. . . She quickly dismissed the thought of the so-called reward for her services, because, in emotional terms, she would have nothing.

Marcus spoke quickly to her as she became unduly silent. 'You must be tired, Amy, and I'm sure Mrs Monahan will see to it that we're provided with refreshment forthwith.'

'Of course, sir,' the woman said at once, clapping her hands to several of the servant girls, who were openly gawping, and more than a mite envious, at seeing their master so solicitous and tender towards the newcomer among them.

And Amy had not the slightest doubt that she would be the cause of much gossip and speculation, no matter how easily the Dublin newspaper article had been worded.

There was more than a little speculation going through her mind too, especially regarding the ladies whom Ronan Kelly had referred to as the Chapman sisters. It wasn't an Irish name, and from his snide reference, Amy guessed that they weren't elderly spinsters of the parish, either. . .

'May I show Miss Finch to her room first, Mr Bellingham?' Mrs Monahan said. 'Then I will have tea and cakes sent to the sitting-room directly.'

'That will be fine, thank you,' he answered.

On hearing their instructions, the maids and other servants scattered to do their various duties, and Amy entered the house for the first time. She was instantly struck by how comfortable it was, and how tastefully decorated. Marcus may have been fortunate in his choice of housekeeper in keeping the house in sparkling order, but the carpets and pictures and other accoutrements all spoke of a man with innate good taste.

'Do you approve, my dear?' he asked her smilingly, as she gazed around her.

'Very much so.' At least she could answer that with sincerity, and there was something else she needed to say. 'I know your aunt would have approved as well. And I am so very sorry that she is unable to see it for herself.'

'So am I. I'm afraid Aunt Maud's expectations of my situation were never very high, and I'd very much hoped to reverse them during her visit here.'

He spoke so sincerely that Amy could hardly doubt his words, and she resisted the cynical thought that it would all have been to his advantage, anyway. The better situated Lady B. had seen her nephew, the more likely she would have been to invest in his madcap scheme. . .

Mrs Monahan stood unobtrusively at the foot of the curving staircase until Amy had taken her fill of the spacious hallway of the house, and had a glimpse of the comfortably elegant sitting-room. A servant had already brought the travelling bags inside, and taken them to the upstairs rooms.

'I think I should like to see my room and refresh myself, Marcus,' she murmured delicately now.

'Of course.' He stood back while she followed Mrs Monahan up the stairs. Amy glanced down, to where he still watched her. One hand was on the banister rail, one foot on the lowest stair, almost as if his dearest wish was to follow her. She dismissed the foolish fantasy, and continued upstairs until Mrs Monahan opened a door with a great flourish and waited for Amy to go inside.

'Oh, what a lovely room!' she exclaimed at once. 'It's so light and airy.'

The housekeeper looked highly pleased with her involuntary reaction. 'Mr Bellingham chose the particular colour schemes for the bedrooms following a sojourn he made to the Scandinavian countries, miss,' she informed her. 'He was much impressed by their light furnishings and thought it would reflect the strong mountain light well.'

'He was perfectly right,' Amy said, moving to the window, to where the view of the mountains was so splendid. 'I know I'm going to love it here.'

She spoke without thinking, as if she was going to stay here always, and she bit her lip almost as soon as the words left her mouth. Mrs Monahan saw the gesture, and put her own interpretation on it.

'You must have very mixed feelings in these early days, miss,' she said sympathetically. 'I can't imagine how you must have felt at Lady Bellingham's demise, but if you'll permit me to say so, your presence here is just what Mr Bellingham needs. I've seldom seen him look so content, despite all.'

With every attempt at reassurance and comfort, she twisted the knife in Amy's heart. And she could no longer deny that for a moment—a very *real* moment—she had accepted that she was here to stay, and that the marriage between herself and Marcus was a love match.

But of course, that was what everyone would believe, and what they *must* believe, if the deceit was not to be exposed. She inclined her head to the housekeeper.

'I shall do my best to be worthy of him, Mrs Monahan,' she said. Whether or not it was correct to say such a thing to a housekeeper, she neither knew nor cared. For Amy Finch, lady's companion, it was a perfectly natural thing to say.

The housekeeper cleared her throat, obviously touched by such humility.

'Your bags are on the stand, miss. And there's fresh washing water in the jug. When you're ready, you'll recall that the downstairs sitting-room is on the right of the staircase, and your refreshments will be ready in about ten minutes.'

'Thank you,' Amy said.

Then, alone for the first time, she suddenly wilted. She had come so far, in every way. The ordeal of pretence had only just begun, and she was only now beginning to realise it. There was an entire township of acquaintances who had to accept her and believe in this engagement, and her heart quaked at the thought of carrying it through.

She squared her shoulders, determined not to be so lily-livered. She had made a promise to Marcus, and she wouldn't renege on it. She would behave like a newly engaged young lady and go through the ceremony of marriage with him. . .and remain with him for as long as was necessary. . . The thoughts ran through her head like a bittersweet refrain. . .

She removed her bonnet and small cape, and turned quickly to her travelling bag to take out her toiletries. The jug and basin stood on a marble washstand, and once she had splashed some cooling rosewater on her face and hands and dabbed them dry with a towel, she felt considerably calmer.

She reminded herself that she didn't face this alone. It wasn't that kind of a challenge. Whatever happened, she would always have Marcus by her side—even if it filled her with a strangely shivery feeling to know it.

Her glance was drawn to the comfortable four-poster bed with its chintzy coverlet and hangings, so in contrast with the heavier fabrics and colours of fashion. In proper circumstances, a bed such as this, in this very house, would have been her marital bed. . . Her face flushed hotly at the thought, and she knew how futile were her dreams that this situation was anything more than a sham.

But she couldn't help remembering some of the things Marcus had said to the newspaper reporter. In particular, that they had corresponded for a very long time, and had formed a warm regard for one another, even before they met. . . At the time she had considered it no more more than a clever twist on the true state of affairs, but she accepted honestly, that on her side, at least, it was true.

She had been intrigued for a very long time by the reckless and adventurous nephew of such a stiff and staid person as Lady Bellingham. She had enjoyed sharing the gentle teasing in his letters that the lady was too poker-faced to see, but which Amy saw only too well, and responded to in such carefully couched terms, since she'd been obliged to read the letters back to Lady B. before despatching them to Marcus.

Yet now, for the first time, she wondered if Lady B. had been so mentally unobservant after all. Or if she, too, had secretly chuckled at the apparent innocence of some of the arch sentences in the letters that went to and fro, while knowing all the while what these two were up to. And being up to a bit of secret foresighted mischief herself!

Had she actually decided to do a spot of match-making a long time ago? It had never occurred to Amy until this minute, but the thought startled her so much that she felt quite agitated by the time she went downstairs to find the sitting-room and a welcome cup of tea.

'Is everything to your liking in your room, Amy?' Marcus said, once the maid had dispensed the drink and departed back to the kitchen.

'Very much so. The whole room is so light and airy, and I understand that the furnishings are a reminder of your Scandinavian travels,' she murmured, for want of something intelligent to say when her thoughts were so disorientated.

And had Marcus but known it, she was trying very hard to get the image of that four-poster bed out of her head, knowing how unseemly it was to let her mind dwell on that one object of furniture.

'Indeed. You would like the Scandinavian countries,' he said casually. 'I'm told they are very reminiscent of your native Scotland.'

'Thank you, but I have no desire to go there,' she said quickly. The thought of another long sea voyage was something she couldn't bear to contemplate.

'I wasn't actually inviting you,' he said coolly. 'Though it would be an ideal place to spend a honeymoon.'

Amy studiously avoided looking at him. He went too far, baiting her like this. He would expect her to colour up, and she knew to her fury that she wasn't disappointing him. But how could she help but see him for the charismatic man that he was, so very much the master in his own home, with an air of gentility that was totally unexpected? And how could she help but fall under his spell?

Her hand jerked on the handle of her cup, and she was in danger of spilling the brew. She replaced the cup carefully in her saucer for a moment, and looked at him unblinkingly.

'I would like to know a little about your friends and acquaintances before I meet them, Marcus. Perhaps you would care to begin with the ladies Mr Kelly mentioned. I believe their name was Chapman.'

She tried to sound casual, even though her heart was pounding at this blatant and embarrassing attempt to solicit information. She found herself hoping he would say they were in their middle years after all, and that Kelly had merely been goading her into thinking otherwise.

But then she saw the glint in Marcus's eyes, and knew he could see right through her need for information. Of course, he would, she seethed. An adventurous rake would know the wiles of women only too well. The thought did nothing to please her.

'Oh, I'm sure you'll like them,' he said, and perversely Amy knew very well that she probably would not. When he paused, she went on irritably,

'Well, that tells me a lot, doesn't it! Are they young, old, married, or spinsters?'

She prayed for the description to be the one she preferred, and was increasingly angry at herself for feeling that way. Dear Lord, if she was going to feel unreasonably jealous of every female Marcus had known before her, she was a poor specimen of womanhood indeed.

She could see the twitch at the corner of his mouth, and knew he was inwardly laughing at her. He treated her like a child, she raged, when her feelings were very definitely all woman. She sipped the hot tea, uncaring if it scalded her mouth as long as it gave her something to do.

'You won't find the Chapman sisters in the least intimidating,' Marcus said. 'The older one, Edwina, is a few years older than yourself, while Julia, although out of the schoolroom, is still something of a scallywag according to her governess.'

'She still has a governess? So how old is she, then—fourteen or so?'

'A little more, I fancy,' Marcus said carelessly. 'I really couldn't say exactly. Her father is a widower, and feels disinclined to control her, even if

he could, and the governess has been with the family
for some years.'

'I see.' The younger girl certainly sounded a bit
of a handful, thought Amy.

'What else do you want to know? The Chapmans
aren't our only neighbours, and naturally they'll all
want to make your acquaintance in due course.'

'I think I prefer to wait until I meet them before
learning anything more about them, after all,' she
said now.

'Perhaps that's wise. Prejudging people can be a
dangerous occupation.'

He spoke without expression, but Amy knew at
once that his words were meant to be taken personally. She felt her face colour up again.

'You can hardly blame me for the impression I
had of you! However much of a rapport I felt we
had through the letters we exchanged—albeit in
your aunt's name—I still had to listen to her
constant derision of you.'

She clapped her hand to her mouth, appalled at
what she was saying. His aunt had recently died,
and here she was, telling him in no uncertain terms
how little the lady had thought of him.

'I'm sorry, Marcus.' Without thinking, she put
her hand on his arm. 'I shouldn't have said that.
Your aunt truly loved you, despite everything, I
know she did.'

Now she was making it worse, she groaned! He
lifted her hand as it rested on his arm and kissed
her palm before letting it go again.

'I know she did, and you don't have to make
excuses for her despair of me, Amy. I was always
well aware of that. All I'm saying is that you

shouldn't prejudge people before you've met them.'

'But I'm sure you must have had a preformed opinion of me before we actually met.'

She spoke quickly, if only to divert the conversation, since the last thing she wanted was for him to suspect that for a long time she'd been half in love with him through his letters. But she immediately wondered if she was being stupid in inviting such a confidence about his feelings for her.

He gave a laugh. 'Oh Amy, you may be young, but you have the most artless way of seeking compliments.'

'I assure you I meant no such thing! I was just curious to know, that's all.'

'And if I were to say that I sensed a long time ago that I was exchanging the most delightful letters with my soul-mate, what would you say to that? And I'm not talking about Aunt Maud!'

'I'd say you were teasing me,' she said angrily.

He didn't answer, and she could almost feel the tension rising between them. He drained his tea and held out his hand to her.

'Do you want to see the rest of the house? I think we'll leave the tour of the grounds and the village until tomorrow, but I'm sure you'd like to get your bearings indoors.'

'Thank you, I would,' she said in some relief.

She had been in danger of exposing too many emotions, and she knew she had brought it all on herself by her probing questions. No matter how many people who were part of Marcus Bellingham's world—and soon to be part of her world—it was best that she learned about them gradually, and didn't prejudge any of them, not even the Chapman sisters.

As she settled into the ambience of the house, Amy began to realise more and more what she had already suspected: that here, at least, Marcus was revered as the kingpin of his world by his staff, who obviously adored him, and with no question of being seen as the rogue his aunt had clearly thought him. How extraordinary, and how very sad, that his Aunt Maud had never got to realise it. She had no doubt that a gentleman with an estate of this size would command respect from all his neighbours. The house was very well aspected and appointed, and it was clearly a gentleman's house. It was so comfortable that Amy began to suspect the very idea that he needed his inheritance at all. And therefore, perhaps, there was no need for the proposed sham of a marriage between them!

When he finally showed her into his wood-panelled study, his sanctuary of sanctuaries, she challenged him.

'Forgive me, Marcus, but since we should always speak frankly to one another—' she began.

He held up his hand, and motioned her to sit on one of the leather chairs in the study, while he remained perched on the long oak desk.

'I wonder why such a remark always prefaces something the listener doesn't want to hear?' he observed. 'So what is it that you're about to chastise me with now?'

Coupled with her vague suspicions, his complacency irritated her.

'I wouldn't dream of chastising you, sir,' she said

with cool sarcasm. 'But I would dearly like to know
how you come to live in such splendour while pretending poverty! And if you think me impertinent
in asking such a question, then I apologise——I think,'
she added.

His eyes flashed for a moment, and then he
laughed.

'I'm not aware that I ever pretended poverty, as
you call it, and nor would I demean myself by doing
so. And since you are to be my bride, I suppose you
think you have a right to probe into my affairs.'

It was Amy's turn to flash her eyes now, and to
know she was going bright red in the process.

'For pity's sake, Marcus, we are hardly the most
normal of couples, and our association is more of a
business one than any other. So, yes, I do have a
right to know what's going on, and why you say
you have this desperate need for funds, when you
live in such luxury.'

He was silent and thoughtful for a few moments,
clearly weighing up just how much to tell her, she
fumed. And then he slid off the desk and moved
behind it to sit on his chair. At once, he was dis-
tanced from her, and she watched him uneasily,
wondering just what lies were to come out now.

She totally despised herself for falling in love
with a rogue and a cheat and a liar. . . The thoughts
were in her head before she could stop them, and
she drew in her breath. At the sound, Marcus's eyes
softened a little.

'You're quite right to wonder, my dear,' he said,
'but had it never occurred to you that all of this was
to impress my aunt? I wanted her to think well of
me, and in doing so, I recklessly entered into an

agreement with Sir Edmund Chapman some while ago now.'

'Is he something to do with the Chapman sisters?' Amy said, remembering Ronan Kelly's snide comments.

'Their father.'

'So what was this agreement? Did he loan you some money to tide you over until you could wheedle your way into your inheritance? If you agreed to take one of his daughters off his hands in return, you've rather exploded that little scheme by being forced into this mock engagement with me, haven't you?'

Horrified at her sudden inability to stop, she heard herself quizzing him, and he gave an expressive oath before he snapped back.

'Dear God, but you've surely got the most vivid imagination of any woman I know! And like most people who let their flights of fantasy run away with them, you've got it all wrong.'

'Have I?' Amy said, as the sick feeling washing over her at the thought of Marcus having fond feelings for some other girl refused to go away.

'Do you think I could possibly own all this?' he said, waving his hands around expressively. 'At least, not with a partner who seems intent on gambling away all our profits before we even find the gold deposits we're seeking.'

'You don't own this house?' Amy said stupidly.

'I do not. It's leased to me, lock, stock and wine cellar, for an extortionate sum from Sir Edmund, and the lease comes up for renewal in two months' time. After that, he'll have me out, since he's got no time for sentiment or dreams.'

'But everyone here is so subservient to you—'

And it gave him yet another reason for getting his hands on his inheritance, Amy thought.

'I've been in Callanby for some time, as you well know, and the agreement is a private one between Sir Edmund and myself. To all intents and purposes I own the estate, but the reality is far from the case. So you see, sweet Amy, my aunt wasn't so far wrong about me, after all. I'm just as irresponsible and reckless as I ever was. And aren't you the sorry one now, for ever throwing in your lot with me?' he added in a rare moment of bitterness.

Chapter Nine

If he'd really cared to read her mind at that moment, he'd be very surprised, thought Amy. She wasn't a fool, and from what Ronan Kelly had slyly hinted about the wealthy Chapman sisters, and from what she had just learned, it was perfectly logical that if Marcus had courted one of them and married her, there would be no lack of funds. . .

That he hadn't done so made her heart begin to pound. Maybe it meant that he did indeed have some standards, and wouldn't marry completely unscrupulously. Not to the extent of making a pretence at love with an unsuspecting wife, who would naturally expect a normal loving and physical relationship.

Amy felt her cheeks burn at the implications of that thought. For in her case, of course, there would be no need for such pretence. Theirs was a cold business arrangement, no more, and she must keep reminding herself of that fact. He had been totally honest with her, and she tried to ignore the self-defensive thought that maybe he could have lied, just a little. . .

When she didn't answer his rhetorical question,

Marcus stood up slowly. He came around to the front of the desk again and drew her to her feet.

'Well, Amy?' he said, in a seductive voice that she didn't want to hear right now when her thoughts were whirling. 'Do you want to renege on me even now, since the world would say that so much of what I am is built on lies and deception?'

'Maybe it's not what *I* would say,' she mumbled, unable to stop herself. 'Not altogether, anyway.'

Because everything that he did, however reckless, was always done with good intentions. She knew that, and she had known it for a long time. She accepted that even this deception over the house had been done with the need to prove himself to his aunt. He was a proud man, and wouldn't have wanted her to think he was a wastrel.

Amy felt him tip up her chin with his finger so that her eyes were forced to meet his. His gaze was unfathomable, but it made her throat tighten. Without warning she closed her eyes lest he should read too much in them. She hardly realised how she was swaying towards him until she felt his arms holding her and his mouth kissing hers. Automatically, her arms clung to him in return, and they stayed locked in an embrace for a long moment.

When he broke away from her, his voice was abrupt, and then he humiliated her with an apology.

'I'm sorry. I shouldn't have done that, since our arrangement, is, as you say, a business one. But you can't expect any red-blooded man to be anything but aroused when you look up at him with those innocent blue eyes.'

'Then I'm sorry, too, since it's hardly my intention to be the coquette! Perhaps it would be best if I kept my distance,' she snapped heatedly, alternately insulted and flattered by his remark.

'I hope you will not,' he said drily. 'How will that look to the people watching us like hawks?'

'What people?' Amy said suspiciously.

'My dear girl,' he said, moving fractionally away from her, 'there are always people who would delight in causing mischief, especially giving a juicy tale to the newspapers in return for having their palm greased—'

'You mean Ronan Kelly, I suppose? I still don't know why you got entangled with the man in the first place, despite his expertise in his work. It seems a singular case of bad judgement to me.'

Amy was perfectly aware how displeased he would be at this censure. But if they couldn't be honest with one another, she might as well pack her things and leave right now. . . Even as the thought entered her mind, she felt a real pang.

For how could she leave this place? Who would take her away from Callanby? Where would she go? What would she do? And how would it look when she had just become attached to the most handsome man for miles around in a fairy-tale engagement?

She was angry with herself for letting all the spineless objections she could think of crowd her mind. Especially when the upshot of it all was that she didn't really want to leave at all.

'I'm sorry you feel the need to question my judgement, but I've already told you about the man's circumstances. He deserves better—or did so,' he added grimly.

'Obviously I'm sorry about his wife and child, and it must have been dreadful for him. Maybe he still has some good points, but for the life of me I fail to see any of them.'

She had sat down again, and she saw a brief sardonic smile touch Marcus's mouth.

'Then your judgement is clearly much better than mine,' he retorted. 'But your inquisitive little mind did insist on knowing it all—'

'Please don't patronise me, Marcus. Since I'm bound to come in contact with him from time to time, of course I was curious as to how you got mixed up with him. A business partner can support or ruin a man, and in any case he's hardly on a social or an intellectual level with you.'

Lord, what a snob she sounded, Amy thought, listening to herself. But it was true. And Lady B. would certainly have hated the man on sight.

'I agree with the second part of what you say, and if there's any double meaning in the first, then I must clearly watch my step.'

She stared at him. 'That I'm bound to come in contact with him from time to time? I assure you the thought doesn't please me—'

'No. That a business partner can support or ruin a man,' he said in a deliberate voice. 'I wonder if you were thinking solely of Ronan Kelly at that moment, Amy. Can I be sure of *your* total support?'

And if that wasn't telling her that all he wanted from her was a business arrangement, he couldn't have put it more clearly. She lifted her chin.

'I never go back on a promise,' she said.

'Good. Neither do I,' he said.

For one wild moment she remembered the sweet words of the marriage service she had attended on Skye such a short time ago. The promises then were said before God, and the contract between them was not to be taken wantonly or lightly. . .and the vows she remembered the most were filling her head now: With my body I thee worship. . . To love, honour and cherish. . .

'May I go now?' she said in a strangled voice, as the tension between them became suddenly stifling.

He looked at her in some surprise, and she was thankful that his usual penchant of reading her mind seemed to have deserted him for the moment.

'You're not a prisoner, Amy. You may go anywhere you like, though I suggest you rest before dinner this evening. Travelling takes its toll. Meanwhile, I shall draw up a list of people to invite to the house for a celebratory evening very soon and we'll go through it together at some stage. I want everyone to meet my future wife as soon as possible.'

She couldn't look at him. In any other circumstances she would have been elated by the very thought, but instead, she felt besmirched at the deception they were playing. If she had been as ruthless as he was, she could have tackled it better. As it was, she had far too romantic a heart, and the situation made her increasingly uneasy. But she had given her word, and she was too honourable to go back on it, however ironic the thought.

The day was still warm, and although Marcus had said he'd take her around the village and the estate tomorrow, she felt a great need to be outside, and to get her bearings alone. And why shouldn't she? As he'd said, she wasn't a prisoner.

She fetched a light shawl from her room, not

bothering with a bonnet or gloves, for she didn't intend going very far. The grounds stretched away from the house and the stables, and a brisk stroll was just what she needed. Seeing no one, she struck out down the gravel drive from which they'd entered the estate, revelling in the clean, fragrant air, and the piquant, unmistakable scent of pine from the wooded valley.

As she walked, she eventually caught sight of the church spire some distance ahead. It made her wonder instantly if it was where Marcus intended them to be married. She had no real religious affinity other than a fervent belief in God and the hereafter, and she hardly thought Marcus was an ardent churchgoer.

So it really wouldn't matter who said the words over them, as long as the deed was done. And what a dismal way to enter into a marriage. . .

She continued walking with no real intent now, and her head drooped down with the thought. She was unaware of anyone else in the vicinity, enjoying the blissful solitude that nevertheless made her examine her own thoughts too minutely.

'Good afternoon,' she heard a female voice say, and she jerked her head up, startled. A woman was coming towards her, on foot, as Amy was herself. A youngish, smartly dressed woman, with dark hair and an attractively vivacious face.

'Good afternoon to you,' Amy said, taken off-balance, and wondering frantically if this could be one of the Chapman sisters. But surely not. The olive glow of her complexion belied that fact. The woman smiled apologetically.

'I'm sorry if I startled you. You were so deep in

thought, and I thought it best to speak before we actually bumped into one another.'

There was surely the merest hint of a foreign accent in the speech, even though it was very slight. The stranger held out an elegant gloved hand to her now, and Amy took it at once, regretting the fact that her own hands were bare.

'My name is Hélène Dubois, and since we get so few strangers in Callanby I am sure you must be Miss Amy Finch,' she said.

Amy knew there was no sense or logic in feeling irritated that news of her arrival had preceded her, but it didn't stop the feeling, all the same.

'Then you have the advantage of me,' she said, inclining her head and withdrawing her fingers from the gloved hand, still wishing she had worn her own bonnet and gloves so that she looked as chic as the stranger. Whoever she was, she was certainly not one of the Chapman sisters.

'I am so sorry, Miss Finch,' the woman said, 'but we have all been intrigued to see the lady who has captured Marcus's heart.'

Amy blushed furiously as she went on coolly, 'I am governess to Miss Julia Chapman—'

'Oh, I see. I had not expected—'

Hélène Dubois laughed. 'You expected a governess to be an elderly and strait-laced lady, no doubt.'

'Well, I know one should never put people into certain moulds like that, but perhaps you are right,' she admitted. After all, when anyone thought of a lady's companion, they automatically thought of a simpering creature. . .and Amy had never considered herself anything of the kind.

'It's no matter, *chérie*,' she said, in what Amy

saw as a patronising manner. 'But tell me, is Marcus at the house?'

'Yes.' And clearly these two knew one another very well if she referred to him in such an intimate manner.

'Then I will go and welcome him home, and issue the invitation I've been charged with.'

She smiled and moved on, sophisticated and sure of herself, and leaving Amy feeling ridiculously inadequate and annoyed to register the sudden jealousy running through her. She had believed the Chapman sisters to be her main rivals, and now there was this rather voluptuous Frenchwoman, who was clearly eager to welcome Marcus on his return. . .

Amy listened to herself with mounting anger. She had no rivals, for heaven's sake. She was the one wearing the magnificent sapphire ring on her engagement finger when Hélène Dubois greeted her. Amy was the one who held all of Marcus's future in the palm of her hand. She was the only one who could save his inheritance. . .or totally denounce and destroy him.

She drew in her breath. If those thoughts had crept into her mind before, they were glaringly obvious now. And so was the insidious thought that once her promise had been given, Marcus would do his utmost to keep her sweet. It was in his best interests. No matter where his heart truly lay, he would flatter and court her, Amy Finch, for as long as it suited his purposes. Even to the extent of marrying her.

She felt a small sob rise in her throat. What a fool she was, to think that all his soft-talk was in any way true. She should have listened more to his

aunt. She should have heeded her own common
sense. She shouldn't have fallen in love. And she
shouldn't be so stupid as to read more into Hélène
Dubois's words than was actually said.

Amy strode on forcefully, knowing she had been
far too gullible, and that the most idiotic thing she
had ever done was agreeing to Marcus Bellingham's
outrageous proposal.

Before she realised it, she had walked through the
woods at the edge of the estate to where the sparkling river meandered in leisurely fashion. It looked
so peaceful as it rippled easily over rocks and shale
that she could hardly credit the fact of it ever being
in torrent. She found herself peering into its fairly
shallow depths, and trying to imagine whether or
not she could see any of the glinting gold it was
reputed to contain.

'Pretty, ain't it?' she heard a voice say, and she
turned with a sigh as she recognised its owner.

'Hello, Mr Kelly—'

'Ronan's the name, little lady. There's no need
for a man's partner and his lady-love to be so formal
with one another.'

'I prefer formality, if it's all the same to you,'
Amy said, uncaring that she was being prim and
standoffish. She didn't like the man, and could never
trust him, no matter how sympathetic she was
regarding his tragedy.

She heard him give a kind of snort. 'You'll find
we don't stand on much ceremony in this part of
Ireland, me darlin',' he said. 'And we'll be seein'
a good deal of each other, I daresay, before the
nuptials are tied. Have you set the date yet? Marcus

won't want to be kept waitin' overlong for his bride,
I'll be bound.'

Amy's dislike of him grew. He was snide and
uncouth, but she reminded herself that she had to
keep up the pretence of the eager bride-to-be, at
least for the immediate future.

'We haven't set a date yet. You must remember
that his aunt has recently died, and society
decrees—'

Kelly snorted again, giving that leering chuckle
she hated. 'I told you, darlin', society don't matter
a fig in Callanby. We left the starched-shirts behind
us in Dublin. They don't belong here.'

Amy glared at him. 'No? Then what about Sir
Edmund Chapman and his daughters—and the folk
who come here for the bracing air in the summer?'

'City folk, all of 'em,' Kelly sneered. 'You won't
want much to do with them, I'm thinking. Sir
Edmund and his sprogs are not much better, but the
French *mam'selle* now, she's a different matter.'

He winked, his meaning clear, and Amy turned
away from him at once.

'Please excuse me. I'm going back to the
house now.'

She moved haughtily, her head held high, aware
that he was watching her. He really was the most
odious little man, she thought, and he was also
someone to fear. If she once let her guard slip, she
was quite sure he wouldn't be averse to putting in
his pennyworth of gossip with the Dublin newspaper
in return for a fat fee. And the last thing she, or
Marcus, or Lady Bellingham would have wanted,
was a scandal.

When she reached the house again, she slipped

inside and went straight to her room. After the simple way she had been accepted here by Mrs Monahan and the rest of the staff, the rest of the day had been oddly unsettling, and she needed to calm herself before she changed for dinner.

She descended the curving staircase as the grandfather clock at its foot was striking seven. She could see Marcus in the drawing-room, a glass in his hand. He turned to greet her at once. He was immaculate in evening attire, every inch the gentleman, and Amy thought at once that the contrast between him and his partner couldn't be more marked.

And she was more than glad that she'd donned one of her favourite gowns of peach watered silk, with a looped richu hem and a *décolleté* neckline. Her dark hair was brushed to a sheen and piled on top of her head, with soft curling tendrils in her nape and at her ear-lobes. Marcus came towards her and raised her hand to his lips.

'You look beautiful,' he said gravely. 'Will you take an aperitif before we go in to dinner?'

'No, thank you,' she said. 'I'm actually quite hungry.'

The minute she had spoken she thought how gauche she sounded. And how very *young*, when she wanted to look as sophisticated as——as——

'I met Mademoiselle Hélène Dubois when I was walking this afternoon,' she said at once. She watched him closely, trying to detect whether his expression or his voice became warmer when he answered.

'So I heard. Did you like her?'

'How can I tell from so short an acquaintance?

She seemed pleasant enough—'

'Oh, Amy.' He began to laugh, and squeezed her shoulder affectionately. 'I assure you there's no need for you to be jealous of anyone—'

'I'm not!' she said hotly. 'I only spoke to her for a few minutes—'

'And now you're wondering just how well I know her, since she came here expressly to see me as soon as I returned from Dublin. Do you deny it?'

She just about managed to resist the urge to scowl. That would *really* have stamped her as the schoolgirl. . .

'I don't deny it,' she said. 'Naturally I'm curious about all your friends.'

He leaned forward and kissed the tip of her nose.

'Then be assured that Hélène is no more than a friend, and never has been. And to set your mind at rest, it wasn't merely a social call. She was delivering a dinner invitation from the Chapmans for tomorrow evening.'

'Oh,' Amy said, feeling more foolish than ever now. It was funny how she'd never recognised she had such a jealous streak—but perhaps not so funny, because she had never had it tested before. And then she felt a sudden fright.

'So I'm to be thrown in at the deep end, am I?' she said. Ignoring her refusal of an aperitif, Marcus had pressed a glass into her hand, and she took a sip of the small amount of fiery liquid now, hardly realising that she did so.

'You have to meet people, Amy. And meeting a few at a time may well be easier on the nerves than meeting the entire curious town. If my aunt were still alive, she'd be only too happy to think I moved in civilised society.'

That was hitting below the belt. But she had to admit that having met Ronan Kelly, Lady B. would be more than relieved to think that Marcus moved in more elegant circles.

'I know you're right, and I'm sorry. This situation is still new to me, and I need a little time to adjust—'

He took the glass from her hand, and she realised she had drunk it all. But she was aware that it had relaxed her, and that a warm glow was coursing through her body.

'I'm the one who should be sorry, my dear, for rushing you into all this when there *was* no time. In normal circumstances, I would have courted you slowly—'

'No, you wouldn't,' Amy heard herself say, her mind suddenly sharp and clear. 'In normal circumstances you wouldn't have courted me at all, so please don't pretend an affection that you don't mean. While we're alone, there's no need for it, and I'd prefer that we simply act as friends.'

He said nothing for a moment, and then shrugged. 'If that's what you wish,' he said, more coolly.

It wasn't, but it was the way she knew it had to be if she wasn't to betray her own feelings for him.

The dinner gong sounded at the moment, saving them from any further discussion, and Marcus offered her his arm and led her to the dining-room. It was almost farcically formal, Amy thought, in mild hysteria, when there were only the two of them here, and the small army of servants who attended to their every whim.

'Do you find something amusing, dearest?' he

asked her through the flickering candles on the table.

The endearment was undoubtedly for the benefit of the staff, but it still had the power to make Amy's heart beat unaccountably fast.

'Not at all. I was just thinking how your aunt would have loved all this, and how very sad it is that she couldn't see it all,' she said, fixing her gaze on him unblinkingly.

He had the grace to tighten his lips, and she knew very well that he'd interpreted her words correctly. If Lady Bellingham had been here, Miss Amy Finch would still have been her mere companion, and the mock engagement would never have taken place.

'Knowing you as I do, then you probably believe she's here in spirit,' Marcus retorted. 'I'm sure your romantic little heart does believe in such things, and that she's smiling down on us benevolently at this very minute.'

She managed not to glare at him. One of the servants was spooning soup into their dishes, wide-eyed at what she evidently thought of as a very tender conversation.

'I'm sure she's perfectly aware of all that's going on, Marcus,' Amy said, with only the slightest touch of sarcasm in her voice.

When they had finished their dinner and were in the drawing-room with coffee and sweetmeats, she asked him to tell her more about the dinner engagement tomorrow evening.

'There's no need to be nervous about it. Sir Edmund is a hard-headed businessman, but on social occasions he's a genial host, and I'm sure his daughters will make you feel welcome.'

And Hélène? But she didn't want to know any

more about Hélène, nor if it was likely that the governess would be joining the party for dinner. If she was no more than that, it was unlikely, but Amy had the feeling that Hélène was looked on more as a family friend than an employee.

'I'm not in the least nervous,' she said breezily, more than aware that she'd taken a glass of wine too many with her dinner, and that her brain seemed to be pleasantly floating now.

But with it came the feeling that she could cope with anything, including a Frenchwoman and the Chapman sisters.

'Do you play?' Marcus said. She looked at him, startled, and her gaze went to the pianoforte in the corner of the room.

'A little, but not very well, and I'd prefer not to do so this evening,' she began.

'I meant chess,' he said calmly.

Her face felt hot, the way it always did when she was caught off-balance and had to admit her lack of knowledge. She saw his half-smile, which did nothing to ease her discomfiture.

'Amy, you have the most delightful colouring in your cheeks that I have ever known in a woman,' he said. 'Don't ever lose that ingenuousness.'

'I'm not sure what you mean,' she murmured. 'But you make me feel singularly inadequate because I am not well versed in every kind of social skill. Your aunt and I did not indulge in such things as chess, and for relaxation she preferred me to read to her.'

'Then you shall read to me,' he said, and she looked at him in astonishment.

'I hardly think that's appropriate.'

'Why on earth should it not be? What could be sweeter than for a man to have his beloved reading to him?'

Amy knew her colour had deepened even more at his words. What could be sweeter indeed? And what could be more poignant too, because his words were said in jest, while she so dearly wanted them to be true.

'I think not, Marcus,' she said.

'And I think that nothing else will suffice for us to end this delightful evening,' he said decisively. 'Wait here.'

He left her sitting bemused for a few moments, striding out of the room, while she wondered what she was supposed to do now. She soon found out when he returned with a slim volume in his hands and gave it to her.

'You can't possibly expect me to read this,' she said as caustically as she could.

'Why not?'

'Because—well, because I would feel foolish,' she said, floundering.

'Then, if it makes you feel less foolish, I won't even look at you while you're reading,' he said calmly. 'I'll just listen to your delightfully soft voice saying the words. How does that suit you?'

He was mocking her again, she thought. How could it be otherwise? Taunting her and baiting her, and it was all so unfair. . .but, of course, he didn't know how her feelings towards him had changed— and seemed destined to change, chameleon-like, by the minute.

One minute she was filled with love for him, and the next, she was enraged by him. She decided it was far safer to cling to the latter emotion, but also knowing that it was easier to say than to put into action.

'What do you propose? That I sit at one end of the room with my back to you, while you sit at the other?' she said sarcastically.

Marcus looked at her steadily. 'Why are you so determined to hold me at arm's length?' he said at last.

The question took her by surprise, and she snapped back a reply, annoyed to know she was sounding more of a shrew with every minute that passed.

'I hardly think you need to ask that, and I absolutely refuse to read love poems.'

He gave a half-smile. 'Oh, well, it's no more than I expected, but it was worth it to see those flashing lights in your eyes, my sweet. Very well, I'll put you out of your misery and allow you to read from a novel instead—with one proviso.'

'What is it?' Amy asked suspiciously.

'Since Miss Austen's words are so evocative I think we should make ourselves comfortable. I shall sit in an armchair, and you will sit on a floor cushion and lean against me. That way you do not have to look at me.'

It sounded both feasible and far too intimate. But before she objected strongly, Amy was caught by his words.

'Miss Austen?' she said.

'You know the works of the lady, I presume.'

'Naturally. Your aunt was also fond of hearing me read them to her. I'm just rather surprised that you would have chosen them,' she retorted.

'A good author is a good author,' Marcus said enigmatically, 'and there were many times on my travels when I happily lost myself in a book of such acute observations.'

Without more ado he produced another volume from his pocket and handed it to her. Amy's lips twisted slightly as she saw the title.

'And just which one of Mr Bennett's diverse daughters do you envisage me to be, I wonder?' she said, before she could stop herself. 'Going by recent experiences, I am surely as reckless as Lydia—'

'And as elegant as Jane, and as beautiful and pithy as Elizabeth,' Marcus said.

'So if I'm such a paragon, it's a wonder no gentleman has singled me out before now, is it not!' she retorted again, refusing to take such arch compliments seriously.

'I am deeply grateful that they have not,' he said.

And if they had, Amy thought, she would not be here now, saving his fortunes, and falling in love every bit as recklessly as the fictitious and headstrong Lydia Bennett.

Marcus placed the deep floor cushion in front of his armchair, and sat down with his arms folded determinedly. There was clearly to be no help for it. And with the sudden feeling that her legs weren't going to hold her up much longer if this conversation continued, Amy sank down on the cushion abruptly, her gown billowing about her in a rustle of silk.

'Lean back against my knees and make yourself comfortable,' Marcus instructed. 'And we'll have several chapters before we retire for the night.'

Please don't make that sound so very seductive and inviting, Amy pleaded silently. So lovely, and so impossible. . .

'*Pride and Prejudice*', she announced in prim 'lady's companion' fashion. She opened the book to the first chapter, and began to read, her voice husky. '"It is a truth universally acknowledged that a single man in possession of a good fortune must be in want of a wife."'

She stopped immediately, swivelling around to look up at Marcus accusingly. It had been some while since she had read this particular book, and she had taken no account of the well-remembered first lines when he'd handed it to her.

'You chose this book deliberately,' she said.

She felt his hand caress the nape of her neck, and a shiver ran through her.

'My dear girl, you really shouldn't read something personal into everything. Miss Austen makes a simple statement of fact, and one that no sane person would dispute.'

He was so smooth and plausible. . .and such a rat, she thought inelegantly.

'Except that in this particular case, the single man is not yet in possession of a good fortune,' she said without pausing to heed his reaction.

And when she did, she held her breath, knowing that, however true, her words were in bad taste in pinpointing their unique situation. She fully expected him to rant at her immediately. But he didn't do so. He merely laughed, stroking her hair and letting his hands caress her slim shoulders in a totally unfair way, sending shivers down her back and drying her mouth.

'Maybe not,' he said, 'but the rest of it cannot be denied. I am very much in want of a wife, Amy.'

Chapter Ten

Lying in bed that night, Amy knew what a mistake it had been to allow the reading to continue. She had always felt a certain warmth for the silly, delightfully feckless character of Mrs Bennett wanting so desperately to get her daughters married off. And in the end she had been helpless to resist the reading, even while she found the situation between herself and Marcus increasingly relevant in Jane Austen's powerful words.

But it wasn't, of course! Not unless she compared Lady Bellingham's clumsy mismanagement of two people's affairs with the hopeless attempts of Mrs Bennett. It hardly mattered, Amy thought wearily, as sleep continued to elude her. Whatever the motive, or the connivings of the ladies concerned, the outcome was the same.

She ignored the eventual happiness of Jane Bennett and Mr Bingley. It was her own situation with Marcus, and that of Lizzie Bennett and Darcy, that interested her the most. Two couples, both mismatched, and set on a collision course that seemed destined to end in disaster and heartache.

In effect, she reasoned, they were poles apart. Mr Darcy, insufferably pompous, yet highly desirable too, considered Miss Lizzie Bennett too far beneath him to propose marriage. And Amy Finch found herself betrothed to a man who didn't really want her, except for the fortune that marriage to her would bring.

When she thought about it more sensibly, there wasn't the slightest connection between herself and those fictional characters. It was just the remembered deviousness in the novel that was unsettling her, and she couldn't get it out of her mind now. And if she was required to read to Marcus again, she would suggest a different kind of novel.

She tried hard to make sleep come, but the newness of the bed and her environment wouldn't let her. And over and over in her mind she kept hearing Marcus's voice when she had rounded on him.

'. . .the rest of it cannot be denied. I am very much in want of a wife, Amy.'

He had spoken with such conviction and sincerity. And if Miss Austen had chosen those words with particular care for their meaning, they were none the less emotive when spoken in a man's sensual voice in the warm intimacy of a candlelit drawing-room.

In want of a wife. . .it was so much sweeter than being told one was in *need* of a wife. *Wanting* someone was longing for them, and loving them. . .and she was being the craziest fool for ever imagining she had detected something personal in Marcus's voice when he had said it. His wants were for a very different reason, and he was merely repeating the words of the novel. She would do well to remember it.

She awoke to find the sun streaming in on her, and a maid was drawing back her curtains. She must have slept, though her bedding was so rumpled it looked as though a team of horses had galloped through it. And she looked in some astonishment at her little clock, to find that it was well past ten o'clock.

'Why has no one woken me earlier?' she exclaimed. 'I'm not normally a lie-a-bed.'

'Mr Bellingham said you were not to be disturbed, miss, and that there was no need to rush at all. He asks you to take breakfast with him in half an hour,' the maid said. 'I've brought you fresh water for washing, and if there's anything else you need, you only have to ask, so you do.'

Amy gave a small smile, for who ever heard of a mere companion being dressed and coiffed by a maid. . .? Or being allowed to lie in bed until half the day had gone! Until this moment, experiencing the luxury, it hadn't fully dawned on her how her status had changed with Marcus's proposal.

'Thank you for the offer,' she said, 'but I prefer to do things for myself—Docherty, isn't it?'

'That's right, miss,' the girl said. She went out of the room, pink-faced with pleasure that Amy had recalled her name so quickly, and leaving Amy to her own ablutions.

They were going to take a tour of the town some time today, she remembered, so she wore a discreet walking dress of green tarlatan that had a matching bonnet and cape. She blessed Lady B. now for always insisting that her companion was turned out smartly, since it displeased her to see a young woman sloppily dressed.

Or had even that been another ploy towards preparing Amy Finch for a more prominent role in life?

She would rather not think so, but now that she had got the idea into her head of Lady B. manipulating her over the years, she couldn't rid herself of it. She tidied her hair and pinned it up neatly, pinching her pale cheeks to put some colour into them, though that probably wouldn't be necessary.

She only had to hear one of Marcus's outrageous remarks, or an unexpected endearment said for a listener's benefit, and her natural colour would inevitably return.

She gave up worrying about it and went downstairs to where Marcus was already in the dining-room. He greeted her with a kiss on the cheek and a squeeze of her hand, and she knew she must get used to this kind of thing while the servants were watching the tender little display.

'Good morning, my love. Did you sleep well?' he asked.

'Tolerably well,' Amy said. 'It always takes me a while to get used to a different environment. And I hadn't expected to sleep so late!'

He nodded, as if this was the most natural conversation in the world for two people sharing breakfast. She supposed she must get used to this too, and also to the way the servants looked on so approvingly. The fictionalised news of their 'romance' had clearly charmed them all.

'Shall you show me the town today as you promised?' Amy said quickly, not wanting to remember the deceit of this whole arrangement.

'Of course, though it must wait until this afternoon, since I must attend to business matters this
morning. I'm sure you can amuse yourself in the
meantime, Amy. We have a fine library in the house,
and I know how you like to read.'

She refused to look at him, knowing he was
reminding her of the book he had presented her with
last night, and the gullible way she had fallen into
the trap. Miss Austen's words were still in her head.
He was indeed in want of a wife, but not for any
loving reason. And when someone wanted to be
wanted solely for herself, the thought of such calcu-
lated need was more than wounding.

'I shan't be bored, I promise you, Marcus,' she
said. 'Nor do I expect to occupy your whole attention every hour of the day.'

'But you know that you do,' he said, so quietly
that she could barely hear him.

In any case, it was only said for the servants'
benefit. . . Even as she thought it, Amy knew it
wasn't so, for none of them could have heard him
either. So he either said it to mock her, since he
could hardly mean it in the way she wished; or he
was merely reminding her of her obligation to him
now that she had given her word to take part in
the deception. She lifted her chin, suddenly full of
daring.

'Then I'm pleased to hear it,' she said in a soft
voice. 'It's what every woman wishes to hear from
the man she is going to marry.'

His eyes widened a little at this small flirtation,
but whatever he might have replied to it was interrupted by the arrival of Ronan Kelly, breezing into

the dining-room and announced brusquely by Mrs Monahan.

'The top o' the mornin' to you both,' he said at once. 'I thought I'd be callin' in to see what your plans are for today, Marcus, though it would be understandable if you lovebirds didn't intend doin' anything more than getting properly acquainted for a coupla days.'

He didn't exactly sway, but Amy was sure she could detect the remnants of the previous night's drinking bout on him, and she turned away with distaste.

Marcus was not so tolerant.

'You're drunk, man,' he snapped. 'And I'll thank you not to come barging in here and making sly remarks about my fiancée. I think an apology is in order.'

'Marcus, it's not necessary—' she murmured, but he raised his hand as if to stop any argument.

Kelly scowled, his face darkening.

'If I said anything out o' place, then I apologise, but I ain't drunk, and it'd take more'n a few snifters to get me roarin'. So you'll be up at the site today, will you?'

'I'll join you there in a little while,' Marcus said, making it obvious that he wished Kelly anywhere but here.

The man waited a moment longer, looking at them both with narrowed eyes, and then turned on his heel and went out of the house.

'I'm sorry, sir,' the housekeeper said, moving forward quickly. 'I couldn't prevent him pushing past me—'

'It's all right, Mrs Monahan. Don't fret yourself.'

As she shooed the servants out of the dining-room, leaving them alone, he turned to Amy. 'He didn't upset you, did he?'

'I think I'm made of sterner stuff than that,' she said, leaning towards him. 'But, Marcus, he makes me very uneasy. The way he looks at us—as if he knows more than he lets on.'

'He knows nothing, and what he surmises would be put down to drunken ravings as usual.'

But Amy sensed that he wasn't quite as complacent as he sounded. They must always be on their guard, for if Ronan Kelly once suspected that this engagement wasn't all that it appeared, he'd be the one to denounce them.

'I'll be back in a couple of hours, Amy,' Marcus said now, preparing to leave. 'We'll have a light lunch and then we'll take the gig into town.'

'I probably won't want to eat another thing,' she protested, 'especially as we're to go out this evening. You haven't forgotten, I suppose?'

She certainly had not. It had been one of the things preying on her mind in the sleepless hours of the night. Meeting the sophisticated Hélène Dubois again, and the unknown Chapman family. . .

'I have not,' Marcus said, pressing a kiss to the top of her head as he passed. 'And get that worried frown off your face, my sweet. They'll love you.'

She had her doubts about that. Whatever he said, she thought it highly likely that Sir Edmund Chapman had earmarked his elder daughter Edwina for Marcus's future bride, and that the lady herself had had aspirations in that direction.

What would the two of them be thinking now,

when Miss Amy Finch, unknown upstart, had captured the best prize in town? Maybe Hélène Dubois, too, had toyed with the idea of becoming Marcus's bride. There had been an undoubted warmth in her voice when she spoke his name. And even the younger Chapman girl, the unruly Julia, was probably awash with puppy-love for him.

Amy brushed a hand that wasn't quite steady across her forehead. This scheme that Marcus had hatched, awful though it was, had seemed so simple, yet the deeper she became involved in it, the more complicated it could become. The last thing Amy wanted to do was to arouse some other lady's wrath because she thought she had a prior claim to Marcus's affections.

The thought was immediately tempered by another one. Because the last thing she really wanted was to discover that Marcus himself had had some prior attachment. She smiled ruefully, knowing how well Miss Austen's fictional words could be twisted to suit her own purposes.

For she was so very much in want of a husband. She was so very much in want of Marcus Bellingham's love.

She spent the rest of the morning browsing about the house, firstly enjoying the pleasures of the extensive library, and later delighting in the sensual fragrances of the garden room that was full of plants and exotic blooms. It was far too lavish to be called a mere conservatory, and had obviously been stocked with loving care by its previous owner.

Sir Edmund Chapman must be a man of some taste, Amy thought, and she found herself wonder-

ing about him for the first time. She had assumed
him to be elderly, but it wasn't necessarily so, and
some of the books in the library certainly suggested
a man of liberal tastes.

She felt a sliver of unexpected excitement. She
had come into contact with few gentlemen, save
for those of Lady B.'s acquaintance, and they were
mostly dour and in their dotage. It would be stimu-
lating to meet someone of obvious good taste with
two lively daughters, who could surely not be a
stick-in-the-mud.

She found that she was smiling, and thought how
ironic it would be if she felt an attraction towards
this gentleman—and even more so if it was
reciprocated. . .and almost at once she caught her
breath, realising where her wild imagination was
leading her. For, of course, it couldn't be so!

Amy was affianced to Marcus Bellingham, whom
she loved, even if he didn't love her, and with whom
she had agreed to enter into a sham of a short-lived
marriage. After that ended, what gentleman would
want her?

She realised she was shaking visibly, and the
scents in the garden room were suddenly as cloying
and overpowering as a hallucinatory drug. She had
to get outside and into the fresh air, while she told
herself not to be such a fool, and that she had to let
things take the course she had agreed upon. When
the marriage ended, she would have means, and
could then make her own destiny. And if the thought
was dismal and shaming rather than exciting, she
let it pass.

*   *   *

Marcus returned in good time for them to eat a frugal salad lunch, though Amy wasn't in the least hungry.

'What's Sir Edmund Chapman like?' she asked him as they left the house and he handed her into the gig.

'In what way?'

'Oh, Marcus, don't be difficult! I have an impression of an elderly, stuffy man who is set in his ways if he can't give you a stay on the house until you've found your gold.'

She heard him laughing. 'Edmund would be mortally offended to hear himself described in that way, Amy.'

At least she'd goaded him into some kind of response, Amy thought resentfully, waiting for him to go on.

'Well? So what's he like? You really should warn me, Marcus, if he's old or infirm—'

'I assure you he's neither,' Marcus said, amused. 'But we'll make a brief call on him this afternoon since you seem too impatient to wait until this evening to meet him.'

She fumed at his careless dismissal of her request. If she already considered Sir Edmund to be something of a tiger, she would like to be properly forewarned.

It took a long while to travel through the main street of the town, which was larger than Amy had at first realised. Or perhaps it was because they were stopped so often, when one and another greeted Marcus and waited to be introduced to her.

'You seem to be a popular figure,' she remarked.

'And that surprises you, doesn't it?'

'Not at all. I was merely thinking how pleased your aunt would have been to know you were held in high regard. Why must you see hidden meanings in everything I say?'

'That's rich, when you constantly do the same to me,' he said.

'And with good reason, I might remind you,' Amy said smartly. She heard him give a heavy sigh.

'Truce, Amy. And I'd be obliged if you would try to pretend, however difficult it is, that you and I are madly in love. It's essential if our story is to be believed.'

She stared straight ahead to where the huddled cottages and shop-fronts, with their bright-painted doors, were giving way to more spacious buildings now. Each end of the town obviously held the more affluent inhabitants with the business and social activities taking place in its heart.

But these things merely flitted through Amy's mind. Of far more import was the way that an educated gentleman couldn't see what was so obvious to the humblest of his household staff! And she thanked the Lord that he could not.

'Well, Amy?' he said, more sharply. 'We'll soon be at the Chapmans' home, and I want them to see that there's harmony between us, if nothing else.'

'Well, sir, I'll do my best to appear madly in love with you, if that's what you instruct,' she murmured. 'I'll keep reminding myself that it's part of the bargain.'

He didn't answer and they continued in silence. When a large house set on the hillside behind the church came into view, she guessed at once that this was the Chapman residence. Hélène Dubois was evidently quite a walker, if she had walked all that way to visit Marcus, a fact that said something very significant to Amy.

'It's very elegant,' she said, when the silence lengthened.

'Sir Edmund is a wealthy man. Until her death, his mother lived in the house I occupy now, and I believe he intended that one or other of his daughters should eventually live there.'

'I see.' With a husband, naturally. It would have been Sir Edmund's wedding gift to Edwina or Julia. It wasn't hard to believe that Marcus Bellingham was intended to be the husband in question.

'No, you don't. Not if you're seeing hidden meanings that weren't meant. They were observations, no more.'

They had neared the house, and a dark-haired young girl came running out of the front door. A girl young enough to have no inhibitions about flinging her arms around Marcus's neck the minute he alighted from the gig, her brown eyes sparkling with mischief.

'Marcus, how lovely to see you! Father said you were coming to dinner this evening and bringing your young lady, but we never expected to see you any earlier. Oh, don't say you've changed your mind about dinner. I've planned a special song to sing for you—'

He extricated himself laughingly, and Amy thought enviously how wonderful it must be to be so young and vivacious, and so careless of observing the usual social conventions. Alongside Julia Chapman, she suddenly felt as old as Methuselah.

She realised the girl was smiling at her, and any

faint sense of resentment fell away. She was a child, no more, and apparently eager to make Amy's acquaintance. As Marcus helped her down, he introduced them to one another.

'I wanted so much to meet you, Miss Finch. You know you'll be the envy of every lady in Callanby, don't you? Your story is so romantic, especially as every lady in town was hoping to catch Marcus's eye.'

Amy laughed at her ingenuousness. 'Then I must be doubly fortunate,' she said lightly, threading her arm through Marcus's with easy propriety. 'And please do call me Amy.'

The first hurdle was over. Julia linked her arm through Marcus's free one, and they went into the house together. Meeting her was like a breath of mountain air, and if the older girl, Edwina, had had designs on Marcus, she didn't show it. More reserved than her sister, she was a perfect hostess, and made the usual condolences over Lady Bellingham without any fuss. Of Sir Edmund there was no sign.

'Father's taken Hélène into Wicklow to collect some painting materials she ordered,' Julia said. 'Somebody could have delivered them, but Hélène never misses a chance to go to Wicklow, and Father wanted to see his lawyer, anyway.'

If it sounded an odd arrangement to Amy for a wealthy employer to escort a governess to town, it was none of her business. They were clearly a bohemian household, and it meant that she wouldn't meet Sir Edmund until this evening after all. But she did see his portrait hanging over the mantel.

'Was that taken some time ago?' she said tactfully, seeing the bold and rakish look in the man's dark eyes.

'No more than two years ago, Miss Finch,' Edwina said. 'My father is a handsome man, is he not?'

'He is indeed,' Amy said politely, although such fleshy features and heavy-lidded eyes were not to her taste. He looked far too indolent, with none of Marcus's refinement. And he was much younger than she had supposed.

When they were on their way back to the house, she turned to Marcus indignantly.

'You didn't tell me how comparatively young Sir Edmund was. I envisaged someone quite different. I suppose it amused you to see me forming quite the wrong opinion?'

'Why not? You seem to form the wrong opinion of everything else.'

She declined to answer such an absurd statement. But she couldn't deny that she had formed so many differing opinions of Marcus himself, that she hardly knew which was the correct one any more. Part of her still despised him for the cheating way he was claiming his inheritance, but a far greater part of her longed for his approval in every way. Ruefully, she supposed that love forgave everything.

She dressed with care that evening. There would be three other ladies beside herself at the Chapman house, and she was quite sure they would all be beautifully dressed. Having now met Hélène Dubois and seen the portrait of Sir Edmund, she wondered if there was more than a business connection between the two of them. It was none of her business. . . But she couldn't help hoping it was so, and for purely selfish reasons. Because if Hélène was enamoured of Edmund, then she wouldn't be concerned about Amy's betrothal to Marcus.

She let herself dream for a few minutes more, before reminding herself severely that in a few months' time none of this would matter. The engagement and the sham marriage would be over, and Marcus would have his inheritance. He would then be free to marry where he chose, without being manipulated into an unwanted alliance. And just where Amy Finch Bellingham would be, she knew not.

Amy's deep-red silk gown rustled about her as she descended the stairs. Marcus was darkly elegant as always, and she couldn't help thinking what a fine couple they presented. Every inch the lovers, she thought bitterly. He put his hands lightly on her shoulders and kissed her cheek.

'Nervous?' he asked. 'You needn't be.'

'Does it show?'

'Only to me. To everyone else you look perfectly poised. If you're quite ready, then we'll go.'

If anything, it occurred to Amy that Marcus himself was less than easy now. Perhaps he wasn't as insensitive as she thought, and presenting her to friends and acquaintances was reminding him that he had a conscience after all. He had to act the devoted fiancé, just as much as Amy did.

But once they had been admitted into the Chapman house, the breezy Julia dispelled any idea of stuffiness. It was no surprise to Amy now that Hélène was included in the dinner party, and her

suspicions that the lady was more than a friend to
Sir Edmund were surely not unfounded.

As for the gentleman himself. . .he raised her
hand to his lips with all the accomplished ease of
the philanderer. The word slid into Amy's mind,
and for all his exuberance, she disliked him and
didn't trust him, and sensed that there was a ruthless
streak beneath the oily charm.

'So Marcus has had his wings clipped at last,' he
said, in a less-than-genteel manner. 'And by the
prettiest little bird to reach these shores since
Mam'selle Dubois. You're to be congratulated,
Marcus.'

Amy squirmed under his scrutiny, and drew her
hand away from those fleshy lips as soon as she
decently could.

'You're making Amy blush, Father,' Julia
squealed. 'Don't bait her already when you hardly
know her.'

If Amy had her way, he wouldn't be baiting her
at all, she thought, and Hélène was more than welcome to him. The lady seemed quite unperturbed
by her employer's attentions to the newcomer,
which could as easily be attributed to her own self-
confidence in their situation as to complete
unconcern.

But all in all, the evening passed pleasantly
enough, and when Julia sang her special song for
Marcus, everyone listened attentively. It was an artless little ditty of unrequited adolescent love, and
when it ended, Sir Edmund gave a throaty chuckle.

'You see what you've done to my daughter, Miss
Finch. You've broken her heart by capturing the
most eligible bachelor in town.'

'I'm sorry. . .' she said, unsure quite how to handle such blatancy. Marcus solved it for her, by leaving the pianoforte where Julia had insisted he stood alongside her, and coming to sit beside Amy on the sofa. He slid one arm around her shoulders.

'I think Julia's fickle heart will be broken many times before she settles down,' he said lightly. 'As for mine, it has never felt more complete.'

He touched her cheek with his forefinger, and Amy felt her throat tighten. If only the look of love in his eyes was real, and not just for effect.

But the evening was less fraught than she had feared, even though she was perceptive enough to recognise Sir Edmund's sly remarks about Marcus's lease being shortly up for renewal. For anyone unaware of the circumstances, the asides passed unnoticed, but since Amy was fully aware of them, she smarted for the way Chapman baited him whenever he could.

Before they left, Marcus invited everyone to a special evening to celebrate the engagement in a month's time, explaining that it wouldn't have been right to hold it any earlier, with Lady B.'s demise still uppermost in their minds. Though as no one in Callanby had ever met the lady, and they were the only two who mourned her, there was no real reason for the delay.

Amy sighed with relief once they were home again.

'Thank you,' Marcus said simply, when he finally said goodnight at her bedroom door.

'For what?' she said, ever aware of the intimacy of their situation, and the longing that she found it increasingly difficult to suppress.

'For being everything that I imagined you would be,' he said.

'Marcus——' she said faintly, feeling his arms go around her. His lips were touching her cheek, and it would take no more than a small movement for them to reach her waiting mouth.

'No matter how much of a business arrangement this is, you can hardly expect me to ignore how very lovely you are, Amy. I already knew the half of it from your letters. I love your bubbling humour, and your funny little spurts of indignation, and the way you blush so beautifully. Most of all I love the way you complement me so perfectly.'

She couldn't move as he went on speaking in that low, seductive voice. She felt as though she were suspended in time, wanting him so much, and willing him to mean everything he said. Willing him to be sweetly seducing her with his voice and his arms and his kisses. . .

She smothered a moue of sound in her throat as that kiss finally reached her mouth, and then she was clinging to him and holding him, and the reckless longings would no longer be denied. This was the man she loved, to whom she was going to be married. . .

The thought sobered her a little, reminding her that it wouldn't be a proper marriage. She wouldn't have all of him, the way a married woman had all the love of her husband. She wouldn't know the physical side of love, because their arrangement was too much of a gentlemen's agreement for it to be otherwise.

If it was wicked and unlady-like to wish that things could be different, then she was wicked. The

evening had been charged with emotion, and it had
been easy to pretend that it was all real—and she
so badly wanted it to be real. She was pressed tightly
to Marcus now, her breasts flattened against his
chest, and she couldn't be unaware of the hardness
of his body against hers. It didn't alarm her. Instead,
it filled her with an almost desperate yearning to
know the more intimate secrets of love.

'I think I had better leave you to your virginal
bed before I'm tempted to do something we'll both
regret,' she heard him say in a slightly strained
voice. 'Goodnight, my lovely Amy, and sleep well.'

He reached behind her to open her door, and then
he pushed her gently through it. It was almost as if
he had been so affected by her that he was in danger
of losing control.

And if he had been, then was that love? Or was
it merely some baser desire that had nothing to do
with love, but was simply lust—the kind of desire
that could be fulfilled for a man by any woman of
the night for a couple of pennies?

Inside her room, Amy leaned against her bedroom
door, feeling as wrung out as if she had run a hundred miles. Her limbs were limp, and yet all her
nerve-ends seemed to be stretched taut in the new
awakening that was taking hold of her. The tran-
sition from being a young girl to feeling all the
desires of a woman were not confined to the wedding night, she thought weakly.

Nor did they only come when that symbol of
respectability was affirmed. They were there all the
time, insidiously undermining the most ardent intention to remain pure. . .and it scared her to know that
a woman could feel desire every bit as much as a

man. Lust and love weren't so very far apart after all, Amy thought shamefacedly.

She tore off the deep red gown that seemed now to have been a totally bad choice for this evening, suggesting as it did the colour of heat and passion. She had worn it for courage, but it had been all wrong, even though she had seen such approval in Marcus's eyes. But she had seen something else in Sir Edmund Chapman's. It was the same as the speculative and lecherous look she had seen in the eyes of the objectionable Ronan Kelly's.

'I won't think of any of them for one minute more,' she said aloud in a sudden blaze of anger and frustration.

She slid out of her undergarments and into the most voluminous nightgown she possessed, as if to ward off the merest suggestion of being considered any man's plaything.

She thought she was in for another sleepless night, but she was so strung-up that she fell asleep almost at once. It didn't help, for she dreamed the most erotic dreams she had ever known. They were dreams that shocked her, containing images that she would not have allowed into her head in her waking hours.

But when she awoke with a start in the middle of the night, the dreams still lingered, and she was guiltily loath to let them go. Not when she had just been clasped in Marcus's demanding arms, and he had been telling her how much he had always loved her, while proceeding to strip away all her inhibitions along with her innocence. . .

Chapter Eleven

After Amy had been in Callanby for several weeks, she was finding it all too easy to slip into the ways of the community. People were very pleasant towards her, and she was quickly falling under the charm of the population. Not for nothing were the Irish credited with having the gift of the blarney, she acknowledged.

And not for nothing was Ireland credited with being so *green*, she thought, on the stickiest summer day she had ever known, watching the rain streak the windows as it came down in torrents, and seeing how the lawns steamed in the sultry air.

It had rained solidly for four days now, and the air was so heavy that tempers inside the house were quickly frayed. Amy was tired of reading and embroidering and keeping her own company. The rain didn't keep Marcus indoors, although she found it hard to believe it was necessary to keep visiting the site in such downpours.

'It's when the river's in flood that the silt gets stirred up, and there's more chance of the gold deposits being found,' he told her with barely concealed impatience. 'I thought I'd explained all that to you.'

'I would have thought there was more chance of finding a needle in a haystack,' she replied testily.

She could feel the tackiness on her skin, and even the weight of her own hair was a trial in the humid atmosphere of the house. All the windows were kept firmly closed as the rain lashed down, accompanied by a wayward wind.

'There's no point in arguing with you,' he said.

'Because I'm a mere woman?' Amy said, knowing she was goading him, and seemingly unable to help it.

'No. Because there's more than one kind of faith in this world, and if I didn't believe we'd find the gold eventually, there'd be no point in going on.'

'Or wasting money,' she reminded him.

'Or throwing away the money I don't yet have,' he agreed stonily, putting his own interpretation on her words.

Amy knew she was being shrewish again, but she had never been a spendthrift, nor had ever had the means to be so, and she couldn't bear to think that all of Lady B.'s inheritance would be squandered on a futile mission.

She'd overheard more than one furious argument between between Marcus and his partner, with Kelly snarling about the unlikelihood of finding gold, but that as long as Marcus was willing to fund it, he was willing to keep on the search. . .and boozing away his own assets.

It was all so unfair, since Marcus sincerely believed in what he was doing, that he had to end up with a rat like Kelly. Remembering it, Amy backed down at once.

'I'm sorry. I shouldn't poke my nose into men's business affairs.'

'No, you should not. It's my place to do the worrying, if there's any worrying to do.'

'And is there?'

Marcus shrugged. 'I wouldn't admit this to everyone, but I'm beginning to have the strongest suspicion that all the pundits were right, and the gold was truly played out centuries ago. But I've never been one to give up until it all seems hopeless.'

'I know that,' Amy said softly, remembering all the other schemes over the years, and the enthusiasm with which Marcus had entered into them. But nobody ever got rich on dreams alone, and without a goal in sight. . .

A sudden crack of thunder made her jump, and a jagged streak of lightning lit the sky. She put her hand on his arm.

'Don't go out in this, Marcus. It's not safe—'

'Your concern touches me, my love,' he said, with barely concealed mockery. 'But I don't care to have my partner call me too lily-livered to go out in a rainstorm.'

'Your partner's a fool if he thinks any man is superior to the elements,' she snapped, losing patience with this egotism. 'And I'd be concerned for anyone out and about in such appalling weather. I'm not that hard-hearted.'

And if he thought her concern for his safety was because of what she stood to gain from their marriage, he couldn't be more wrong. It was the man himself that she cared about, though he was doing precious little to enchant her at this moment.

'Attend to your woman's doings, Amy, and leave me to deal with mine,' he said, infuriating her further with such insufferable male arrogance.

He strode out of the house without another word, and she fretted and fumed for the rest of the day. There had been visits over the past weeks from the Chapman girls, and one or two others in the town, and she had been quite pleased to make return visits, with or without Marcus. But on a day like today only a fool would venture out of doors.

'You've no need to bother your pretty head about Mr Bellingham, miss,' Mrs Monahan said an hour or so later, when Amy had called for more drinks to cool her parched throat, and stabbed her fingers a dozen times with her embroidery needle.

She put down the wretched tapestry with a sigh, knowing she was making a botch of it in her impatience.

'Is it so obvious?' she asked the housekeeper.

''Tis only natural to see you so concerned about your man, miss. And if it's any consolation to you, I know he's as anxious for you to not be restless in these dismal days.'

'Does this weather happen often?' Amy said, not wanting to dwell on the sincere words, and happy enough to keep her talking.

'I'm afraid it does. We're in a basin in the mountains here, as you know, and sometimes it seems as if the Blessed Mary's seen fit to open the heavens directly over our heads.'

Amy felt less than benevolent to any supernatural

being who could pour such a torrent down on a community. And there was something else on her mind too.

'Well, I hope it won't prevent people from coming to the party next week after all your preparations.'

'Folk will always turn up for a party, miss, never you fear. Especially one to celebrate such a happy occasion.'

But would Thomas Varley come all this way? He had been sent an invitation and accepted with alacrity—just as if he was determined to see for himself that there was a proper engagement to celebrate, Amy had told Marcus.

After Mrs Monahan had gone back to her duties, she remembered Marcus's reply.

'Of course it's a proper engagement, and it will be a proper wedding. Aunt Maud would have wanted it, and so will the community hereabouts. They all love an excuse for dressing-up and dancing in the streets,' he'd said steadily. 'What happens after that is between ourselves and no one else.'

'Dancing in the streets?' Amy had said with a laugh, ignoring the rest.

'Of course. The old boys will get out their fiddles and escort us from the church to the house with music, and the townsfolk will be following and dancing and wishing us well. It's a Callanby tradition.'

It sounded charming and wonderful for two people who loved each other to be escorted and fêted in such a way. For these two, it sounded less than honest, Amy thought, but rather than say as much she made the feeblest of objections.

'Won't it be disrespectful to your aunt to make such a show of things?'

'Hardly, when it's my aunt who's brought it all about,' Marcus retorted.

The comment just about summed it up to Amy, dispelling any foolish romantic thoughts from her mind. Lady B. had dictated the terms of this marriage and would have expected a show. And Marcus would carry it through.

The banging of a door made her jump, and she turned her head to see him enter the drawing-room where she was sitting. He had shed his heavy outer garment, but his face was wet and his dark hair was shiny with rain that trickled onto his collar.

Without thinking twice, she exclaimed at once, 'How mad you men are to be out in such weather. If you care to come to my room, I'll dry your hair with a towel before you catch your death of cold.'

If it sounded like an invitation that could be construed as compromising, she dismissed the thought at once. She could hardly have said otherwise, when he was literally dripping all over the costly Axminster carpet.

'I accept your invitation, ma'am,' he said with mock humility, and she knew how much like a scolding wife she had sounded. 'But don't you want to hear my news?'

'What news?' she asked.

'We may have found something,' he said, so cautiously that she recognised it for the understatement it was. Her eyes sparkled.

'Gold? You mean there actually *is* gold up here?'

She blushed, realising how sceptical she had been all this time. But she had been well indoctrinated by

Lady B.'s scepticism of Marcus for a long time. . .

'O ye of little faith,' he said lightly. 'But perhaps it was unwise of me to say anything just yet, since we're not counting any roosters. There's certainly something there, and once we've isolated it Kelly will take it to the assay building in Wicklow. Though I'm not sure how wise it is to trust him with the mission on his own, and he'll have to be charged not to tell the world, or to start gambling away the profits before we've even registered our claim.'

'And once you do, and you're rich, then you can buy him out,' Amy stated.

And if it all happened, maybe he wouldn't need his aunt's money at all. . .but he'd want it, since it was rightfully his. And he could buy Amy out too, quickly and neatly, and no harm done. Except to her heart.

'Probably,' Marcus said. 'But there are more pressing things to do at present, unless you've decided to let me drip here all afternoon.'

Amy turned to leave the room and he followed her upstairs to her bedroom. Whether it was proper or not to admit him she neither knew nor cared. Engaged couples had a certain leeway in their relationship, and anyway, who was there here to comment or criticise?

She felt suddenly reckless and made no objection when he closed the door that she had left slightly ajar. He sat on a chair near the window, where the rain still shimmered down its surface, enclosing them in a steamed-up atmosphere made fragrant with Amy's pot-pourris and lavender sachets.

She fetched a towel from her wash-stand and

stood behind Marcus, rubbing the dripping hair and massaging his scalp. It was a far more sensuous, intimate task than she had anticipated, and she felt an almost irresistible urge to bend and kiss the exposed skin at the nape of his neck.

'Do you see us?' he suddenly said softly.

Amy looked at him, startled, and then followed his gaze to where their two images were reflected in her dressing-table mirror. Only a fool could have missed the intimacy of her actions as she caressed his head with the towel, his hair tousled and boyish. Embarrassed, she dropped the towel and made to snatch her hands away from him, but he reached up and captured them so that she couldn't move away.

'Please let me go, Marcus,' she said, her breath a whisper away from his cheek. He merely held her tighter and she bit her lips together tightly.

'If we had met before my aunt made her ridiculous ultimatum, I would never let you go,' he said, more roughly. 'But while we're so cleverly manipulated by her, we have to abide by the arrangement we've made, and I won't try to persuade you otherwise.'

It was hardly the best of compliments, if compliment it was meant to be. If it was meant to be some obtuse way of saying he cared for her, then she had no intention of asking, and throwing herself open to a possible rejection. It wasn't done for a lady to admit to a man that she loved him until the man said so first. And the two of them were simply stifled by Lady B.'s directions. She pulled her hands away from him at last.

'I think it's time you left my room now,' she said, stiffly formal. 'I'd hate the servants to suspect there's anything improper about our relationship, and for any scandalous rumours to start.'

She knew how stuffy she sounded now, but it was the only way she could deal with the situation. He looked at her steadily for a moment, treating her to that long penetrating stare she found so disconcerting.

'You haven't been listening to a word I've said, have you?' he said at last. 'All right, my sweet, I'll leave you to your chaste thoughts, but I trust you'll be in a more loving mood at the party, if only for our guests' benefit.'

'I'll do my best,' she said without expression.

Thomas Varley would be arriving here on the Friday, the day before the party. Marcus had been told he had other business in Callanby during the afternoon, and would be arriving here in time for dinner. On Saturday morning he and Marcus would be ensconced in the study, and in the afternoon Marcus wanted to show him the gold site. The imagery of the so-correct Thomas Varley wallowing about in mud on a riverbank was enough to make her smile.

'Does the thought of acting as my beloved amuse you so much?' Marcus asked.

'Not at all. I was merely imagining your Mr Varley getting his feet wet and giving that famous tut-tut at being brought to such a Godforsaken place!'

For a moment she thought he was going to be angry, and then his face relaxed, and she could see the laughter dancing about in his eyes. And he was suddenly the Marcus with whom she had had such fun in their mutually guarded letters.

'The sight of him mincing about is one I shan't want to miss. That walrus moustache will surely bristle with disapproval too,' he agreed. 'I'm only sorry you can't be there to see it as well.'

'Why can't I?'

'Because, my love, I want you to be serene and lovely for the evening, and not mud-spattered. I want to show you off to the world. But have no fear. I'll be sure to describe the gentleman's reactions to you at some suitable time.'

She had to be satisfied with that. She hadn't really expected him to invite her along to the site. It was men's business, and it was clearly desirable to Marcus that Thomas Varley should believe in what he was doing. For a man who had always been an adventurer, he needed approval, she realised, just as much as anyone else. He needed hers.

Over the next few days, the weather improved dramatically with what Mrs Monahan called 'the little people's summer mischief', and the hot sun began to steam the grounds even more, filling them with an ethereal-like beauty. And Amy realised that somehow she and Marcus had recovered much of their old camaraderie. It was a great relief, for she hated being on bad terms with anyone, especially Marcus.

Besides, there was beginning to be great excitement generated in the house for the imminent party. None had been held here since Marcus took up residence, and for the staff to be sharing in the celebrations for their favourite gentleman was putting a smile on everyone's face.

*   *   *

Amy was very nervous waiting for Thomas Varley to arrive, but when he did, wearing a voluminous cloak that was far too hot for summer, and perspiring heavily, his relief at actually reaching Callanby made him expansive. This relief would surely be added to by the fact that she and Marcus looked such a happy and united couple, Amy thought briefly, as they waited in the drawing-room with arms linked, while Mrs Monahan showed him in.

'My dear young people,' he said by way of greeting. 'This is indeed a happy occasion, and from the glow about you both, I trust you have both recovered from the shock of Lady Bellingham's demise.'

He was not quite as formal as before, and at his words Amy realised with a little shock that she hadn't really thought of Lady B. in days. It was sad, and yet inevitable, with everything changing so rapidly in her life.

'With the mutual help of each other, I believe we have,' Marcus said gravely. 'It's a great comfort to me to have Amy with me.'

Varley's sharp gaze remained on him for a minute, and then he turned to Amy.

'And how are you settling down, Miss Finch? Shall you like living in the depths of the country when you're married?'

She felt Marcus's grip tighten on her arm for a second before they all sat down, and she glanced at him with a warm smile before answering.

'I know I shall. I like the people hereabouts, and I have already settled in here quite nicely.'

'Then let us hope it all continues as happily. I should imagine the recent inclement weather stretched your inner resources to the utmost.

Although I'm told it's easy for one to view the world through rose-coloured glasses when one's in love.'

Amy didn't dare to look at Marcus after such an unexpected remark, but she heard his easy laugh.

'That's probably true, isn't it, my love?' he asked, and Amy found herself agreeing with a blush.

It was also amazingly easy to pretend that all this was real, she thought, as the evening developed. Thomas Varley became far less of a stuffed-shirt when fortified with Marcus's good wine and brandy. He was almost human. . . And before bidding them good-night and retiring to his guest room, he gave a small chuckle that sounded odd coming from that normally sober gentleman.

'I must confess, Marcus, that I had a few wee suspicions about your sudden attachment to Miss Finch. But now that I see you together, well, it's obvious that I was wrong. And I'll say no more lest you start to think that this hard-headed lawyer is turning into a sentimental old fool.'

He had already been shown his room, and he left them together in the drawing-room. In the small silence following his departure, Amy was suddenly nervous. She too had taken a glass more wine than she normally did, and had felt easier in conversing with the two gentlemen.

But had she unwittingly gone too far in allowing the pretence of their love to appear so real? And if so, would Marcus be alarmed, wondering if she intended to keep him to the marriage bargain long after they could reasonably end it?

'I hope I did nothing to embarrass you,' she murmured.

He looked at her in some surprise.

'On the contrary. I was about to thank you for complementing me so superbly. If it was all an act, then you are a consummate actress, Amy.'

He was an accomplished actor too, she thought mournfully, for she had truly been carried away by the ambience of the evening... And tomorrow would be even more emotive, with friends toasting their health and wishing them every happiness for the future. The euphoria of the evening vanished like will-o'-the-wisp.

'Perhaps that's where my vocation lies,' she said in a strangled voice. 'Perhaps when we finally go our separate ways, I should attempt to follow in the footsteps of those legends of the stage—'

'Don't talk nonsense. Those people are shallow and affected, and I wouldn't care to see you emulate any of them, Amy. You're a beautiful and desirable woman, and your future should be with a man who loves you.'

She said nothing, keeping her eyes lowered and her hands clenched, certain that he couldn't be telling her more plainly that he wasn't the one.

'Well, if this is the only time I ever need to exercise my acting skills, I promise not to let you down, Marcus,' she said. 'Now I'll bid you goodnight.'

He caught at her hand as she went to leave the room, and she looked up at him, filled with misery but doing her best to hide it.

'Whatever the future holds for us, I hope we'll always be good friends, Amy. And it's the normal practise for friends to kiss one another goodnight.'

She was in his arms before she could protest, even if she had wanted to. But she was so limp now from the wine and from relief that the evening that had gone more successfully than she could have hoped, that she remained perfectly passive in his arms, her eyes closed, willing herself not to respond in any way that might be misconstrued.

'I might have wished for a little more enthusiasm, even from a friend,' he said when the kiss ended. 'But it's no matter. Go to bed now, Amy, and don't rush to get up in the morning, for we'll have a late night ahead of us.'

Their whole situation was more than frustrating, Amy thought. Having to pretend to be in love with Marcus when they were in company was no hard-ship to her. It was far harder on the nerves to pretend that she *wasn't* in love with him when they were alone. But she did as she was told and spent a leisurely morning on the Saturday of the party, knowing the evening would be something of an ordeal.

By now she had become acquainted with most of the guests who would be coming, and the initial curiosity about her had died down a little. But not entirely.

The Callanby folk were nothing if not intrigued, some of them to the point of being downright inquisitive, she thought with a smile. And she couldn't really blame them when she had appeared out of the blue, not as a lady's companion, but as the betrothed of the most eligible man in town.

She had seen nothing of Marcus and Varley for the rest of that day. And when it came to dressing for the evening, she found that her hands weren't quite steady. This should all be so very different. A girl's engagement party should be one of celebration and happiness. . .and instead, it was the beginning of a path that was destined to have no proper ending.

She resisted the temptation to become maudlin, knowing she must appear bright-eyed and as radiant as a bride-to-be was expected to be. The maid, Docherty, helped her into her gown that evening, a beautiful shot-silk in a shade of midnight blue that she adored. Then she teased out her hair until it shone like a dark cloud about her face.

'You look a real picture, miss,' Docherty said enviously. 'Mr Bellingham will be so proud of you, so he will.'

Right on cue, there was a tap on the door, and she ran to answer it. Marcus stood there with a jewellery box in his hand. The maid gawped at him fatuously, then scurried out of the room, leaving them alone.

He said nothing for a moment, and Amy felt tongue-tied and nervous. Surely he, too, was realising the magnitude of this undertaking at last, and was wondering, even now, if it was wise to go through with it. But of course he would. He *needed* her. . .

She spoke in a scratchy voice. 'Well? Will I do? I'll not disgrace you, will I?'

A wild thought flashed through her mind that she could disgrace him with the most outrageous scandal if she opened her mouth and told this illustrious company the true state of affairs. But she never would, of course. She needed him too, in quite a different way. . .

'You could never disgrace me,' Marcus said. 'I was just thinking what a great honour you do me in agreeing to go through with this charade, Amy, and wondering how I ever had the temerity to suggest it of you.'

'It was necessary,' she said woodenly. 'We both know it, and we both accepted it at the time.'

He nodded, and moved towards her. Without thinking, she stepped back a pace as if to ward off any thought of him taking her in his arms. Not now. Not right now, when all her nerve-ends were stretched so tight at the thought of being greeted with so many congratulations for their future happiness. They didn't only deceive Thomas Varley and his lawyers. They deceived friends and servants too, and it was a thought that constantly pained Amy.

'I have something for you,' he said. 'It's an engagement present.'

'Oh, you shouldn't have done that,' she exclaimed. 'Really, Marcus, I wish you hadn't—'

He didn't answer. He merely opened the long box in his hand and took out the most exquisite sapphire necklace Amy had ever seen. She swallowed hard as he stood behind her and fastened it around her neck. It was a perfect match for the ring she wore on her finger and the gown she had chosen for this evening, and she was fairly sure it hadn't been one of Lady B.'s pieces.

'Before you ask, my sweet practical Amy,' he said, just as if he could read the whirling thoughts inside her head, 'while we were in Dublin I obtained a catalogue from a high-class jewellers in the town and instructed Varley to purchase this piece for me especially for this occasion. He was happy to do so, knowing he could offset the cost from the inheritance.'

She didn't miss the mocking note in his voice
and half-wondered if it was a kind of defence. She
couldn't be sure, but she guessed that being charged
with such a purchase would have pleased Varley, if
only to prove Marcus's good intentions towards his
intended bride. She bit her lip. It was all so awful,
when it should have been so wonderful. . .and she
had been silent for too long.

She felt Marcus's hands caress her shoulders, and
then his kiss on the nape of her neck.

'Won't you please accept it in the spirit in which
it's given, Amy? It's a token of love and friendship.'

'And undying gratitude,' she murmured, knowing
she was spoiling the moment, but compelled to do
so before she twisted into his arms and begged him
to say that the love was real.

'That too,' he agreed. 'Now, if you're ready, shall
we go down together, or do you want to make an
entrance alone? Most of the guests have already
arrived.'

She felt her heart jump in fright. She had dawdled
in her room, and now there was no turning back.
She fingered the necklace for a moment and then
gave a tremulous smile.

'Together,' she said. 'And if I've been ungracious
in my response to your gift, I'm sorry. It's truly
lovely.'

'But no lovelier than its owner,' Marcus said.

As they went down the curving staircase, she
glimpsed a crowd of people already in the drawing-
room and spilling out into the reception area at the
foot of the stairs. Varley was standing with the
Chapmans and the governess, and seemed on good

terms with them. They were obviously old acquaintances, and Amy had discovered he had already
called on them before coming here.

As soon as the guests caught sight of Amy and
Marcus a ripple of excitement seemed to reach out
towards them. The next moment everyone had
poured out of the drawing-room and were applauding the couple madly.

'Oh, Lord, this is too embarrassing,' Amy murmured, clinging tightly to Marcus's arm.

'No, it's not. It's just the Irish way. They relish
a good celebration, so smile and look happy, the
way you should. Think of it as the first step of your
budding acting career.'

He said it to calm her, but she wished she'd never
made such an idiotic comment. He'd think she was
acting the whole time now, and while it was sensible
for him to believe it, it was one more thing to offend
Amy's sense of integrity.

But she was so quickly swept into the throng of
guests that she soon forgot such disturbing thoughts.
The Chapman girls were at their most sparkling,
especially Julia, who had recently discovered astrol-
ogy and was flitting prettily about the room trying
to gauge everyone's Zodiac sign and matching or
mismatching them.

'Are we a match, I wonder?' Marcus whispered
to Amy, under cover of the general babble of noise.
'Or would a lifetime together prove to be completely
incompatible?'

'We'll never know, will we?' she said flippantly,
moving on to where Sir Edmund Chapman
was waiting to pump her hand, his eyes assessing her far more lasciviously than she liked. But if

Mademoiselle Hélène Dubois truly had her sights set on him then, however rakish the gentleman, he would soon have his wings clipped.

And why not? The landed gentry had been known to marry governesses, and it was just as feasible as an adventurer marrying his aunt's companion.

She pushed the thought out of her head and found herself standing near Ronan Kelly. Naturally he was an invited guest, and she knew Marcus had insisted on them preserving absolute secrecy for the time being about the possible gold findings. But Kelly knew she would have been told, and his greedy eyes lit up as he approached her, a glass in his hand as always.

'Good news, little lady, and not only about the engagement, if you get my meaning,' he said, involving her in a private little conspiracy that she didn't care for.

'I think that's men's business,' she said quietly.

'So it is, but it'll certainly involve you if it proves as good as we suspect,' he said. 'Marcus's wife will be getting even more fine jewels for her pretty neck.'

He raised his glass to her, and she felt an active dislike for the man, stronger than she had ever felt before.

But then, she was learning so much about herself in recent weeks. And in doing so, she was discovering a wealth of emotions inside her that had been dormant until now. She knew she was capable of strong hate, and even stronger love, and she couldn't deny it.

'I'm sure you know that ethics demand that you don't talk about it, Mr Kelly,' she said, trying to appeal to his better nature, if he had such a thing.

He gave a kind of snort that disgusted her. He really did nothing to enhance this company.

And when she was mistress here, she thought indignantly, she'd have words to say about who was invited and who was not. . . She suddenly registered her own thoughts, and gave a rueful smile. Seeing it, and thinking it was for him, Kelly pressed her hand in his.

'Don't you fret none, pretty Amy. I'll not let your man down by gabbing on the findings too soon.'

Amy snatched her hand away, just managing to resist the urge to rub it against the skirt of her gown to rid herself of the odious feel of it. She was more than thankful when one of the elderly spinsters of the town called her name and gushingly told her how pleased they all were that dear Marcus had found his true love at last.

'Thank you, Miss O'Neill,' she murmured.

'And when's the wedding to be, my dear? We're all looking forward to it so much,' she went on.

'We haven't settled on a date yet—'

'But it will be quite soon, dear lady,' she heard Marcus's voice behind her. 'I hardly think there's a man alive who'd want to wait a minute longer than he had to to claim such a beautiful bride.'

Amy accepted his kiss on her cheek and heard the older woman give a sentimental sigh. But Amy was suddenly too tense to respond. The playacting simply deserted her. It was all so wrong. . .so terribly wrong. . . And then she caught the sharp, speculative look on Ronan Kelly's face, and she smiled up at Marcus in a kind of desperation.

Chapter Twelve

It was quite a large party of thirty or more guests. The evening was interspersed with eating and drinking, and much jollity was provided by the Irish fiddlers Marcus had hired for the occasion, and the younger folk who were persuaded to dance a few jigs. If they were nothing like as accomplished as the dancers who had performed in the Dublin hotel, the whole atmosphere was friendly and cheerful. When it was nearing midnight, Marcus took centre stage and asked for a little quiet. He drew Amy to his side, and her heart began to thud more quickly as he made a small formal speech.

'My friends, you all know why you're here tonight, and I thank you all for helping me to celebrate my good fortune in capturing the heart of the wonderful lady who has done me the honour of agreeing to be my wife.'

He had to pause then to the sounds of cheering and clapping and foot-stomping. Callanby folk were certainly uninhibited, thought Amy. But it gave her time to gather herself, and to try to ignore the deepening flush in her cheeks that would be construed as perfectly normal in the circumstances. She had known this announcement would be made, but it was none the less emotive when it did.

'I now ask you to drink to my lady's health and future happiness, which I shall do my very best to ensure,' Marcus went on gallantly.

When it was done, someone thrust a glass of wine into each of their hands, and before Amy knew what he was about, Marcus had threaded his arm in hers so that they were linked.

'And we will drink to one another as a promise and a pledge of our love,' he said.

It wasn't easy to take a sip of wine this way, but it was evidently a well-observed custom, and brought roars of laughter when it was finally accomplished with the minimum of spillage.

By now Amy began to feel as though she were living out a fantasy, and that none of this was real at all. She could see a sea of smiling faces, but in the midst of them, there was one face that hardly smiled at all. Ronan Kelly wore his usual mocking look that disturbed her so. She wished they hadn't had to invite him at all, but as he was Marcus's partner, to leave him out would have been an insult.

She daren't let him suspect things were less than above-board, she thought now, or that this wasn't a real love-match. She hugged Marcus's arm, whispering quickly that his scowling partner looked anything but congratulatory. Marcus held up his hand again to quieten the babble.

'My fiancée and I thank you all for your good wishes and gifts,' he said. 'But there is someone missing here tonight, and I cannot let this occasion go by without paying due tribute to her. In fact, if it wasn't for Amy's association with my dear aunt, we would never have met at all. We both owe a great deal to her, and if there has been an occasional shadow over our faces, it's because Aunt Maud isn't here to witness our happiness.'

There were murmurs of sympathy and understanding, and Marcus raised his glass again.

'But I also know how Aunt Maud would object to this celebration turning into a wake, so I ask you all to join me in a toast to her memory, and then continue making merry.'

After they had all complied, the fiddlers began playing another intricate tune at once, and Amy turned to Marcus gratefully.

'Thank you. That was just the right note to strike, and I'm sure it will have allayed anyone's suspicions.'

'Then let us continue to allay them by appearing as the loving couple we're meant to be,' he said softly.

She smiled up into his face, abandoning any thought of being stand-offish. This was no evening to be a shrinking violet and pretending an undue modesty. This was her evening as much as his, and she intended to enjoy the rest of it.

Marcus's attention was caught by Thomas Varley at that moment. Varley had been deep in conversation with Hélène Dubois, and Amy turned as the governess joined her now, as elegant as ever in pale lemon silk.

'That was a very sweet gesture for Marcus to make to his aunt,' she said. 'You must have been very fond of her too, Miss Finch.'

'I was. She was a good friend to me, and it was

a great sadness to me when she died in such terrible circumstances.'

'But rather fortunate that such a circumstance should have such a happy ending, you must agree!'

'I hardly think the death of a good lady could be construed in any way fortunate—'

'But perhaps you would not be in the position you are in now, if it had not happened?' Hélène said. 'I only mention the fact because I know what a confirmed bachelor Marcus had been until your arrival, much to the regret of the townsladies, of course. To share in mutual sadness and have it turn so quickly to romance must have been very rewarding.'

The inference was obvious. Hélène assumed that Amy had somehow wheedled her way into Marcus's affections after Lady B.'s death. The irony of it was so ludicrous as to make her almost laugh out loud.

'Oh, very rewarding,' she said in a spurt of mischief. 'I couldn't have stage-managed a happier ending myself, even though I do miss the lady dreadfully, of course.'

'Of course,' Hélène said, with no idea of the double meaning in Amy's words. 'But there are always compensations.'

She smiled conspiratorially as Sir Edmund moved towards them, and her voice became more vampish at once. Amy's face flamed, realising now that the Frenchwoman had been comparing their circumstances. Watching the governess flit about the room, Amy half-revised her thought that she had set her sights on becoming Lady Chapman, since it seemed she couldn't resist flirting with any male in the vicinity.

And then she deliberately forgot her. Such behaviour didn't concern her, and she wouldn't let it. But she had never thought of herself as a fortune-hunter, and she didn't like the inference that she was.

'Don't let that one ruffle your feathers, little lady,' Ronan Kelly said, sidling close by. 'We all have to look out for ourselves in this world, and our Mam'selle Dubois is only doing the same. She's after anything in trousers,' he added crudely. 'But you need have no fear, since 'tis clear that you and Marcus were made for each other.'

He winked, and she moved quickly past the obnoxious man to find herself face to face with Thomas Varley now.

'Well, Miss Finch, you do Marcus's engagement gift proud. I've complimented him on his good taste on all counts.'

And from that, Amy assumed he had forgiven them for the unfortunate scenes in his chambers, and was prepared to believe they were marrying for love after all. He wasn't old, even if his stiffness had sometimes made him appear elderly, but he seemed to have mellowed considerably, she thought in some surprise. Or else he was able to show another side of himself at a social gathering.

She was both thankful and regretful when the evening was finally over, although many folk lingered into the small hours of the morning. But despite her determination, she found it impossible to relax to order, and it had been as much of a strain as she had expected.

All she wanted now was to be alone. She dismissed the faithful Docherty, a little dismayed to find she had been waiting up all this time to help her undress, and told her to get to her bed or she'd be good for nothing in the morning.

And then she simply wilted. She unfastened her gown and let it drop to the floor, unpinning her hair until the weight of it curled about her shoulders. She caught sight of herself in the mirror, no longer flushed and radiant as she had been told by one and another, but pale-faced and wan.

Around her throat the glorious sapphires of Marcus's engagement gift shone and sparkled in their pure perfection. They seemed to Amy at that moment to be a mockery of all that was decent in life, and to emphasise the extent of their deceit. She made to unfasten the clasp, but her hands were shaking so much she couldn't manage it.

The frustration of it all, and the release of tension after the evening was suddenly too much, and she sat down heavily on the edge of her bed in her undergarments, weeping.

She didn't even hear the tap on her door. The next thing she knew was that the bed dipped, and then there was the feel of someone's arms around her, turning her into him.

'Dear God, Amy, don't do this. Don't make me feel any worse than I do already for leading you into this,' she heard him say in a low, desperate voice.

She leaned heavily against him, unable for the moment to break away from his warm and loving embrace. His words were hardly the sweet nothings to someone you professed to love with all your heart. . .but she knew that condition didn't apply in his case.

And she was increasingly aware of the compromising situation between them now. A certain indulgence between betrothed folk was accepted, especially here in more liberal country surroundings. . .but that hardly meant sitting on her bed in her undergarments and being held so closely in his arms that she could feel every beat of his heart against her body. . .

It added insult to her bruised feelings to register anew the humiliation of his words. To Amy's mind they meant that he regretted ever making the outrageous proposal to her. . . She struggled feebly to release herself, trying to find the words to send him packing, but he was holding her tighter, as if he couldn't bear to let her go.

'I guessed you'd be having some kind of reaction by now, though I didn't expect to find you in quite such abject misery. I can't leave you for the night like this, Amy,' he murmured. 'You and I have always been so close in mind and spirit, and you'll never know how bitterly I despise myself for wrecking that closeness. I need your forgiveness.'

'What for?' she whispered. 'If there's any blame attached to anything we've done, then we share it. You have no need to ask my forgiveness.'

She looked up into his face, and heard him catch his breath. Slowly, he bent his head and his mouth found hers, and she couldn't and *wouldn't* resist his kiss. She wound her arms about him and held him close, and somehow they were falling back on the bed, and his hand had found her breast and was caressing its softness.

And, heaven help her for her wickedness, but it was more than she could do to protest, when the exquisite sensations the contact evoked were like nothing she had ever known before in her life.

'My sweet, sweet Amy,' Marcus whispered against her throat. 'Do you have any idea how often I've longed to do this?'

'No,' she said faintly.

'And does it offend you so terribly?' he went on with relentless seduction.

'No——' she said, knowing that it should. 'Oh, I mean yes, yes it does——but I can't——I can't——'

He lay half over her now, and she was finding it difficult to breathe. Not only because of the weight of him, but because there was a deep longing coursing through her that screamed out for fulfilment. She *wanted* him as much as it was evident that he wanted her.

'I won't compromise you, my dearest, much as I'm desperate to know all your sweetness,' he said softly, and she knew at once that it could only be the wine and the ambience of the evening that was making them both so free and relaxed.

Amy somehow managed to remind herself wildly that their arrangement was strictly a business one, and for the marriage to be annulled there must be no consummation. . .and certainly not before the wedding. . .

'Please go, Marcus,' she whispered now. 'I don't think I can bear much more of this.'

He didn't demean either of them by asking if his attentions were obnoxious to her, and Amy thought ruefully that he must surely know that they were not. A long while ago, one of Lady B.'s kitchen maids had told her that a man always knew when a woman was ready for him, and that she couldn't hide it. And the evidence of Marcus's own desire was all too clear to her.

He nodded as if to acquiesce, and then he bent his head to where the petticoat revealed the swell of her breasts. His fingers found and released one rosy tip, and his lips had covered it before she could think what was happening. A sharp shooting sensation, as sweet as honey, soared through her loins, and she gasped both with shock and unexpected pleasure.

When he looked at her again, she saw that they were both breathing as heavily as each other.

'My task will be made all the harder in trying to keep my hands off my bride now that I've tasted some of your sweetness, Amy. But I'll leave you to your bed now, with some idea of how it might have been if things had been different.'

When he had gone, she rolled over on to her stomach for long moments, still shocked and hardly able to think straight. She knew she should never have permitted such intimacy, but she had been powerless to resist. And now she was reluctant to break the spell of his caresses, or to ponder too deeply over his words. She knew that in his heart Marcus was an honourable man, and would never have suggested this marriage if it wasn't for his birthright and Lady B.'s conditions.

But he was a young and virile man too, and the piquancy of their situation was clearly having an effect on him too. It gave her a small, guilty feeling of satisfaction to know he found it impossible to remain immune to her.

Slowly, she undressed properly and climbed into bed, wondering just what a capricious fate really had in store for the two of them. She didn't dare to hope for a happy ending, for there could be only one happy ending for her, and that wasn't part of the plan.

The person flitting about downstairs and tidying up the remnants of the party in the drawing-room glanced up when a door on the landing opened. Soft light spilled out of the room on to the landing, and the maid could see that it was Mr Bellingham who emerged, and she knew full well that the room in question was that of Miss Finch's.

It didn't bother her. Such things happened, but it would be an interesting titbit to tell the grand widower fellow she had her eye on. Her eyes sparkled. Ronan Kelly was always interested in a bit of gossip and the goings-on of other folk, especially when it involved his partner.

Amy was relieved to say goodbye to Thomas Varley during the following morning. Though if she had always thought he saw too much before, then what was he seeing now, when she could hardly look at Marcus without embarrassment over what had happened last night!

'It's been a pleasure to meet you again, Miss Finch,' he said as he took his leave. 'And I look forward to hearing news of your wedding.'

'You'll be sure to know the date as soon as it's arranged,' Marcus said.

And of course he would expect an invitation, if only to see that the terms of Lady B's Will were carried out properly. Amy tried not to be cynical, but Marcus was so brisk this morning that she thought he must surely be regretting coming to her room. And remorse on her part had set in quickly.

She should never have allowed it to happen. . . But no matter how many times she told herself as much, it *had* happened, and she couldn't forget it.

But once Varley had gone back to Dublin, the two of them were alone and Marcus looked at her anxiously.

'Are you all right?' Marcus asked. 'You look very pale this morning.'

She had a great urge to say facetiously that she always looked this way when a man had come to her room and seduced her. . .but this wasn't the time for funning, and anyway, he hadn't, not completely. . .

'I'm well enough,' she said. 'But, Marcus, I think we need to get a few things settled between us.'

'Oh? What things are those?'

She should have been warned by the ominous note in his voice, but she blundered on, because it had to be said, and now was as good a time as any.

'After the wedding,' she said, 'you won't—we won't—what I'm trying to talk about are the sleeping arrangements. We'll still have our separate rooms, won't we?'

'Is that what you want?'

'It's what has to be!' she said in a panic. 'Marcus, if I thought any differently—'

What she meant was that she knew she would find it impossible to be sharing a room, a bed, with him, and not let him know her feelings. She couldn't let him make love to her without reciprocating. . .

'You mean you'll want to be sure of having your pound of flesh when the marriage is dissolved with no fear of your being tainted. Only in this case, the flesh in question is the settlement I've promised you.'

In the silence of the room, Amy could hear her heart beating. It wasn't what she had meant at all, but she might have known he would put his own interpretation on it.

'You make it sound so sordid, and may I remind you that none of this was my doing, and nor was I the one who schemed a way to get round Lady B.'s bequest,' she said heatedly.

'Nor you did. As for the other business—the sleeping arrangements as you call them—no, my dear, we will not continue to have separate rooms. I wouldn't care to have it bandied about by gossiping servants that Marcus Bellingham was less than a lusty bridegroom who didn't sleep with his wife.'

As Amy gasped, he went on.

'But rest assured, there's nothing so offputting for a man than to have an unwilling woman in his bed. Since the plan is to have the marriage annulled as soon as convenient, we'll be as brother and sister—unless you decide otherwise. Does that satisfy you?'

She snapped her agreement, but inwardly she seethed with outrage. Who ever heard of a woman taking the initiative in such a situation? In her innocence, Amy was sure it never happened, and therefore they had reached another stalemate.

And at that precise moment, a gossiping servant was down by the river, relating all she had seen on the previous night, and embroidering it with her own brand of blarney to an attentive Ronan Kelly.

'Well now, this is something to ponder on, and

you're the grand wee girl for bringing me this news, Maureen. I always thought this attachment was too sudden, but our man didn't believe in wasting any time in getting his oats.'

'You'll not let on that I said anything, will you, Ronan?' she said anxiously. 'I've me job to think of, and if Mr Bellingham suspected I'd told you, I'd be out like a shot.'

' 'Course I won't let on, me darlin'. And the last thing I want is for you to be slung out, when there might be even more titbits to discover.'

'Like what?'

'I don't know. All I've got is a gut feeling that summat's not quite right, and the old girl snuffing it like she did was the best thing that could have happened—'

'Don't say such things,' Maureen said, quickly crossing herself. ' 'Tis a sin to speak ill of the dead—'

'Ah well, let's forget the lot of them and have a wee bit of sinning ourselves,' he said with a chuckle, and rolling her in the grass. She'd catch pneumonia, so she would, Maureen thought weakly, with the ground still a wee bit damp after all the rain, but it would be worth it if she could persuade Ronan Kelly to marry her. . .

Once the weather improved again, the days passed more agreeably. Most of the party guests sent thank-you messages to Amy and Marcus, or called on Amy with invitations of their own. She was in demand for afternoon teas, and she and Marcus were invited as a couple to card parties. It was easy to pretend this would never end, and now that they had resumed a less intense relationship, it was easier on the nerves.

Though, Amy had to admit, if she was feeling more serene than before, Marcus was not. But the reason was inevitably on account of his partner, more than herself.

'The man's an idiot,' Marcus stormed late one afternoon when he'd walked down to the town to bring Amy back from the Chapmans'. The summer evenings were warm, and they had both discovered a great pleasure in walking.

'What's he done now?' Amy said.

'We're not ready to take the findings into Wicklow for assaying, but he's been insisting that we should. There's not enough to go on, and frankly I'm not convinced that what we've found is gold at all. But when he gets into one of his pig-headed moods, there's no arguing with him.'

Amy just managed to refrain from saying they seemed to be well matched in that department.

'But surely it has to be a joint decision?' she said.

'You would think so. And I've said adamantly that we should wait a while to collect enough samples to give ourselves every chance. But that's not good enough for Kelly. Now he's gone off half-cocked into Wicklow with the samples we've got, and if there's any chance of it being the real stuff, we'll both be going into Dublin for further advice.'

'And you're doubtful of the outcome?' she said, hardly needing to ask. His look told her as much.

'He's promised to come straight back with the news, but I don't think he knows the real meaning of partnership,' Marcus said. 'I don't mind telling you, Amy, the sooner I can buy him out, the better I shall like it.'

She didn't answer. If she had ever dreamed for a moment of not going through with this marriage, she knew she couldn't do it. Whatever his reasons for it were, she was marrying for love, and when you loved someone you wanted to help them all you could. Marcus needed her help in this, and she wouldn't let him down.

'You must rue the day you ever met the Bellinghams,' he said, obviously misunderstanding her silence.

'I certainly do not! I was very fond of Lady B., and—well, you must know that I'm fond of you too, Marcus.'

Dear Lord, how lukewarm that sounded, when what she actually felt for him was a glorious and uninhibited passion. She felt him press her arm against his in a friendly manner.

'I'm glad to hear it. I'm fond of you too, Amy,' he said in a glib voice.

A messenger arrived from Wicklow a few days later. Marcus received the sealed envelope in his study, and after a while he sent for Amy to join him there. She knew from his set and angry face that it wasn't good news.

'What is it?' she said quietly.

He handed her the document from the assay office, but she couldn't make much sense of it. It was a mass of figures and words she didn't know, and she admitted as much.

'I don't understand—' she began.

'The only thing you need to understand is that there's no gold,' he snapped. 'The material we so laboriously sifted and collected was pyrites.'

Amy looked blank, but hearing the flatness in his voice she knew how bitterly disappointed he must be.

'You obviously don't know the word,' he said.

'I'm afraid I don't.'

'Then let me put it more clearly. It's what's commonly called *fool's gold*, Amy, and it's virtually worthless. The name for it is self-explanatory, and the biggest fools of all are those who go chasing after gold in an area when they should have the sense to know the gold has long since been played out.'

'Oh, Marcus, I'm so sorry,' she whispered, wanting to go to him and put her arms around him, but seeing from his hard, tight expression that he wanted no soft sympathy.

'I'm sorry too, but that doesn't help the situation. Nor does this note from Kelly.'

He almost flung it at her, and she read the scrawled, careless writing with a feeling of distaste as the unwelcome phrase 'deserting a sinking ship' came readily to her mind.

''Tis the worst of findings, Marcus, and I'm off to Dublin to drown me sorrows and have a wager or two. I'll be back in a week or so.'

'How could he act like this! Any decent partner would be here trying to decide what you should do now.'

Marcus shrugged. 'Maybe it's not what we have to decide, but more likely to be what's already been decided for us. You can't fight fate, Amy, and if fate has decreed that there's no gold to be found, we might as well give up. Maybe Kelly's got more sense than I have in that respect.'

'I'll never agree to that! And when did you ever

give up on a project? It's not like you, Marcus. Remember all the times you've tried things before and kept your enthusiasm until the end—'

Her voice died away at his look. She didn't mean to condemn him. Rather, she meant to bolster his confidence, because he had always had such faith in his projects. But she could see she was doing him no good at all now.

'You know me too well, of course, and I can't blame you for seeing this as the end of what my aunt would no doubt call a wildcat idea, instead of my researching the area thoroughly. She never credited me with any serious intent.'

'But I'm different,' Amy said passionately. 'I always had faith in you, Marcus, you must know that!'

She stopped abruptly, knowing that if she went on she was in danger of telling him that she loved him and that she would always stand by him, no matter how his fortunes changed for better or worse. She swallowed drily.

'Your faith is touching, Amy, but it would have been far easier for my peace of mind if this had been a successful venture—and if we hadn't discovered it while you and I are set on our present course.'

'What do you mean?'

'I mean that if we had really been able to make a gold claim, it might have seemed less manipulative for you to know I wasn't entirely dependent on my aunt's fortune.'

Her conditions would still have applied though, Amy thought cynically, but he wouldn't have needed to pretend such a passion for her as he had displayed last night. . . Her spirits plummeted at the thought, and her voice was flat when she replied. 'I'm sorry. I wish I was anywhere but here, but I'm afraid there's little I can do about it for the present.'

He looked at her as if she had been speaking in a foreign tongue.

'I thank God that you *are* here, Amy. You're the one thing that cheers me, but I'm the worst kind of company right now. I need to be alone to do some hard thinking. Please try to understand.'

She was feeling claustrophobic in the study by now, in any case, and she also needed to be alone with her thoughts. To weep silently over his disappointment, and to rage over the insensitivity of a partner who chose to opt out of a proper discussion and confrontation, and to go off drinking and gambling instead. Kelly had never disgusted her more.

But it was obvious that Marcus wanted no one at all at this moment. His pride was like that of a wounded animal who preferred to lick his wounds without witnesses, and she couldn't help him.

'I intended going for a walk this afternoon, anyway. I'll see you in time for dinner, Marcus.'

She left him alone, and went outside the house without bothering to fetch a bonnet or gloves since the day was so gloriously warm. She pushed the last half-hour out of her mind, knowing there was nothing she could do to help, and tried to concentrate on the beauties of nature instead.

In so short a time from the rains, everything seemed to have shaken itself out and dried out again. Today, the sky was a clear vibrant blue and everything about her seemed to have benefited from the recent heavy downpours. Flowers blossomed in profusion, the lawns and trees displayed brilliant shades of green, and the surrounding mountains were friendly and benevolent sentinels.

The entire area was truly beautiful, and in any other circumstances, Amy knew she would never want to leave it. The thought made her catch her breath, knowing she had little choice. Once the marriage and eventual annulment was a *fait accompli*, there would be no reason for her to stay, and she had too much pride of her own to stay on sufferance with a man who only married her for gain.

'Amy, *Amy*! I've got such news!'

She jerked up her head at the sound. She had been walking aimlessly over the sloping hillside, and was halfway to the town when she saw the slight figure of Julia Chapman waving madly at her. She smiled in some relief at having her thoughts diverted, since the girl was clearly agog about something.

'And good afternoon to you too, Julia,' she said, amused that the other's exuberance had made her quite forget her manners.

'Oh yes, good afternoon! But I'm far too excited to waste time in apologising for startling you—'

'I think you're already doing so, and you had better calm down before you have a fit,' Amy said, with a small laugh. 'Let's sit down on the grass and you can tell me what's happened to excite you so.'

Fanned by warm breezes, the grass was tinder-dry now, and they sat down together, their skirts spread out around them, and Amy waited expectantly.

'Hélène—Mademoiselle Dubois—has just told us she's become engaged!'

'Oh yes? And who's the lucky gentleman, I wonder?' Amy said, indulging her.

So Hélène had caught her prospective husband, she thought cynically. She had no doubt that the gentleman in question was Sir Edmund Chapman, and the Chapman girls would be acquiring a new stepmother. Though it seemed odd that Hélène should have been the one to tell them and not Sir Edmund himself. . .

'You'll never guess in a million years,' Julia said with a giggle. 'It's all so odd, and they don't seem at all suited to me, but Hélène says she's looking forward to living in Dublin. She's always gone there as often as she could, and she's just come back from a few days there with her news.'

'For pity's sake, Julia, will you stop prattling and tell me who she's engaged to!' Amy said in exasperation.

'Haven't I said? Why, it's that stuffy lawyer fellow who was paying her such attention at your party. Apparently they've known one another quite well for some time, the sly old things.'

'Not Thomas Varley? You *surely* don't mean Thomas Varley?' Amy said in total astonishment. What an ill-matched pair. . .and yet Varley had certainly been paying Hélène a lot of attention at the party, now she came to think about it. And Hélène might well think of him as quite a catch if she yearned for Dublin society. Well, well.

'That's him,' Julia said carelessly. 'Rum, isn't it? But I can't say I'm sorry she'll be leaving some time. I'm far too old to need a governess any longer, don't you think?'

Chapter Thirteen

Amy couldn't wait to get back to the house to tell Marcus this astonishing news. He was in his study and looked up with some irritation when she burst in unannounced. When she blurted out Julia Chapman's information, he looked at her sceptically.

'You must have heard wrongly, or else this is no more than idle gossip on the part of a child,' he said shortly. 'I can't believe a shrewd lawyer like Varley would have been taken in by such an obvious young woman as Hélène Dubois.'

Amy had never felt any particular love for the young woman in question, but since it seemed to her that Marcus was damning the entire womanhood of Callanby by his tone, she found herself rising quickly to her defence.

'Why do you say that? Hélène is very attractive.'

She could even be generous now, since the governess clearly had no further interest in Marcus, if she ever had done. 'Why shouldn't there be genuine affection between them?'

'There may well be,' he said drily. 'And any

affection on Varley's side would be for a voluptuous young woman who's turned his head. But for Mademoiselle Dubois, I suspect the affection would be there for somewhat different reasons.'

'Oh? And are you going to explain to this simple female just what you mean by that?' Amy demanded, hearing the superiority in his voice.

He didn't rise to her bait. 'You haven't been here very long, Amy, and you don't know people the way I do. Mademoiselle Dubois has set her pretty bonnet at various gentlemen in the past, to no avail. At one time it was even thought Sir Edmund would succumb, but he's far too wily an old fox to be caught in the marriage stakes again.'

'I've certainly been here long enough to suspect that much for myself!' she said. 'And did Hélène never turn her attentions to you?' she dared to ask.

He gave a short laugh, his face relaxing momentarily for almost the first time since Ronan Kelly had sent him the news from Wicklow he'd been dreading.

'Oh, yes, the lady tried her wiles on me too, but her style wasn't to my taste,' he said carelessly, and with monumental male arrogance.

Amy forbore to ask just what style *was* to his taste, demanding again to know just what he meant by Hélène's affection for Varley being somewhat different from true love. Admittedly, she also found it hard to believe in such a condition existing between the two of them. But didn't they say that love was frequently blind?

'I mean the lady likes the bright lights, which is why she goes to Dublin whenever she can as a respite from her duties in Callanby. I presume that's where she and Varley have met at various times, and as a well-travelled woman she'll have realised the potential for a good social life with him. A wealthy bachelor with a solid law practice is always considered quite a catch.'

'So you see her as a fortune-hunter?'

'What else?' Marcus said.

'And is that how you still see me?'

The moment she had said it she knew it was the wrong time to ask such a provocative question. Until she had come bursting into the house with Julia Chapman's news, Marcus had warned her he was unlikely to be at his best over the next few days, and that she would be wise to keep out of his way.

While she sympathised with him over the desperate disappointment of the assay report, she couldn't see the point of bottling up the frustration of it all. There was no sense, either, in brooding over what couldn't be changed, but she accepted that it was the way of the male ego to hate admitting failure, even if it wasn't of his own doing.

And of course it was all still uppermost in his mind, and of far more importance than a gossipy report of the impending nuptials of his lawyer and a young girl's governess.

'I'm sorry. That was foolish of me,' Amy said quickly.

'And quite unnecessary. If you don't know by now that I think nothing of the sort, then you must be wearing blinkers. Now, if you would kindly leave me, I have to compose an important letter to despatch to Dublin.'

'And before you ask,' he added at her look, 'I'm

not about to offer my congratulations to Thomas
Varley, at least not until I hear confirmation from
the man himself. I'm sure it will be reported as an
item of social interest in the newspaper, even if he
doesn't send me prior information. The letter I'm
composing is to send to the inn where Kelly always
stays in town, dissolving our partnership.'

Amy was shocked. It seemed hardly right to do
such a thing in a letter, even though she freely admitted that Marcus owed few favours to the man.

'Surely you can't just do that!' she said. 'Isn't
there a legal contract between you or something?'

'There was no formal contract, since Kelly has a
great mistrust of lawyers and the like. There was a
gentlemen's agreement, if such a thing could be
applied to a rogue like Kelly. It was agreed between
us, albeit in writing, that if no gold was discovered,
the partnership could be instantly dissolved by either
one of us on payment of a token penny as compensation. And right now nothing will please me
more.'

'Will he accept it just like that?' Amy said
uneasily.

Marcus shrugged. 'He'll have no choice. Regard-
less of his careless attitude, I lodged the signed
agreement at Varley's chambers. If there's any dispute, it will simply be brought to court. I foresee
no difficulty, except for the delay in getting the
letter to him,' he added pointedly.

Amy left him to it. It sounded simple enough. . .
but her sixth sense told her Kelly wasn't the type
of man to be fobbed off with a token payment that
was downright insulting. There could be trouble
brewing, and she prayed that Marcus would word

his letter carefully, though in his present mood she
doubted it very much.

She had to admit that once the deed was done, and
the letter had been despatched by the regular
Callanby-to-Dublin messenger, Marcus was easier
to live with. It was as if a great weight had been
lifted from him, not only because he had parted
company with Kelly, but because he had finally
accepted that this particular project was over.

Although 'being easier to live with' was something of a misnomer, Amy thought, because she
hardly ever seemed to see him except at mealtimes.
He spent hours tramping the fields or riding with
his grooms and stable-lads, and never once invited
her to accompany him. If her pride was bruised, she
was forced to accept that it was his way of dealing
with matters, but she was obliged to spend far too
much time alone.

A few days later there was a small item on the
social page of the Dublin newspaper, announcing the engagement of Mr Thomas Varley and
Mademoiselle Hélène Dubois. She brought it to his
attention over their evening meal.

Marcus nodded. 'I received a note from Varley
to tell me of the fact before it appeared in the
newspaper.'

'You didn't tell me!'

'I didn't think I had to,' he said. 'You were quite
convinced it was true, anyway—'

'And you were not.'

'I was, actually. I spoke with Hélène at the
Chapmans' a few days ago, and she's now dis-

playing a ring on her engagement finger.'

Amy was indignant on two counts now. One, that he hadn't told her he now accepted that her reportage was true; and two, that he'd been to the Chapmans' and conversed with Hélène Dubois, and hadn't thought it of sufficient import to tell her that either. It all pointed to one thing in Amy's mind. *She* wasn't of sufficient import to him, and once this enforced association between them was brought to its necessary conclusion, they would go their separate ways and his life would hardly have been ruffled.

'Have I said something to upset you?' Marcus said now, when she sat staring at her plate without touching her meal. 'I thought you'd be pleased to know Hélène was firmly betrothed now, since you seemed to have some idea that the lady was after me.'

'How inelegant you make that sound,' she said swiftly. 'But I was thinking nothing of the sort. I was merely thinking what a poor sort of life you and I would have had together if you can't be bothered to tell me about the trivial details of your day as well as the major ones.'

His eyes glimmered with amusement. 'At least you now accept that Hélène is, and always has been, one of the trivial details in my life, my sweet.'

'Oh, I do!' Amy said, feeling an inexplicable sense of despair, and stabbing her fork into her succulent chicken dinner with some viciousness. 'And no doubt I am destined to be another. Easily disposed of when I've served my purpose, and never thought about again.'

He didn't answer for a moment, then said, 'You couldn't be more wrong, Amy. I owe you an enormous debt, and I shall never forget that. As for disposing of you easily, I assure you it won't be easy. I should be totally bereft if I thought I had to let you go out of my life completely. You've been part of it for too long.'

Please don't say these things, she begged him silently, for you'll never know how they twist my heart.

'So when the parting comes, shall we revert to writing letters to one another again?' she said, not trusting herself to think what cold comfort such a suggestion was giving her. She didn't want his words on pieces of paper. She wanted all of him, in her heart and in her life.

'If that is what will please you,' he said.

'It will be rather strange writing to one another in a more personal vein,' she said, determined now to keep the conversation at this level. 'I was always writing as your aunt in times past, remember, and dictating her words.'

'But it was your personality and your humour that came through the letters, and that was what I found myself looking for so often,' Marcus replied.

'Oh well,' she said brightly, 'as long as you're sure I won't bore you with my doings, I'll resume writing as soon as I have an established address.'

She listened to herself, making ridiculous small talk now, and planning for a future she didn't want. She ate her meal while tasting none of it, and thinking there was precious little humour between them these days, with all the varying tensions of their relationship.

'You have never bored me, and you never will, and it doesn't become you to demean yourself,

Amy,' he said, with a note of irritation.

She knew it wasn't a bad idea to get him riled, exhausting though it might be. For while they annoyed or baited one another, it stopped her constant longing for his caresses and his kisses. It stopped her from remembering the night of their engagement party, when he came to her room and so nearly seduced her. And it stopped her remembering how much, and how badly, she had wanted that to happen. . .

They retired to the drawing-room after the meal, where they were served coffee and then brandy, which Amy declined as usual. And she picked up her needlework while Marcus continued to thumb through the newspaper.

She thanked heaven he had lately agreed that she could discontinue reading to him, pleading that she much preferred to read silently than to read aloud. In reality she found the works of Miss Austen far too emotive for comfort, and Marcus's other choices had been too heavy for her taste.

'Good God!' he suddenly exclaimed aloud, startling her. He made no apology for his words, and stared fixedly at a small item in the middle pages.

'What is it?' Amy said.

'I wondered why there had been no word from Kelly after my letter. It seems the fool has broken his leg after a drunken gambling bout and is now laid up at the Dublin Inn.'

'Oh, the poor thing—'

'Don't waste your pity on him. His type usually comes up smelling of roses. It seems he was in collision with a runaway vehicle in the main square. The gentleman in the vehicle is full of remorse, and by way of compensation is paying for his stay in Dublin and for all his medical needs for as long as necessary.'

Amy couldn't help but smile at the indignation in Marcus's voice now.

'Well, why not look on the bright side?' she said. 'At least he's gaining a bit of importance by being pampered and getting his name in the newspaper, so he won't be bothering about losing your partnership, at least for the time being.'

'True. And he won't be coming back to Callanby for a while either, from the sound of it.'

So there were to be no immediate confrontations between the two of them. Remembering what a vicious tongue Ronan Kelly had, Amy couldn't be more thankful. By the time his leg had mended and he returned here, time would have softened any resentment he had for Marcus's high-handed dismissal of him. They could wash their hands of him.

'I'm very relieved, Marcus,' she said softly. 'I always had a nagging feeling that he might have found a way to cause trouble, but now that he's experiencing a bit of the soft life—even with a broken leg—I don't think we need fear anything more from him.'

It was a week later when she discovered that she couldn't have been more wrong.

A perspiring person Amy instantly remembered was shown into the drawing-room. Her heart sank, wishing Marcus was here to deal with this, but since he wasn't, a silently disapproving Mrs Monahan handed the man's card to Amy, and she had no option but to speak with him.

'Good morning Mr O'Donnell. May I offer you some refreshment?' she said.

'Thank you, ma'am. A glass of cordial would be very welcome,' the newspaper reporter said.

His practised gaze took in the genteel ambience of the room, and the easy way Amy seemed to act as its mistress. He gave the habitual sniff Amy remembered, and while they awaited the arrival of the cordial she felt obliged to enquire after his health, since he looked near to being apoplectic. He sat down heavily on a chair at her invitation, placing a document case on the floor beside him.

'I'm well enough, Miss Finch,' he wheezed. 'Though the thinness of the air in these parts does me no good at all.'

'And do you often travel this far on newspaper business?' she asked in some surprise.

'I do indeed, if the story warrants it,' he said.

She had forgotten how ferrety-faced he was, and how irritating was that constant sniff. But she surmised that he probably wanted to quiz Marcus on the break-up of his partnership, which Kelly would no doubt have told him.

'Your man is away from home now, then, is he?' O'Donnell said, when he had taken a great gulp of his drink.

'Mr Bellingham is not here at the moment,' she said, more formally. 'If you have any other business to attend to in the town, it might be best if you returned later.'

'Thank you, no. I prefer to wait, if 'tis all the same to you. 'Tis a matter of some importance that I wish to see him about.'

'If it's anything that I could help you with—'

'I'm thinking you'd prefer it if I dealt with your man, Miss Finch, since 'tis something of a delicate matter, do you see.'

Amy didn't see at all, and nor did she like the inference that Marcus had committed some misdemeanor, which was the impression she was getting from this odious man.

'Perhaps you'd care to look around the conservatory and the gardens while you wait,' she said. 'It's far too nice a day for staying indoors, and I'm afraid I do have some domestic chores to attend to. May I show you the way?'

How much like the grand lady of the house she sounded now! Amy wasn't addicted to putting on airs and graces, but in his case she didn't care. He hadn't been invited here, and he wasn't a person she cared to encourage. She was quite sure Marcus wouldn't encourage him either.

O'Donnell nodded as she rose from her chair, waiting pointedly for him to comply with her suggestion.

'That will be very agreeable, Miss Finch. And may I say how well you to fit into these surroundings, almost as if you had been born to them.'

'Well, since you know very well that I wasn't, I prefer not to enter into a discussion about my personal life,' she said smartly, unable to hide her displeasure any longer.

Amy knew it was part of his stock-in-trade to probe for information, but he was getting no more out of her. His presence disturbed her, making her recall the last time they had met, and all the lies she had been forced to tell. None of it sat easily on her conscience.

She moved to the long windows and opened them wide, letting in a welcome breath of air.

'If you care to visit the conservatory first, you'll find it to the far left of the house,' she said, 'and please feel free to wander outside as you will. I'm expecting Mr Bellingham back quite soon.'

She breathed a sigh of relief when he left her, and went straight to her room on the pretext of having matters to attend to. From her window she could see when he left the conservatory a short while later, where the humid atmosphere was probably far too warm and sticky for his comfort.

She watched as he strolled among the shrubberies, his document case still firmly held beneath his arm, which was presumably to give him an air of some importance. And then her heart leapt as she saw him wave a hand in greeting and call someone's name.

Amy moved back in the shelter of her curtains as Marcus appeared in her field of view, but even from this distance she could see the darkening frown on his face as he was obliged to shake hands with the reporter.

It was well known that eavesdroppers never heard any good of themselves, although Amy had always thought it was a foolish adage. Why on earth shouldn't they overhear compliments as well as slanders. . .not that she could hear anything of the conversation that was going on—no, *raging*—now, between Marcus and O'Donnell.

But she could see the gestures. Whether or not Marcus had intended inviting him back to the house, Amy didn't know. But in any case, the man had immediately opened his document case, taken out a large sheet of paper and shown it to Marcus. This was followed by what looked like a copy of a newspaper.

If fury could have been transmitted through the air, Amy knew she would be registering its full impact. Marcus had torn the paper into small pieces, but he was staring hard at the newspaper now. Whatever was in it had shocked and infuriated him—and everyone knew that once words were in print they were there for all to see.

Amy's heart thudded wildly at the look on Marcus's face. For one ghastly moment she thought he was going to throttle O'Donnell. He lifted his hand as if to strike him, but as the man backed away he seemed to change his mind and gesticulated that he should come to the house.

Amy dodged back further, seeing the triumph on O'Donnell's face, and the murderous anger on Marcus's. Her mouth was so dry she couldn't have spoken to anyone, and when there was a knock on her door a few minutes later, she jumped visibly and croaked to someone to enter the room.

The maid bobbed briefly. 'Mr Bellingham requests that you join him and the other gentleman in the study at once, miss,' she said, her eyes wide.

Amy swallowed. So whatever the trouble was, it concerned her. Had O'Donnell somehow found out that the engagement was all a sham and was about to expose them? There was no way that he could know, as far as she knew, but she couldn't think of any other reason to make Marcus so angry.

She sped down the stairs and into the study after a peremptory knock on the door. That Marcus was holding the meeting in his sanctuary at all was ominous enough, when she knew all his instincts would be to send the reporter packing.

The two men sat in stiff silence, but there was a look of speculative satisfaction on O'Donnell's face.

'Sit down, Amy,' Marcus said.

She did so abruptly, feeling as though her legs weren't going to hold her up for much longer until she knew what all this was about.

'I would much prefer not to have brought you into this meeting at all,' he went on, 'but since it involves you so personally, it's only fair that you should see the rag that O'Donnell has brought here for my comments.'

He reluctantly handed her the newspaper. It was open at the inner pages, and one paragraph in the so-called Gossiper's Column was heavily ringed in black. She read it quickly, her face blanching as she did so.

'There's a more-than-cosy domestic arrangement at a certain house in Callanby, where a gentleman has installed his future bride. What would his aristocratic aunt have had to say about this, we wonder, had she still been alive to see it? Gossiper has it on good authority that the gentleman sees the lady's bedroom door as no barrier to his attentions.'

Amy was numb with shock. No names were mentioned, but anyone reading it who had seen the previous details of their so-romantic engagement would be in no doubt as to who the parties were. And it was all so wrong. . .at least, in the sordid way it was being portrayed here.

'Do you have any comments to make, Miss Finch?' O'Donnell said silkily, watching her closely.

She found her voice with difficulty. 'I don't know

who informed you of this pack of lies, but I demand, as I'm sure Mr Bellingham does, that you retract it immediately.'

She assumed that, apparently having had his say, Marcus was prepared to let her have hers. And her eyes burned with indignation at this odious newspaperman having so much of the whiphand over them. There was surely a law against printing slanderous gossip. . .but since no names had been mentioned, presumably the law was helpless to act. But she couldn't imagine that Thomas Varley would be any too pleased in seeing his client's respectable image so badly dented.

'I can't do that, Miss Finch, not unless you and Mr Bellingham want to give me a prepared statement saying that no impropriety has taken place,' he said, oozing blandness. 'But I must warn you that such statements often have the opposite effect from the one the parties concerned were hoping for. Most folk would see it as a case of protesting too much, and they'd simply assume that it was all true anyway.'

'That's infamous! And who was it who gave you this misinformation?' Amy said, her eyes blazing.

Even as she said it, she knew. It had to be Ronan Kelly, and this was his way of taking revenge on Marcus for his high-handed dissolving of their partnership. It could only be guesswork, but no doubt he could twist O'Donnell's scandalmongering brain with his snide words. It was sickening, especially after Marcus had helped him back on his feet after his earlier tragedy.

'The piece of paper you tore up, Marcus,' she said, turning to him. 'Was that—?'

She ignored the fact that he'd know now that she'd been watching from her window. It didn't matter. Nothing mattered now but restoring his good name—and hers.

'It was a scrawled letter with the facts as they are presented here,' Marcus said.

'Then without that as evidence—' Amy said hopefully.

O'Donnell laughed. 'My dear Miss Finch, do you think I would bring the original here with me, when I fully anticipated Mr Bellingham's reaction? That was a copy, dear lady, and the original is safely back in my office.'

Amy felt physically sick. And then he reached into his document case and brought out his pencil and notebook with the flourish she remembered, licking the lead several times with some relish.

'So now, my dear sir, do you have some statement to make for our readers?'

Sir Edmund Chapman called at the house during the late afternoon, his face dark with disapproval, and demanding to see Marcus at once. For a rakish gentleman, with certain persuasions of his own, he had a strong inner sense of morality regarding his tenants, of whom Marcus was one. He had also self-styled himself as the lord of the manor, as far as Callanby was concerned.

Mrs Monahan asked him to wait in the drawing-room while she informed Mr Bellingham of the caller, muttering beneath her breath that the whole house seemed to be disrupted with comings and goings and upsets today.

'And get a move on, woman,' Sir Edmund

snapped, with unnecessary displeasure.

Amy was sitting motionless in the drawing-room with a book in her hands that she was making a pretence of reading. She heard Sir Edmund's words as the door was opened, and she looked up in surprise as the gentleman was shown in. She had never heard him so testy before, and she registered that he eyed her with a very narrowed look as she rose to greet him with an outstretched hand. Her heart sank as he took it ungraciously and dropped it immediately.

'Good afternoon, Sir Edmund,' she murmured. 'I trust you are quite well?'

'I would prefer not to answer that question just now, Miss Finch.'

'Your daughters, then?' she enquired. 'I haven't seen them for a few days. Are they well?'

'You'll forgive me, madam, but I didn't come here to make idle chit-chat. It's Mr Bellingham that I came to see, on a matter of some importance.'

Amy felt her face flood with colour at the reprimand. Sir Edmund was known for his flirtatious ways and his liking for a pretty woman, and this astonishing attitude filled her with alarm. Whatever had happened on Sir Edmund's horizon was apparently something dire. And if it was to do with Marcus, then that involved *her*. . . The wildest speculations flashed through her mind.

Maybe Sir Edmund had somehow lost all his money, and he was calling in the lease on this house immediately.

Perhaps one of his daughters had found herself in the worst possible trouble that could befall an

unmarried lady, and was putting the blame on
Marcus. . .

Whatever it was, Amy simply refused to face up
to the worst possibility: that he had seen the newspaper article, and was coming here, hell-bent on
finding out the truth of things. Perhaps they should
have gone to him first, she thought wildly, but why
should it be any of his business?

When Marcus came into the room, she looked at
him wordlessly. He came straight to her, ignoring
Sir Edmund for the moment, and drew her to her
feet, his arm firmly around her shoulders.

'Good afternoon, Edmund,' he said. 'I can guess
what you've come here about—'

'Can you, you young scallywag! And what do
you have to say about it? I warn you, I'll not have
a scandal going on under my roof, and I'd always
thought better of you, Bellingham.'

'If you will allow me to speak, Edmund, I will
tell you exactly what I've told that scumbag of a
reporter from Dublin.'

Sir Edmund smiled slightly at the term. For all his
pomposity, he had a liking for the more earthy terms.

'Well? I'm waiting,' he said, seating himself on
a chair, and folding his arms across his chest.

'I have given O'Donnell a statement, which Amy
and I have both signed, and you may see a copy of
it in my study in a moment. It states that there is
no truth whatsoever in the disgraceful reportage of
our relationship in Gossiper's Column. And that we
hope very much that the good folk of Dublin and
Callanby and the outlying areas will wish us well
in our forthcoming marriage in two weeks' time.'

Chapman stared at him without speaking for a moment.

'Is this true?' he demanded. 'Have you and Miss Finch set the date for the wedding?'

Amy felt Marcus's arm tighten on her shoulders, and she thanked heaven that he had been quickwitted enough to do this so that O'Donnell had been obliged to leave the house with the signed statement and a promise to publish it.

'It has been decided for some time, but we saw no reason why folk should know just yet. My aunt's death made us feel the need for discretion before making a formal announcement too soon,' he said deliberately.

Hearing this, Edmund slowly nodded as if understanding. How gullible he was, Amy thought fleetingly. How thankfully, wonderfully gullible. . .

'I trust that when this news gets about, Amy's good name will be vindicated,' Marcus went on more forcefully. 'There's no scandal in our relationship, I assure you.'

'My dear boy, I shall see to it personally that both of you will continue to be held in the highest regard.'

His gushing remorse that he could ever have felt ill towards them was almost worse than his instant condemnation, thought Amy.

'And you will allow me to hold your wedding breakfast at my home,' he went on. 'It will let everyone know that you have my protection, and will always do so.'

'That's extremely generous of you, Edmund, and we will be pleased to accept. But we want no great fuss. All we want is to be together.'

He turned to Amy and pressed a light kiss on her

forehead as if to underline his sincerity. The gesture obviously reassured Edmund, and he cleared his throat noisily.

'Then I shall leave you two young people now, as I'm sure you have much to discuss. I certainly don't need to see your copy of the statement for confirmation, Marcus. But I want you to know you have my full support. And Miss Finch—Amy—I trust you will not let this unfortunate incident cloud your future happiness in any way.'

'I'll do my best not to, sir,' she murmured.

When he had gone, she wilted against Marcus. This had been such a terrible, terrible day, and she had not believed that even Kelly could have been so vindictive towards Marcus. And now they had been pushed towards a much earlier wedding than either of them had envisaged. But perhaps it was better so. The sooner the marriage, the sooner the annulment. . .and the thought was enough to break her heart.

Without warning, she was sobbing in Marcus's arms and he was holding her very tightly.

'I'm so sorry, so very sorry,' she found herself blubbering.

'What on earth have you got to be sorry for? None of this was your fault, my dear girl,' he said roughly.

'But if I hadn't agreed to come to Ireland with your aunt—if we had never met—'

'And I thought you were such a believer in fate!' he said in an attempt to tease. 'Isn't it written that a meeting between soulmates is destined to happen

sometime, somewhere, no matter what how we try
to avoid it?'

'I'm not sure I choose to believe in such things
any more,' Amy said slowly.

He tipped up her chin so that she was forced to
meet his gaze.

'Then you let me down,' he said. 'You, of all
people, should keep the faith, Amy. Aunt Maud is
also going to get her way sooner than she may have
thought. And even though fate had to work through
the devious machinations of my ex-partner, a
marriage *will* shortly take place, won't it?'

'Yes,' she said weakly.

He folded her into him, and she could feel the
thud of his heart, as rapid as her own. Today's
trauma hadn't been as easily overcome for him as
he pretended now, she realised. It had been his good
name, as well as hers, in danger of ruin.

'Are we going to stand here like this for the rest
of the day?' she heard him say a few moments later.
'Not that I have any objection to holding a lovely
woman close, you understand, especially one so
fragrant and pliant in my arms. But we have
much to do.'

'Do we?' Amy said. She felt his clasp on her
tighten a little more and he kissed the tip of her nose.

'Of course we do. We have a wedding to arrange.
Don't tell me you've forgotten already! We'll go to
see the priest as soon as you've dried your eyes
and made yourself look presentable. Then there's
considering the guests to invite, which will take a
little thought. Two weeks doesn't give us very much
time, my love.'

'You could have said a little longer,' she

said, but realising his voice had lightened.

'Except that when you want something very badly, and the opportunity for it is presented to you, it's going directly against fate to ignore it. I'm sure your romantic little heart won't disagree with that, my dear Miss Finch.'

It didn't, of course. Even though the reason he wanted this marriage so badly had little to do with romance, Amy thought. But then she gave up thinking at all, since it was something she wanted so very badly too.

Chapter Fourteen

Sir Edmund Chapman was nothing if not thorough. By the end of the day, anyone who amounted to anything in Callanby knew of the disgraceful attempt of Marcus Bellingham's ex-partner to discredit the gentleman and his future bride. They also accepted that the wedding had been planned for some time, and was now imminent. Since it was Sir Edmund himself who spread the news, there was none who doubted it for a moment.

Even as Marcus and Amy emerged from the priest's cottage, with all the arrangements confirmed, they were being greeted by one and another, congratulating them warmly and wishing them well on their forthcoming marriage.

'God bless Edmund,' Marcus breathed irreverently. 'He can be a contrary cuss at times, but this time he's undoubtedly saved the day.'

They saw Hélène Dubois bearing down on them, and Amy held her breath. For some reason the governess always rattled her, and she clung more possessively to Marcus's arm.

'So we are all to be congratulated, Miss Finch,'

she said brightly. 'And it seems that you two will be tying the knot sooner than Mr Varley and myself.'

'When is your own wedding planned?' Amy said, asking out of politeness and for no other reason.

'Perhaps at the end of the year. It has not been decided yet, but we shall want to go away on an extended trip abroad, and it all takes a lot of discussion and planning.'

'What she means,' Marcus said conspiratorially as they moved on, 'is that she's still trying to persuade Varley to take her around the world on some wildly expensive excursion.'

Amy laughed. 'You understand the lady very well, Marcus, though a similar thought had crossed my mind.'

'That's such a good sound, Amy,' he said unexpectedly.

'What is?'

'Your laughter. I was beginning to think I'd lost the capacity to make you even smile any more.'

'There hasn't been too much to laugh about during the last few days, has there?' she pointed out. 'Anyway, you've had a constant scowl on your face ever since you had the assay report, and then seeing that awful O'Donnell man.'

She shivered, knowing that things could have ended up so much worse than they had. Because of Kelly's vindictiveness, they could be outcasts in society by now.

'I'll make everything up to you, Amy,' he said quietly. 'You have my word on that. And we must appear to be the devoted couple from now on, with our wedding day so near. So let the world enjoy your beautiful smile as much as I do.'

He squeezed her arm more tightly to him, and his free hand covered hers on the stroll back to the house. Whenever they stopped to chat with other people she did as she was told and forced a smile to her lips, even though her feelings were in a constant state of turmoil.

One minute she was ecstatic with happiness, almost able to forget the farcical circumstances of this marriage, and simply looking forward to it as eagerly as any other prospective bride. . .and in the next, she was remembering how soon the fairy-tale had to end. As soon as it was reasonable for Marcus to be rid of her, the marriage would be annulled, and she would be paid off handsomely.

'I'll arrange for a dressmaker to call as soon as possible to measure you for your wedding gown,' he said next.

'Oh, Marcus, I'm sure I have something suit-able—' she protested, thinking this an unnecessary expense.

'And I'm sure I've no wish for my bride to wear a gown that wasn't especially made for the occasion. Aunt Maud would certainly have expected it. She'd have been outraged if she thought we weren't doing the thing properly.'

His words silenced her. Aunt Maud. . . Lady B. . . . She could have had no idea of what she'd begun through her meddling in the lives of the two people who were closest to her.

'You are going to indulge me in this, aren't you, Amy?' Marcus said now.

'I'll do whatever you decide,' she said, suddenly as limp as a leaf in the wind, and feeling as though she had no will of her own any more. What Lady

B. had begun, Marcus was simply taking over. . .

She walked on with her head bent, hardly noticing how far they had gone until they were approaching the house. She was aware that he glanced down at her often, but he had said nothing for a long while.

'There's something I wanted to discuss with you, but I don't think this is the time,' he said, after what seemed like an endless silence between them.

'Whatever it is, I'm sure you'll make your own decision in the end,' she said, dredging up a little spirit.

'Do I seem so dictatorial to you?'

She almost laughed at the genuine surprise in his voice. Did he really not realise how her whole life was being dictated by him!

'Only sometimes,' she said in a muffled voice, since she hardly wanted to begin an argument when they were so near to the house now, and supposedly such loving companions.

'Then I'll try to curb it,' he said gravely, with what seemed to Amy to be remarkable restraint. She looked at him unblinkingly, forcing out the words.

'It seems a little late for either of us to try to hide our true feelings, Marcus. At least when we're alone, let's not bother keeping up the pretence of being in love.' As she almost stumbled over the words, she rushed on. 'We both know we're only doing this for gain, so at least let's be honest about it when no one else is around.'

She walked quickly ahead as they reached the imposing front door and couldn't bear to look at him, lest he should see the misery in her eyes. Her true feelings had never been exposed to him, and nor would they be, she vowed. With every word she

said she knew she was losing him. . .but he had
never truly been hers, and that was something else
she should keep firmly in her mind.

The next afternoon a maid knocked on Amy's door
to say the dressmaker was here. So Marcus had
wasted no time, she thought. Indeed, he had been
gone all day, arranging all the things they had listed
last evening when they were ensconced in his study.
All the thrilling lists of things to do that any normal
bride and bridegroom had to arrange. . .

'Would you ask her to come upstairs, please?'
Amy said with a sigh, knowing she would have to
put up with being measured and pinned, pulled this
way and that, and assessed for style and colour.
This, too, should be exciting, she reminded herself.

She was aware that the girl was still fidgeting by
the door. 'Was there something else, Maureen?'

Her words burst out. 'Miss, I didn't know he was
going to do such a thing, surely to God I didn't.
'Twas only a harmless remark, so it was, but maybe
I coloured it a bit—'

'What are you saying?' Amy said sharply. The
girl took a deep breath and Amy saw how her hands
shook as she clasped them tightly together.

''Twas all Ronan's doing, miss. Sure and he's
got the wickedest tongue on him when he's well in
the drink, but I never thought he'd go to the newspaper, and I'll not have anything more to do with
him now—'

'Are you saying you told Ronan Kelly the lies he
passed on to the newspaper?'

'Not in those words, miss! And by all that's holy,
I never meant that to happen! We're all fond of you

and Mr Bellingham, but I daresay you'll be tellin' me to pack me things and go now, and who could blame you!'

She was a real drama queen, thought Amy, seeing her agitated face. But what was the point in sending her packing? The damage had been done, and anyway, it had only precipitated what had to happen. The marriage...the annulment...the eventual loneliness...

'I shan't send you packing,' she said wearily. 'You've been honest enough to tell me the truth, and it had better remain our secret.'

'You mean you won't tell Mr Bellingham?' Maureen said hopefully, clearly not believing her luck.

'I think not,' Amy said, imagining his reaction.

To her embarrassment Maureen came back into the room and grabbed her hand to clutch it between her own.

'You're a real saint, so you are, miss, and I'll be your devoted slave for ever.'

She turned and sped out of the room to fetch the dressmaker, while Amy dried her hand from the contact with the girl's clammy ones. Whether she'd done right or wrong, she didn't know, and cared even less. All she knew was that she couldn't have faced another upset with Marcus, knowing how volatile he still was over the situation. No, there were times when things were best left to settle.

And, after all, she wouldn't have been a woman if she hadn't had her head turned by the dressmaker's compliments and the swatches of beautiful bridal fabrics brought for her approval. Mrs Brodie had the knack of swathing them around her client's body to best effect, and they finally agreed on a beautiful heavy cream brocade.

It would have a high waist and low neckline, but not too low, considering the modesty of the occasion. The sleeves would be long and fitting and the skirt would billow out to show the lovely fabric to perfection. Mrs Brodie had no qualms about her ability to get it finished in double-quick time.

For such an important client as Mr Bellingham, known to be under Sir Edmund Chapman's patronage, she would work day and night if need be. . . and there were three other possible clientele in that Chapman household, she thought, with a speculative gleam in her eye.

'You must carry yellow roses to represent true love, Miss Finch,' Mrs Brodie declared. 'If you wish it, I can do the ordering for you. Some young women mistakenly overdo the size and shape of the bridal bouquet, but if you leave everything in my hands, I promise that you'll be the most beautiful bride the county has seen.'

'Thank you,' Amy said faintly, knowing she was being swept along by the woman, but finding no will to resist.

She hated her own feebleness, for it was totally out of character, or at least, the character she'd always believed she had, until now. But she hardly knew herself any more.

'I'll be back in three days for the first fitting,' Mrs Brodie said.

'Thank you,' Amy said again.

When she had gone she let out her breath, feeling as if she had been holding it in for ages. As indeed she had while the tape measure was being pulled ever tighter around her waist and bosom. After all the restrictions she needed to get some fresh air into her lungs. She needed sunlight.

Walking always restored her, and she walked briskly away from the house and grounds until she found herself at the river's edge. It was so beautiful now, with none of the rain that had swollen it almost to a torrent a few weeks ago. Now it was gentle, rippling over stones and rocks, and crystal clear. She stood gazing down into its shallow depths, with the dazzle of sunlight on it, seeing how the glint of minerals fragmented the water to shimmering silver and gold.

Amy caught her breath. This must be just the way it had been from time immemorial when the search for gold was uppermost in men's minds. Then, and now, always searching. . .and for the lucky ones, making their fortunes. For the rest, there was only fool's gold. . . Almost mesmerised as she stood staring down at the shimmering water, Amy found herself identifying with that worthless metal.

For she was surely the fool, for falling in love with a man who only wanted her for the gold in his inheritance.

She turned away, angry with herself for allowing herself to fall into such a low frame of mind. She had never been a pessimist, and she wasn't about to start now, hard though it may be to see what the future held. And then her heart leapt as she saw Marcus watching her from a short distance away.

'You startled me,' she stammered. 'I thought I was here alone.'

He strode towards her. 'And I thought you might

have been contemplating throwing yourself into the river to solve all our problems.'

Her mouth twisted. He was teasing, but his words wounded her all the same.

'Then you were sadly mistaken. I don't intend to let them be solved for you that easily!'

'It's the last thing I would want. Besides, you could hardly drown in this part of the river. It's far too shallow.'

She moved away from the edge. 'I'd prefer not to talk about drowning if you don't mind. It has a particularly upsetting inference in my mind.'

'Dear God, Amy, how could I have forgotten, even for a moment?' he said, near enough now to take both her hands in his. 'These last weeks have been so full, and now the wedding plans have taken precedence over everything. I'm so sorry to bring up unpleasant memories for you.'

'It's all right,' she murmured. 'We can't spend the rest of our lives in a state of mourning. Life has to go on.'

If it was a trite cliché, it was none the less true, and she was too confused to speak otherwise. She felt so close to him, standing here in the sunlight holding hands. So close in body, and yet so far in spirit. To any casual onlookers they must look like the epitome of young lovers on the brink of marriage, unable to bear being apart, even for a moment. . .but there were no onlookers, and this winding stretch of the river was blissfully private.

'That's what I wanted to talk to you about,' Marcus said slowly. 'I have some plans, Amy—'

She pulled her hands away, biting her lips. 'I

hardly think your future plans are going to affect me—'

'Nevertheless, I would like to discuss them with you, the way we always did in the past through my aunt's letters. You always made such sane and sensible comments.'

Which made her sound about as desirable as an old shoe, she thought. But at least he didn't do her the indignity of pretending she was going to be included in whatever plans he was hatching up now. . .plans that were presumably going to come to fruition once his aunt's legacy was his. She said nothing, but waited for him to go on.

'I want to show you something,' he said abruptly.

They walked for some distance to where the ground levelled out before it dipped back towards the woods and the house. From here Amy could just see the rooftop with the sun shining on it, and far beyond it, those of the town buildings. Callanby was little more than a large village, really, and nestling as it did in the basin of the protective mountains, it was idyllic. In any other circumstances, she knew she would never want to leave this place.

'What do you think?' Marcus said, spreading out his arms to encompass the huge grassy area.

'I don't know. What am I supposed to think?' she said.

'I've spoken with Edmund Chapman, and once Varley has signed over my aunt's money to me I've agreed to purchase the house and grounds. And this area here lends itself perfectly to what I have in mind.'

For one wild moment Amy felt as if Lady B. was standing at her shoulder and telling her scathingly that her young scallywag of a nephew was about to embark on some new hare-brained scheme that would come to nothing.

Impatiently, Amy mentally brushed the lady aside. Marcus was a man, not a young scallywag, and by now she thought she knew him well enough to sense that he would have thought something out very deeply before telling her.

'Go on,' she said quietly, at which he leaned forward and kissed her lightly on the mouth.

'Thank you. For one moment I thought I sensed the ghost of my aunt hovering near. I should have known you'd be more tolerant, and at least give me a hearing.'

Amy looked at him with a mixture of suspicion and guilt. He was perfectly right in thinking she'd been aware of Lady B.'s disapproval, but as for herself being more tolerant. . .that rather depended on what he was planning.

'Oddly enough, it was Kelly who inadvertently gave me the idea with his penchant for gambling on the horses,' he said with heavy irony.

'Oh, Marcus—'

'No, my darling girl, I don't intend to turn into a professional gambler, though with all my aunt's dire predictions about me, it was something she never discounted. What I propose is using this land for breeding valuable bloodstock. Horses, Amy. There's a huge future for racing stables, and we have the perfect venue for it here.'

She couldn't have been more startled if he'd suggested flying to the moon. It sounded so feasible, so logical. . .and far more practical than any other scheme he had proposed so enthusiastically, she admitted. The land here was lush and green and flat, and with his aunt's money behind him, she was sure that this time it would be a success.

This time. . .but she wouldn't be here to see it come to fruition. For, of course, once their business arrangement was satisfactorily concluded, she would have to leave. She wouldn't be anywhere in the vicinity to share in his success. It would be far too humiliating to admit to the failure of their marriage, which was how the world would see it, of course. And she couldn't bear their pity, or their speculation.

'I've obviously shocked you,' Marcus said when she made no comment. 'You think I'm mad.'

'No, I don't. I think it's probably the most sensible thing you've suggested, and I wish you every success with it. And if it's not impertinent of me to say so, your aunt would be pleased that you're using her money sensibly.'

But she was distancing herself from it with every word, and she knew he would sense it. The rasping note in his voice told her so.

'Of course it's not impertinent. You were the one who said we shouldn't bother hiding our true feelings from one another when we're alone, and we've come too far for any of that coy nonsense. I need your approval, Amy.'

'Why? To be sure I won't back out of our arrangement, even at this late stage?'

The words were out before she could stop them, foolish, meaningless words, said with a bitterness borne out of frustration. Their approaching wedding should be such a joyful occasion, and instead it would be a day of deceit, and she was ashamed of her part in deceiving all the good people they would invite. And her true feelings were in such a state of disarray she hardly knew what was truth and what was fiction any more.

'I never believed for a single moment that you would back out,' Marcus said. 'And if you don't know by now how highly I regard you, then you've had your eyes and ears closed all these weeks.'

'Well, for what it's worth you have my total approval of your new plan,' she said steadily, refusing to be drawn into a more personal conversation. 'I'm going back to the house now, and I'm sure you have things to do.'

He gave a smothered exclamation of annoyance, and then strode away from her in the opposite direction.

Two weeks could sometimes seem like a lifetime, and sometimes no more than the blink of an eyelid. For Amy, it was a mixture of both, and both she and Marcus were swept along in a whirl of preparations for their wedding. It was so very easy to pretend it was all real. . .as indeed, it was, even if it was destined to be for such a little while. But pragmatically she decided to put such thoughts behind her and to savour the moments, knowing they would never come again.

The modest list of invitations had gone out, for it was already known that the wedding would be a quiet one, due to Lady Bellingham's demise. The lady was useful on all counts, Amy thought cynically. She had brought this wedding about and was instrumental in keeping it modestly observed.

But not everything would go her way. Lady B.'s

well-meaning intention had been for Amy and Marcus to stay together, and to live happily ever after. What happened after the wedding was entirely due to themselves.

Docherty helped her into the beautiful cream-brocade wedding gown on the afternoon of the wedding. Amy was thankful to have her help, for her hands shook so much she could never have managed the fastenings by herself. The lace veil for her head was held in place by a coronet of pearls and yellow rosebuds to match the bouquet that had been delivered earlier.

Mrs Brodie might be an old fusspot, Amy thought, but she had an expert eye for a total bridal ensemble, and she had been absolutely right in this case.

'You look a real picture, miss,' Docherty breathed. 'Mr Bellingham will be that proud of you, so he will.'

Amy looked at her reflection in the mirror and saw a stranger. A beautiful stranger, whose eyes could no longer deny the fact that she was going to marry the man she loved. For better or worse... and the parting that would come long before death did them part, she reminded herself.

'The gentleman is waiting downstairs for you, miss, and 'tis time to go.'

Amy nodded. It wasn't seemly to appear too eager, but nor was it proper to keep her bridegroom waiting. And the gentleman in question was Thomas Varley, who had come to stay for a night or two before the wedding, and in the absence of relatives was going to give her away.

It also gave him the ideal opportunity to see that Lady B.'s wishes were carried out, she had told Marcus. And she knew very well that once the marriage certificate was signed, Varley would release all the money Marcus would ever need.

She wished such cynical thoughts didn't keep entering her mind, but perhaps it was a good thing that they did, for they helped to keep her feet on the ground. Otherwise she could easily be carried away by the magic of it all.

She moved carefully down the stairs, to where Varley awaited her. He complimented her in his dry, so-correct manner, and Amy had a quick mental vision of him and the voluptuous Hélène Dubois in a passionate embrace. The oddity of such a union did much to calm her nerves. At least everyone said how well-suited she and Marcus were. . .

On the drive to the church, Amy was touched to see the streets lined with people waving to her and wishing her luck. She waved back, unable at last to resist the excitement of the day. If none of it was real, at least she could pretend that it was, just for a little while.

And when she was finally inside the coolness of the church, she saw none of the sea of faces turning to greet the arrival of the bride. All she saw was one face, Marcus's face. She moved down the length of the church as if in a dream, until she was at his side, and the lovely service began that was to bind her to him.

It was a solemn occasion, and the priest intoned over them for what seemed like an interminable time, but once it was over and they went outside into the warm sunlight again, the onlookers showered them with rose petals, and the air was filled with perfume and gaiety.

The moment they were out of the church grounds the fiddlers appeared, striking up a tune and leading the entire procession through the town and up the hill towards Sir Edmund Chapman's home.

'Are you happy?' Marcus said, as he pressed Amy's hand to his side in the crook of his arm.

She looked up at him. Happy? Oh yes, she was happy. Happy enough to let the dream continue, for just a little while longer.

'Yes,' she said honestly. 'It was a beautiful wedding, wasn't it?'

'The only one I could have wished for,' he said. 'Aunt Maud would have loved it.'

'I'm sure she did,' Amy said. And for once he didn't scoff at such fanciful words.

They led the procession to where the Chapman staff were outside the house to greet them, and once inside they were surrounded by congratulations and kisses and gifts.

Edmund had provided a fine wedding feast and insisted on making a lengthy speech before inviting Marcus to speak. Amy kept her eyes lowered as he rose to his feet, wondering exactly what he was going to say. After he had thanked Edmund for his generosity towards them, and Thomas Varley for presenting him with his beautiful bride, he paused.

'There's someone else I especially want to thank, and those of you who were at our engagement party will know who I mean. My aunt is not with us today, though I know my beautiful bride will say she's very much here in spirit. Most of you also know that if it hadn't been for my Aunt Maud's association with Amy, we wouldn't be in this happy state now. So please raise your glasses to my dear departed Aunt Maud.'

There was a *double entendre* in his words that only the two of them and Thomas Varley understood. But when the toast was done, Marcus held up his hand for silence, and Amy realised that he hadn't finished yet.

'I'm not a lover of long speeches, but the most important person I want to thank today is my lovely wife.'

Her heart leapt at his use of the word, and then he drew her to her feet, one arm around her waist, and looked deep into her eyes.

'Gentlemen are sometimes reluctant to reveal their true feelings, even to those who mean the most to them. But today of all days, I think it's important to say what's in your heart. So, since we're among good friends, I'm telling Amy publicly that I will always love her and will do my utmost to abide by the vows we've made before you all.'

He pulled her to him and kissed her amid cheers and wild applause from the assembled guests. The romantics among them clearly appreciated the fact that this was no pompous English gent, but a man who was passionately in love with his wife. And as such, no red-blooded husband would want to spend an hour longer than need be in company, when his wedding night beckoned.

When they were all replete with food and drink, they eventually escorted the couple back to their own house in the same celebratory way they had gone to Edmund's.

By now the sun had gone down, and a pale sliver of the moon rose in the sky. Thomas Varley was returning to Sir Edmund's house to spend some time with Hélène before departing back to Dublin the next day. The farewells were a repetition of all that had gone before, with everyone applauding the newly-weds before they went indoors.

And when they were finally alone inside the house, Amy slowly let out a long breath.

'Was that sigh for any special reason?' Marcus asked.

'No. It was just because it was such a lovely day. No woman could have asked for more on her wedding day,' she said, and then stopped abruptly. Because there was so much more she could have asked for, if she dared. She would have asked for his love. . .all of it. . . She drew in her breath again.

Remembering what he had said in his wedding speech could almost tear her heart apart now. And yet, at the time, it had been said with such sincerity that she had allowed herself to believe it. *He loved her.*

'It doesn't have to end here,' Marcus said.

She looked at him, and her heart began a slow pounding. He took her in his arms, and suddenly she couldn't bear it if there were to be any more lies between them. He had got everything he wanted, and the need for any pretence in private was surely over.

'Please don't do this, Marcus,' she said in a low voice. 'I can't bear it.'

'Is it so very objectionable to you when I touch you, Amy?' he said.

She swallowed. This was her wedding day, and

it should be the happiest day of her life. Instead of which, it was the shallowest. . .

'Of course not,' she mumbled, unable to lie.

'Then I think we should go upstairs to our room.'

Her eyes dilated. 'Marcus, no——'

His arms tightened around her. 'You know very well that it would look very strange if my wife and I slept in separate bedrooms on our wedding night. All your things have already been transferred into our room, Amy. But I promise you there's no need to be afraid.'

She looked at him wordlessly. The only thing she was afraid of was betraying her feelings in the intimacy of his room. How could she sleep next to him, touching his skin and breathing his breath, and not beg him to love her. . .?

'I'm not afraid,' she said, since he seemed to be waiting for her to speak. 'I know you're a gentleman, Marcus, and I trust you.'

'Then you're more of a fool than I took you for,' he said roughly, 'because I'm not sure that I can trust myself any more. It all seemed so uncomplicated at first.'

'Please don't try to explain, Marcus,' she whispered. 'I'm well aware that it's in every man's nature to be roused by a woman, and perhaps if we put a pillow between us——'

'Dear God, do you think that's what I want? Or that you have ever been just any woman to me?' he said.

'What are you saying?' she said faintly. She was still held tightly in the circle of his arms in the drawing-room, which was bathed in moonlight now. It was light enough to see that his eyes were blazing, and she couldn't miss the passion in his voice.

'I'm saying that it's time for truth between us, my lovely Amy. No more pretences. We both know this marriage was arranged out of necessity, and I persuaded myself that it would end amicably and no harm done. But I was wrong.'

'Were you?'

She wouldn't help him, and nor could she, since she was too afraid to hope that he meant what she thought he did.

'The harm would all be done to you, Amy. Your reputation, your shame. A man can get over those things, but a woman would always feel slighted and rejected.'

At his words, her spirits plunged again. He cared more about her reputation than about *her*, and this wasn't about to be a declaration of love after all. She squared her shoulders and lifted her face to his.

'You needn't worry about me, Marcus. I'll survive without you——'

'Will you? Then you're made of stronger stuff than I am, because I'm not sure I could survive without you. I know we had an arrangement, Amy, but arrangements can be broken, if the two parties concerned want it that way.'

He cupped her face in his hands and looked down at her. Even though his face was half in shadow now, she didn't need to see it to know every expression in his eyes, and to recognise every nuance in his voice.

'Amy, did you really think I made that ridiculous statement at our wedding feast just for show? Didn't you know that I meant every word of it? Didn't you know how much I love you, and always will?'

'How could I know, when you never told me!'

'Nor I did. But whatever else you may have thought, I married you for love. If you still want to stand by our original plan, I'll be forced to agree, but not without a fight, Amy. Because I warn you, I'm going to do my damnedest to make you stay married to me.'

For a moment she was too elated to speak, and when she did, it was in a soft, tremulous voice.

'And you have my promise that you won't even have to try. I married for love too, Marcus.'

If they were very different vows from the formal ones they had made earlier that day, they were no less emotive, and just as meaningful. And it was Marcus who drew in his breath then as he took in her words.

If any thoughts of his manipulative aunt flitted in and out of either of their minds at that moment, it was only with a fervent gratitude. But all such inconsequential thoughts were suppressed as Amy clung to him, and he kissed her waiting mouth with a soaring passion. And they were still holding one another as they swiftly climbed the stairs and closed the door of their bedroom behind them.

Historical Romance™

Coming next month

A LORD FOR MISS LARKIN
Carola Dunn

Alison Larkin thought the most romantic thing in the world would be to have a lord falling at her feet and pledging eternal love.

With the arrival of her recently widowed and wealthy aunt, Alison's dream could become a reality. She was granted a Season and would be introduced to the *crème* of the ton.

How vexing that the first eligible gentleman she was to meet was a plain *Mr* Philip Trevelyan who had a way of making Alison forget that it was her dearest wish to marry a lord.

THE IMPOSSIBLE EARL
Sarah Westleigh

Having been reduced to working as a governess, Leonora was left her uncle's fortune and fine town house in Bath. But she also inherited Blaise, Earl of Kelsey! Her uncle had leased the ground floor to Blaise, where he ran a gentlemen's club.

Leonora's hopes for a respectable life in Society and the possibility of marriage would come to nought without a compromise, particularly when the Earl was so clearly *not* a candidate in the marriage mart.

MILLS & BOON®

Makes any time special™

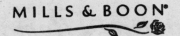

4 FREE

books and a surprise gift!

We would like to take this opportunity to thank you for reading this Mills & Boon® book by offering you the chance to take FOUR more specially selected titles from the Historical Romance™ series absolutely FREE! We're also making this offer to introduce you to the benefits of the Reader Service™—

- ★ FREE home delivery
- ★ FREE gifts and competitions
- ★ FREE monthly newsletter
- ★ Books available before they're in the shops
- ★ Exclusive Reader Service discounts

Accepting these FREE books and gift places you under no obligation to buy, you may cancel at any time, even after receiving your free shipment. Simply complete your details below and return the entire page to the address below. *You don't even need a stamp!*

YES! Please send me 4 free Historical Romance books and a surprise gift. I understand that unless you hear from me, I will receive 4 superb new titles every month for just £2.99 each, postage and packing free. I am under no obligation to purchase any books and may cancel my subscription at any time. The free books and gift will be mine to keep in any case.

H8XE

Ms/Mrs/Miss/Mr..................................Initials ....
BLOCK CAPITALS PLEASE

Surname ....

Address ....

....

....Postcode...............................

Send this whole page to:
THE READER SERVICE, FREEPOST, CROYDON, CR9 3WZ
(Eire readers please send coupon to: P.O. BOX 4546, DUBLIN 24.)